1

*W*agria, Fall, AD 976

Something was wrong.

The morning's rain had dwindled to a light drizzle, and we could see the Danish raiding party clearly now. There were about twenty of the bastards, some armored, some not. Behind them in the tree line huddled the captives and livestock they had taken from nearby steadings. They were a common sight, those Danes. Though we had defeated an army of them several summers before, Danes still came oft from their lands to take what they could from the small Slavic kingdom called Wagria on their southern border. The kingdom we protected.

Normally, Dane raiders such as these would scatter like rats when they saw a force of our strength gather against them, for we were nearly thirty men, all mounted, armored, and well-weaponed. But this group stood fast, and I liked it not.

Mind you, I had no issue bloodying my blade with Dane marauders, but this day was different. This day, we escorted Wagria's pregnant princess, Geira, to her home in Plune. She who was betrothed to my friend and charge, Olaf, and carried within her womb their child.

I scratched at my black beard, my eyes scanning the trees for other signs of trouble, but I could find none. "Why do the fools stand against us?" I wondered aloud.

Olaf's sky-blue eye winked at me. "Because they are fools, Torgil."

"Aye," added a burly, yellow-haired warrior. "The bastards will feel our steel for their mistake. We were right to follow them here, eh, Olaf?" He grinned at our lord.

I scowled at the arse-licker, whose name was Berse. Summers ago, when we lived in Gardariki far to the east, he had been Olaf's second-in-command, but he had lost that position to me. Ever since, he had been a bootlicking fool whom I trusted as far as I could spit into a strong wind, and I was not timid to show it. It had been his witless idea to follow the Danes this day. His, and that of the man called Oskar who rode behind Prince Olaf. A seid-man they called him, a man who could divine the will of the gods through the bird bones he cast on the ground. Olaf had met Oskar the summer before and shown a deep appreciation for his craft, if you could call it that. Anything to give him an advantage over his enemies. It seemed to me that much of what Oskar "divined" could be reasoned, but then, who was I to say? The gods never spoke to me. Still, Olaf liked the man.

"The gods foresaw this, did they not, Oskar?" The raven bone in Olaf's amber beard jiggled as he turned to the strange man. It was because of that bone that Olaf had earned his byname of Crowbone. Crows, of course, were the lesser cousins of Odin's mighty ravens, so the name was partly in jest, which was why we did not call Olaf Crowbone to his face.

Oskar looked the part of a man who spoke to the gods. He wore a simple leather tunic and breeks, a necklace and wristbands fashioned from raven feathers, and circular earrings of wood. And he was totally lacking in hair. It was not just missing from his head — it was missing

RIDDLE OF THE GODS

OLAF'S SAGA, BOOK 4

ERIC SCHUMACHER

BODN BOOKS

RIDDLE OF THE GODS

OLAF'S SAGA, BOOK 4

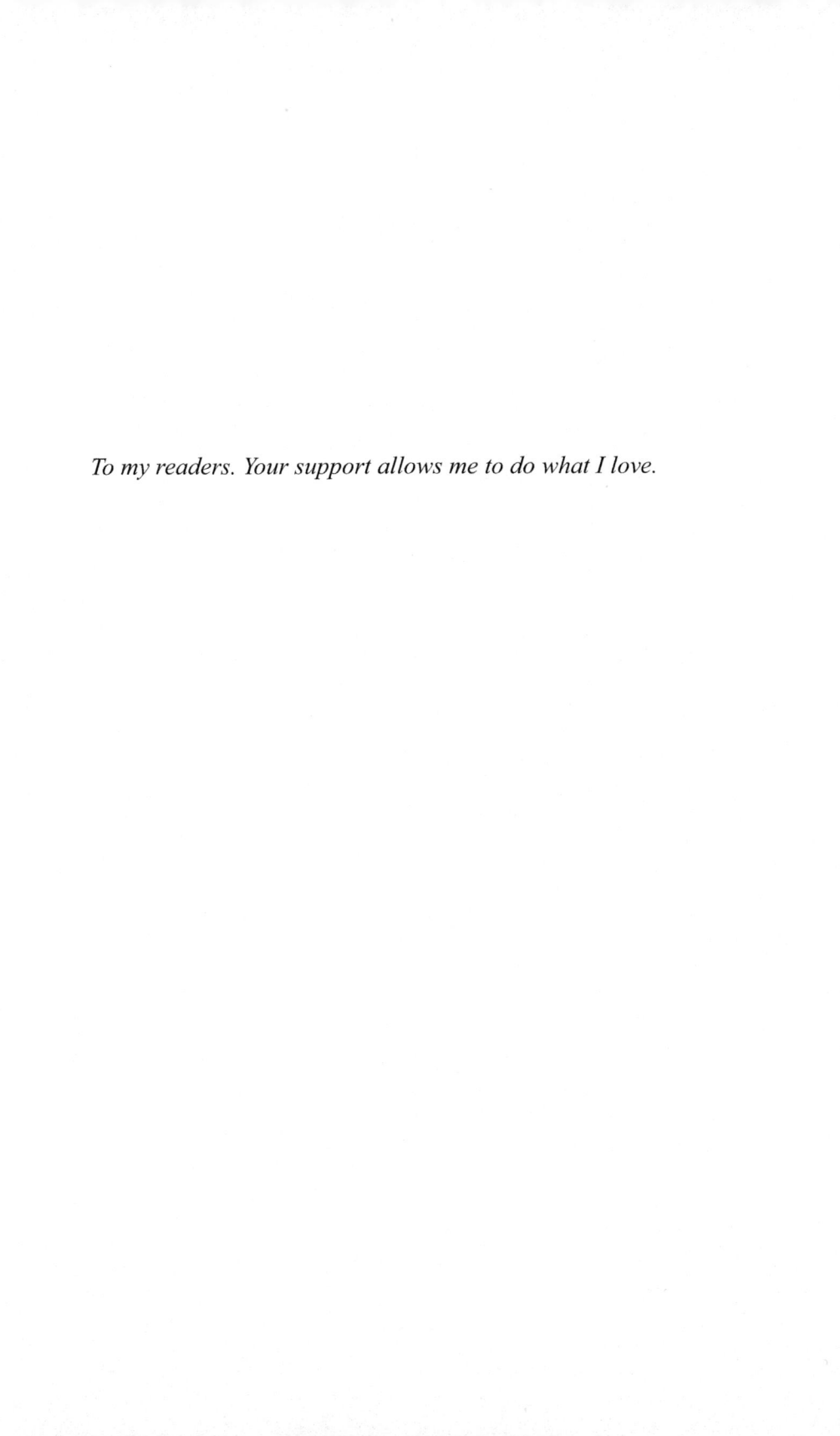

To my readers. Your support allows me to do what I love.

BOOKS BY ERIC SCHUMACHER

Hakon's Saga

Prequel – *Mollebakken: The Rise of Bloodaxe*

Book 1 – *God's Hammer*

Book 2 – *Raven's Feast*

Book 3 – *War King*

Olaf's Saga

Book 1 – *Forged by Iron*

Book 2 – *Sigurd's Swords*

Book 3 – *Wolves of Wagria*

Book 4 – *Riddle of the Gods*

Do you want to know when Schumacher's books are free or discounted, or have access to exclusive content and blog posts? Join his Readers Club at www.ericschumacher.net.

ACKNOWLEDGMENTS

Long ago, I never thought I would one day be writing acknowledgments to the many people who've helped me turn my faint ideas for stories into physical and digital books. It has been a dream of mine since I was a boy, and it would still be a dream if not for you, my readers. It has been your emails, your nudges, your reviews of my work, and your comments on social media that have kept my fingers tapping on the keys of my laptop. As always, I hope this novel brings you hours of enjoyment.

I want to thank my family, who puts up with my ramblings about early medieval history, the Viking shields on my walls, and my hours of sitting alone at my computer with only my ideas for company. I again want to thank Marg Gilks and Lori Weathers, whose attention to detail transform my attempts at proper use of grammar into something that makes me sound better than I am at it. With each book, I endeavor to present a cover that helps set the tone and vision for the story. Thankfully, I have the mastery of David Brzozowski for layout, and the dedication of Andrew Dodor, who even in the midst of war-torn Ukraine is willing to transform my ideas into works of art. It is to you all, and to the countless others who have accompanied me on this journey, that I owe a huge debt of gratitude.

I am a lucky man.

GLOSSARY

Aldeigjuborg – The Old Norse name for a trading post located where the Volkhov River flows into Lake Ladoga.

ardri – A royal title in Gaelic Ireland held by those who had, or who claimed to have had, lordship over all of Ireland. Middle Irish: *ardrí*.

bonder – Free men (farmers, craftsmen, etc.) who enjoyed rights such as the use of weapons and the right to attend law-things. They constituted the middle class. Old Norse: *baendr*.

borg – The Old Norse word for fort or stronghold.

Bolgaraland – The Old Norse name for Bulgaria.

Borysthen – An island settlement at the mouth of the Dnieper-Boh estuary. Today it is known as Berezan Island.

Bryttas – Anglo-Saxon word for "Briton."

Burgundaholm – The Danish island of Bornholm. Old Norse: *Burgundaholm*r.

byrnie – A (usually short-sleeved) chain mail shirt that hung to the upper thigh. Old Norse: *brynja*.

Danavirki – Old Norse for "earthwork of the Danes," a system of Danish walled fortifications that stretches across a portion of present-day Schleswig-Holstein, Germany.

dirham – A silver coin used in the Byzantine and Iranian empires, and used in the land of the Rus as currency.

drekar – A dreki is a Viking longship. Drekar is the plural form of the Old Norse word.

draugr – An undead creature who lives near its burial site and guards its treasure.

Dyflin – Old Norse name for Dublin.

Dyflinarskiri – Old Norse name meaning Dublinshire, an area that stretched to today's Skerries and to Condalkin.

Éireannach – Old Gaelic word for Irish people.

Ellan Vannin – The Man-Gaelic name for the Isle of Man.

Eoforwick – Old English word for York. Old Norse: *Jorvik*.

Estland – Also Eistland. Old Norse name for Estonia.

Fenrir – A monstrous wolf in Norse mythology who attacks the gods on Doomsday (Ragnorak). Old Norse: *Fenrisúlfr*.

Frisland – Old Norse name for Frisia.

fylke – Petty kingdom or county.

Gardariki – The area that formed the land of the Rus. The name means "the realm of towns." Old Norse: *Garðaríki*.

Gura mie ayd – The Manx phrase for "thank you."

Hammaburg – Old Saxon for the city of Hamburg.

Hel – The place most people go when they die. It is also known as Helheim. Hel is also the name of the ruler of Helheim.

hird – A retinue or warband. Old East Slavic: *druzhina*. Old Norse: *hirð*.

Hjaltland – the Shetland Islands in Old Norse.

Hnefatafl – A Viking board game.

Holmgard – The original Rus stronghold situated near the point where Lake Ilmen flows into the Volkhov River. It is often referenced as "Novgorod," though the town of Novgorod and the stronghold are in two separate places. Old Norse: *Holmgarðr*.

Irland – Ireland in Old Norse.

Island – Iceland in Old Norse.

Jomsvikings – Warriors of the settlement of Joms, an all-male society located on the southern shore of the Baltic Sea. Its location and existence are still disputed.

Jorvik – Old Norse name for York.

Keel – The mountain range that divides the eastern Norwegian districts from the western Nowegian districts. Old Norse: *Kjølen*.

Konugard – Kyiv, or Kiev. Old Norse: *Kønugarðr*.

Midgard – One of the nine worlds of Norse cosmology and the only world inhabited by and visible to mankind. Old Norse: *Miðgarðr*.

Miklagard – The Great City, or Constantinople. Old Norse: *Miklagarðr*.

Mjolnir – Mjolnir is the hammer of the thunder god, Thor. Old Norse: *Mjǫllnir*.

Nepr River – Believed to be Old Norse for the Dnieper River.

Nidhogg – The serpent that gnaws at the root of the world tree, Yggdrasil. Old Norse: *Níðhöggr*.

nithing – A nothing. A person of no value.

Njord – The Norse god of wind and water. He was also the patron god of sailors and fishermen. Old Norse: *Njǫrðr*.

Nygard – The Old Norse name for Novgorod, which means "new town." Old Norse: *Nýgarðr*.

Olsborg – An island fortification that formed the nucleus of the city that is now called Ploen in Schleswig-Holstein.

Orkneyjar – The Orkney Islands in Old Norse.

Ostergotland – A district in the kingdom of the Swedes, located in the east of the land and south of present-day Stockholm. Old Norse: *Östergötland*.

Ostman – A general term for any person hailing from someplace to the east of Ireland. It means, "man of the East."

Ox Road – This road stretches from Hamburg up to Viborg in the north. The Danes referred to it as Hærvejen, which means the army road, while the Franks called it Ox Road. It was primarily used as a trade route during the early medieval period.

pogost – A Rus stronghold that acted as the administrative center within the Slavic regions that were subject to Rus rule. The strongholds were there to keep the peace and collect tribute.

poliudie – The Rus process of collecting tribute from the Slavic tribes.

Presota-Tun – The Anglo-Saxon name for present-day Preston, meaning "town of the priests."

Ragnarok – The battle at the end of times. Old Norse: *Ragnarǫk*.

Rippel – The old Celtic name for the River Ribble.

Saxland – The land of the Saxons, i.e., 10th century Germany.

Schlei – A narrow inland waterway that flows from the Baltic into Jutland. Danish: Slien.

seid – Magic. Old Norse: *seiðr*.

seid-man – A shaman or male seer. Old Norse: *seiðr-man.*

Shoh Slaynt – Manx for "here's health," used as "cheers."

Starigard – The Old West Slavic name for Oldenburg in Holstein, where the Wagrian had their main fortress and settlement.

Sudreyjar – The Old Norse word for a kingdom whose name meant "the southern islands," which included the Hebrides and Man. It is also known to history as "the Isles and Man."

Svartahaf – Believed to be the Old Norse name for the Black Sea.

terp (pl. terpen) – A Frisian town, usually walled, that sits on an artificially raised mound and is surrounded by the sea and marshland.

thrall – Old Norse for slave.

Valhall (also Valhalla) – The hall of the slain presided over by Odin. It is where brave warriors chosen by valkyries go when they die. Old Norse: *Valhöll.*

Valland – Normandy in Old Norse.

ves heill – Old Norse greeting meaning roughly "be in good health."

Vestmann – A general term used by the Northmen to describe Irish locals. It means, "man of the West."

wergeld – Also known as "man price," it was the value placed on every being and piece of property.

whale-road – The ocean or sea.

Yule – A pagan midwinter festival lasting roughly twelve days. It later became associated with Christmas. Old Norse: *Jōl.*

NORTHLAND

Sigurd's
Hall

Kaupang

VINGULMARK

SKOTLAND

DANELAND

SUDREYJAR

Ribe

Hedeby

WAGRIA

IRLAND

Jorvik

Amounderness

FRISLAND   SAXLAND

Dyflin

ENGLAND

FRANKLAND

PART I

"At the same moment rose without,
From the contending crowd, a shout,
A mingled sound of triumph and of wailing."

The Saga of King Olaf
Henry Wadsworth Longfellow

from his body. He had no brows. No eyelashes. No hair on his arms or chest. It was as if the gods had forgotten that detail when bringing him to life.

I knew not if the gods had foreseen this moment, but I did know that I was concerned. "Lord," I growled at Olaf. My steed pranced restlessly beneath me, sensing my agitation. "The princess is pregnant. If something happens —"

"I can handle myself," interjected the princess, who tilted awkwardly in her saddle with her bulging belly. The coldness dripped from her response like the rain from the rim of my helmet.

"Suit yourself," I muttered, then spat in the mud beside my horse.

Put plainly, my relationship with Olaf's spouse was as brittle as spring ice. I respected her well enough. She had strength and courage and a mind to match, but still, I harbored a simmering resentment toward her for the loss of my own wife, Turid. You see, I had sworn an oath to protect Olaf and to not leave his side. The plan when we left Gardariki had been to raid and then return to the North, where my wife waited for me with our child. But Geira's betrothal to Olaf had kept me here in her kingdom much longer than expected. Thinking my absence meant my death, Turid turned to the affections of my friend and former lord, Sigurd, whom she married. I suppose it had been the prudent thing to do. After all, Turid had a newborn and needed support, and I had not been there to give it.

None of that would have happened, of course, had Geira not married Olaf, and so I blamed her for my misfortune. She reacted to that resentment with a coldness that was as predictable as it was unpreventable. And so our relationship became a bitter truce of sorts, with Olaf as our buffer. Truth be told, I cared not a whit if a Danish spear took her life. But I did fear for her unborn child, which was Olaf's child.

"Well said, my lady," Olaf declared with a flourish, then smiled that mischievous smile of his. By now, we all knew the look. He was not smiling at us, or at me, or even at his spouse. The bastard was grinning at danger. Spitting in its face. I hated that look. Since we were lads, Olaf's disregard for peril had led to more misadventures than I cared to count, and that grating smile had preceded them all.

"Remain here, Oskar," Olaf called over his shoulder as he prodded his mount into motion.

I spat again to display my disgust.

"Be of glad spirits, Torgil," my friend Sveinn called to me as he kicked his mount forward to follow Olaf. "You could be fighting with one hand instead of two." He waved his wooden right hand at me. Sveinn was a master with wood and had carved the prosthetic himself after losing his real hand to the swipe of a sword.

I sighed and joined the line of horses that Olaf was forming, then I adjusted my helmet and the shield upon my back. Off to my right, the barrel-chested Ulf belched and a few men laughed. Others joked or made bets about the number of Danes they would kill that day. We did these things because, to a man, we were veterans — Olaf's hird or, as he liked to call us, his wolves. We had oft faced death and did not fear a skirmish such as this. Only our mounts seemed agitated as they pranced and snorted beneath us. Perchance they were more keen to the impending strife than we were.

Olaf gazed down the lines to either side of him, then pointed his blade at the Danes and roared. His men echoed his cry. And as one, we kicked our steeds into action. Mud flew from the hooves of our mounts as we charged down the gentle slope. Birds took flight at the thunder of our cries. That alone would have frozen the hearts of most men, but the Danes did not run. Instead, they raised their shields and tightened their ranks, and as their spear tips dropped to meet us, they let loose with a defiant call. It was too late for vigilance. Too late for cowardice. We were all committed to the bloodshed now and would see it through, no matter the outcome.

As we drew closer to our enemy, my reservations gave way to a thrill that was uncontainable. A thrill that shot through my veins and from my mouth in a loud howl. A thrill from which I could not retreat until my blade had slaked itself and the threat of death was defeated.

"Archers!"

Dragomir's hollered words registered in my mind. Though we were well-armored, our shields were on our backs and we were vulnerable, yet we could not turn now. No true warrior could die with an arrow in his back. Besides, we were too near the enemy. So we charged into the storm that was about to be unleashed.

An arrow streaked past my head. I flinched and lowered myself in my saddle. A man to my right tumbled over the back of his steed. Another warrior cried out in pain. The Danes on the field roared all the louder. I shouted my own curses and raised my blade to strike.

And that was when Geira shrieked.

An arrow was protruding from her thigh, just below the reach of her byrnie. At the same moment, a bare-headed beast of a man rose and tossed his spear. The weapon struck Geira's mount fully in its chest. As the animal plunged snout down into the mud, Geira launched from her saddle and rolled toward the enemy. A man advanced to finish her, but Olaf cleaved his head from his body before the Dane could bring his weapon down.

Another Dane came to slay Olaf as he leaped from his saddle to save his wife. I charged at him to save my friend. He saw me at the last moment and turned his blade to protect his head from my strike. Mounted as I was, the momentum of my sword drove the man to his knees. I tried to use my horse's hooves to pummel him, but he scurried away.

To my right and left, our warriors crashed into the Danes. Spears poked upward. Horses whinnied and kicked at the sky. Blades swung down. Men screamed and collapsed or jumped from their saddles and lunged into the enemy's lines.

I spun the shield from my back and galloped to Olaf. As my friend knelt beside his battered wife, I dismounted and held my shield to his back. Olaf heaved Geira into the arms of Sveinn, who had remained on his mount.

"Get her to Plune!" Olaf shouted.

Sveinn hauled her onto his saddle, lowered his body over her, and raced back across the field. Arrows streaked past him, though none found their mark. I turned to face the Danes and the first man in my vision. He was more lad than man, really. Wounded as he was, he could barely hold his spear, but my bloodlust was upon me, and so too was my anger. I stepped inside his feeble spear thrust and hewed into his young frame.

The man behind him saw his friend's body severed and lost all nerve. He scurried for the trees, and I gave no chase. Instead, I charged the archers who were still targeting our men. One loosed an arrow at me, which I blocked with my shield. The man turned to run, but I opened a deep gash in his back, then thrust my sword into the whoreson's spine as he hit the muddy turf.

I spun quickly to check for other Danes but found none. If they were not already dead, they were retreating into the shadows of the forest. I moved to the captives, but I need not have. They all had been tied to trees and now leaned lifelessly against their ropes, their throats slit, their soiled hair falling about their faces. And as their blood drained from their wounds, so also did the vigor from my veins. In its place rose a vast weariness. A sickness, really, for the loss of innocents. It was one thing to kill a person threatening you with a blade. It was another to kill a man, woman, or child who posed no threat. I had seen enough of it to fill a thousand lifetimes.

I turned to Berse. "We will bury the Wagrians here and take our wounded or slain back to Plune. Leave the Danes for the wolves." And because I could not resist, I added, "Let us hope she and the child survive this fool's errand."

2

The rain had returned by the time we reached Plune. Heads downturned and bodies steaming, our weary steeds clattered across the wood-planked bridge toward the fortress, which sat on a small island in a large lake not far from Saxland's northeastern border. High timbered walls encircled the entire island, which one could only reach by boat or the long, narrow bridge we now crossed in single file. On the shore behind us was a small Slavic settlement, which was also called Plune. In times of trouble, the people of the settlement could retreat to the island and find refuge behind its palisade. It was a fascinating place and had everything we might need — a royal hall, barracks, a smithy, storage and food sheds, a barn, servants' quarters — but despite that, I liked it not. Though it was protected by high walls, I felt exposed in that island outpost and cramped within its confines.

The borg's guards and citizens bowed as we appeared in the puddled courtyard, but Olaf did not notice. His mind, I knew, had paced ahead of him. He kicked his mount into a trot and climbed from the beast's back before it had stopped. Then he ran the last few steps to his hall and pushed past the young maidservant who was exiting. Had he stopped to greet her, he might have seen in her hand a bucket filled with bloody water.

I glanced at Sveinn, who stood on the hall's porch, his eyes on his feet. I then looked at Berse, who rode beside me. His stony face studied the scene from beneath his sodden shags of hair. He then glanced at me, and in that gaze, I saw my own fears, which angered me all the more. It need not have been like this.

"See to the horses, Berse, and the men," I snarled at him.

I turned to the lass, who had just stepped into the muddy yard. "What word of Princess Geira?"

The young woman gazed up at me, shook her head, then hauled her bucket away. Its rocking splashed crimson waves upon the puddled courtyard.

I climbed from my mount and strode into Olaf's hall, passing Sveinn without a word. What I found in the gloom of that place gave me pause. Outside the door to Olaf's bedchamber, behind the veil of wavering firelight and floating dust mites knelt three tonsured monks, their heads bowed, their murmured prayers blending with the footfalls of busy maidservants and the crackle of the hearth fire.

When the Danes invaded Saxland and Wagria two summers before, Prince Burislaf and his Wagrians — with Olaf's aid, of course — helped the Saxons drive the Danes back beyond the Danavirki. This was their reward for that alliance: more Christian monks in Burislaf's realm and more pressure on the pagan prince and his people to convert. To their credit, the Slavic prince and his daughters clung staunchly to their faith and, when Saxon nobles weren't present, barred the monks from entering their royal halls. Which was why I found the sight of them now so odd.

I grabbed a passing woman by the arm and inquired again about the princess. Startled by my advance, the woman responded in stuttered fits. "Not well, lord. Her body is broken. We removed the arrow, but she continues to lose blood and strength. She is fighting, but..." The woman's eyes teared and she dropped her head.

I let go of the woman's arm, and she fled. Then I wiped my face and sat on a nearby bench, my back to the warm hearth fire and elbows upon my knees. I let my thoughts float to Olaf. He was no stranger to women. Large, small, fat, thin, ugly, attractive, he lay with them all. They were a conquest for him, and he had always enjoyed the challenge they presented. But Geira was different. He loved her. Since his betrothal to her several winters before, he'd had eyes only for her. She was his match in wit and intellect and speech, and as bold as her father on the field. Too bold. Now she was fighting a different sort of battle — one for her life and that of her child — and I worried for her loss and its effect on my friend.

I thought to go to Olaf to console him and quickly cast the thought aside. He would want to be alone with her. Besides, words did not come easily to me and I feared saying the wrong thing. But even if I could find the right platitudes for the moment, I knew my words would be hollow, and so too would Olaf. My friend knew of my harbored resentment and would see through my lies of concern.

I then thought to go to the men, but they would require news and I had none to offer. And so I did the only thing I could think to do: I sat and waited. I thought to pray, but I knew the gods could do little to change the weave of someone's fate. Those callous bitches we called the Norns wove our destinies at our birth, and there was nothing a person, or god, could do to stay their hands. If they had already woven Geira's death for here and now, she was doomed.

Olaf emerged from the chamber, interrupting my reflections. But rather than move to the hearth as I thought he might, he stopped to gaze upon the monks. So lost were they in prayer, they did not notice him until he grabbed two of them by their cowls and hauled them to their feet.

"Enough of your curses. Out!" he roared as he lifted each into the air and walked them to the hall's door.

"Unhand us," yelled one of the monks.

"What is this?" called the third monk, who had risen to his feet and scurried after Olaf. "We pray for the princess. Can you not see?"

"And now you will pray elsewhere," called Olaf over his shoulder. "All of you." He nudged open the door with his boot and tossed the befuddled monks out onto the porch.

"The prince will hear about this indignity!" growled the third monk. "You can be sure of it."

Olaf bared his teeth in what might have been a smile, were his eyes not so menacing. "Out! Or I will cut off your balls and feed them to the hounds." His hand moved to the hilt of his seax.

The protesting monk blanched and clamped his lips shut, then ushered his companions from the doorway.

Olaf slammed the door after them, then came over to me and sank his long limbs onto the bench. It creaked in protest under his muscular frame. "Bastards," he spat.

"How fares Geira?" I asked abruptly, yet softly. I knew the answer, of course, but I wanted to shift his mind back to what mattered most.

The lines etched on his face spoke more clearly than any words he might have uttered.

"I am sorry," I said. The words came easier than I thought they might.

He turned away.

"Mayhap now that the monks are gone, we will see some improvement in Geira."

Olaf swiveled his head to look at me, and in his blue eyes, I saw the grief that had settled upon him. "Mayhap," he said distantly, then turned his eyes back to the dark hall and rubbed his face. "Mayhap."

Through the afternoon and into the night, we waited. Maidservants came and went. Some brought us food and ale. Others stole glances at their sorry lord as they hauled their buckets and rags hither and yon. Olaf sat, then paced, then sat again. I added wood to the hearth and coaxed it into a flame. I whittled, and for a time, I closed my eyes to nap. Anything to keep my eyes off my friend and his woman. The other warriors of Olaf's hird wisely stayed away.

At some point, I awoke to the sound of whispers. The hall was dark save for the orange glow of the hearth. My eyes traveled the shadows to the door of the bedchamber, where Olaf conversed with Brana, the head of Geira's maidservants. I saw her shaking her head. I saw Olaf's own head bow. Brana laid a brief but gentle hand on Olaf's arm, then retreated back into the room.

Olaf shuffled to a nearby bench and collapsed. He bent his head and buried his face in his hands, his hulking form shaking in silent sobs. My own eyes filled with tears. Not because the loss of Geira touched me that deeply — it did not — but because my friend's grief tore at my own emotions. And so, together and in silence, we cried.

And then, suddenly, he rose and stormed from the hall, moving with a purpose that bespoke of violence.

"Olaf," I called to him, but he either did not hear me or chose not to react.

As the hall's door slammed behind him, my mind flew to the monks, and I instantly understood. They had cursed Geira with their prayers, and now the sorry bastards would feel the pain of Olaf's wrath. I thought to give Olaf chase but restrained myself. What did I care if he hurt the Christian fools?

But I was wrong.

We found Oskar hanging from the walls of Plune in the morning, a raven pecking at the soft tissue of his eyes. As I stared at his dangling body, I wondered if he had missed the signs of his own demise as horribly as he had missed Geira's.

I turned to Berse, who stood to my right, gawking at the corpse. "It's a good thing you don't cast lots." I spat in the mud and stalked away.

3

Prince Burislaf and his family buried Geira in a grove of old oak trees that stood to the south of Wagria's main town, Starigard. The town's citizens often gathered beneath these ancient limbs, carving messages in the bark or leaving tokens at the roots as offerings to the Slavic gods. Under the mantle of one particularly large oak lay the graves of Burislaf's grandsires and sires. And now, sadly, it shielded the remains of his eldest daughter.

The funeral was a somber affair, made all the gloomier by the incessant rain that pattered on the leaves overhead. Though the oaks protected us somewhat from the downpour, thick drops still tapped upon our hooded heads and collected in puddles around our boots. It was not all bad, though. It did mute the howls of the Slavic holy man who prayed over Geira's grave, though it did little to erase from my sight the congregation of Christian priests huddled nearby.

In addition to his governors and supporters, the gathering included those of Prince Burislaf's kin who yet lived in Wagria. There were not many. The prince's two remaining daughters now lived with their husbands, Jarl Sigvald of Jomsborg and King Harald of Denmark, respectively — the former to win the support of the notorious warriors and the latter as an arrangement to keep the peace with Wagria's former enemy. That left only the prince's wife and a smattering of uncles and cousins who were governors and representatives of nearby Slavic tribes.

Olaf was there, of course, though he stood on the outskirts of the gathering. It was a clear rebuke of the man who had so recently been Burislaf's son-in-law. The Northman had co-ruled the western region of Wagria with Geira, and the expectation had been that their son would eventually rule all of Wagria after Burislaf. Many of the governors had resented that. After all, Olaf was a Northman and the Wagrians had suffered mightily at the hands of his kind. To his credit, Burislaf had seen past that. But Geira's death at the hands of Danish raiders had changed things. Olaf had failed to protect her and had failed to give Burislaf a direct heir. Just what would befall the throne now, and what would befall Olaf for his failure, was anyone's guess, though Olaf's physical location at this funeral was a clear indication that he stood on perilous ground.

My mind meandered over these thoughts as the Slavic holy man droned on. Behind me stood the remainder of Olaf's wolves. Out of respect for Olaf, they held their tongues. It was one of the few times I had ever heard them so devoid of improprieties. I had become so used to living with their quips and squabbles and verbal flatulence that their silence made me uneasy.

Off to our right, the hooded monks frowned and clutched their crosses, perchance to shield them from the wickedness that lingered under that oak. The thought of a Slavic spirit attaching itself to one of those priests made me grin. I wondered if they perceived it as a blemish. A smudge of dirt that attached to the skin. I had heard that Christians, unlike Northmen, rarely washed. Mayhap this ceremony would force them to scrub themselves. I hoped so. They stank.

When the service finally ended, we shuffled back to the high earthen walls of Starigard, past the town's heavy gates, and into a fenced estate that belonged to Burislaf. The town's citizens lined the walls and muddy streets, watching us pass. Some cried, for Geira had been a popular princess. Others called out condolences to the prince. I glanced at Olaf, wondering how he was taking the attention, but I could not see his face under his hood.

Within the walls of Burislaf's halls, we found fire and food and ale to warm us, though we found little cheer. Instead, the cavernous space thrummed with hushed whispers and muted conversations, creaking benches, and shuffling footfalls as guests seated themselves. I sat beside Sveinn. Beside him sat many of the veterans of Olaf's hird — Berse, Orm, Ulf, Dragomir — as well as the twelve Slavic Wagrians who had once served Geira.

"When I die, you'd best celebrate with cheer, or I will haunt you," Sveinn whispered. "I want cups hoisted and laughter and song. None of this silence." I marked the irony in his words, for he was a quiet man, known more for whittling by himself than for boisterous merriment.

"Worry not," said the young Dane, Ulf, through his smirk. "We will all be glad when you die."

The table erupted with laughter, drawing the reproachful eyes of the other guests. Our mirth died quickly.

"Damned Slavs," grumbled Orm. "About as fun as mud."

"Hey now!" said Dragomir, a young, blond-haired man whose mother was an eastern Slav but whose father was a Swede. Several summers ago, he had shaved his head and his chin, leaving only a thick mustache to warm his face. He said it was to honor his Varangian roots, for his father had been a member of that elite class of Rus warriors. "I am a Slav."

Orm snorted. "You are only half Slav, Dragomir, which makes you half fun."

Dragomir picked up a crumb and tossed it at Orm, who deftly knocked it away.

I might have smiled at the men's banter had my mind not been on Olaf, who sat somberly at the end of the head table on the dais. In truth, I worried for my friend. It was not like him to keep silent and look so grim. He was a man of emotion and action, be it cheer or anger or speech. Rarely had I seen him sit so hunched and morose, as if dazed by life. Even as Burislaf rose to speak, Olaf barely moved. Barely blinked.

"Welcome, my dear guests," called the prince to the silent room. "My wife and I thank you all for coming." He cleared his throat and shifted his stance. "It is not easy to lose a child."

At that moment, my mind turned to my own young daughter, who grew in the household of my former wife. Though I had seen her but once in my life, the thought of that girl's innocent face turning cold in death left a lump in my throat.

"As you all know, Geira was a woman of intellect and wit and cheer. She was as a flame is to a dark room." The prince breathed deeply, then forced a smile to his lips. "She would not be comfortable with so many downturned faces. So let us hoist our cups," he lifted his silver goblet to the room, inviting his guests to lift theirs to him, "and celebrate the woman whose life brought cheer to us all. To Geira!"

I forced myself to lift my cup if only to appease Olaf, should he be watching.

"To Geira," we called back to the prince, then drank to the woman's memory.

The prince then motioned to the musicians standing in the shadows. "Let us have music. And food!"

"Thank the gods!" said Ulf as he filled his cup from the pitcher of ale on the table.

At the head table, Olaf rose and excused himself. The guests did not notice his departure, but I did. I followed him out into the yard.

I did not expect him to go far, but I was wrong. He pulled his hood over his head and exited the prince's estate. I thought he might head for the town's walls, but my hunch failed me again. Instead, he exited the town's gates and stalked toward the oak grove south of the town, back to Geira's grave site. And there he stood for a long time, looking down.

I watched him from a safe distance, giving my friend the space and privacy he needed to mourn. Though in truth, I was torn. Olaf was a skilled fighter and was known to the townspeople. I doubted he had much to fear from them. But to thieves, he was a target. A man with a heavy purse. To Burislaf's enemies, he carried something more: the prince's favor, waning though it might be. As his protector, I was beholden to my oath, and so I stood near my friend, feeling foolish for doing so, yet knowing I should.

After a time, he ran his sleeve across his eyes, then turned to leave. He stopped, though, when he saw me. "What is it you want, Torgil?"

I stood my ground. "It is not wise for a prince to be out here alone."

He snorted and swept past me, and I let him go because I knew not what to say to stop him or to make him feel any better.

4

I swiped at a bead of sweat as it ran down my cheek. Despite the chill outside, it was warm in Burislaf's hall, and the heat was annoying me. So too was the drone of voices.

I glanced once more at the dais, where Burislaf's wooden throne sat empty.

I was not here by choice. I was here to guard my friend Olaf, who sat mutely beside the other governors of the prince's realm. Olaf was normally easy in nature and glad with speech, but not here. Not now. Here, he no longer had friends. Though he had done the realm a great service protecting its borders and turning aside the threat of the Danes, the governors had never fully embraced the Northman as Burislaf had. And now that he had lost the prince's favor, there was no telling what they might say or do.

There was another reason for Olaf's silence. I knew my friend as I knew myself, and his stillness told me that he mourned Geira greatly. For him, sitting among these chattering men who had no such relationship with Geira must have grated on his nerves. It certainly grated on mine.

There were eight governors, all of them responsible for some small slice of Wagria's small realm, and all of them kin to Burislaf through blood or marriage. The prince had no brothers, and so his closest relatives were two uncles, both with sons of their own who stood, like me, in the shadows. Olaf had never officially been given the title, nor had his wife, though she had ruled Plune and the area around it in Burislaf's name and had been welcome at these councils. It was why Olaf now sat in her place.

The prince came soon enough, dressed in finery that bordered on ostentatious. Gold rings glistened on his fingers. Gold armbands encircled the forearms of his fine wool shirt. A gold band sat firmly on his brow, pressing his combed brown hair tightly to his head. He made a show of organizing his blue cloak before settling into his throne. But all of the finery did nothing to mask the prince's drawn features and the deep circles under his eyes.

The governors halted their prattle, and the mood turned dour. A servant scurried forth with a silver goblet, which he presented to the prince.

"Governors," Burislaf began as he hoisted the goblet. "My kin and friends. Thank you for coming. It is with a heavy heart that I gather you here, though such are the burdens of a prince and the requirements of a realm. I have heard your questions, both spoken and silent, and I know what is on your minds, now that my eldest daughter is dead and there is no child."

Olaf's head bowed at the prince's words, though in grief or shame, I cannot say. Had it been me, it would have been both. It did not help that all eyes shifted to my friend, some more blatant in their regard than others. The bastards were salivating at Olaf's decline.

"I am in no mood for pleasantries, so I will get straight to it. As you all know, my remaining daughters now live in Jomsborg and the Danelands, which leaves the throne of Wagria open should I die. Therefore, I have decided to make Slavomir," Prince Burislaf gestured to his oldest uncle, "my successor."

The reactions to his information were mixed. Most cheered the news and congratulated the graying governor with backslaps and calls of affirmation. Others held their tongues or grumbled something to their neighbor. I suppose I should have known that this would be the case. Every man has his plans and his ambitions. While the news of Slavomir's rise benefited some, it no doubt shifted the calculations of others.

As for me, I did not know Slavomir, save that he had joined us in our fight against the Danes and seemed capable enough. And for that, I held no malice toward him. His son Udo, however, was a different matter. He was a conniver and a coward — a man who had lived off the graces of his father while whoring and drinking and, if the stories were true, beating his wife. I had no patience for men of his ilk.

Burislaf held up a palm and waited patiently for order to return.

"Should Slavomir die before me and I die next, Slavomir's oldest son Udo will assume the throne."

I frowned. Others grumbled, for all knew the tales of his repugnant deeds.

"All here have heard my words. Will all here honor them? We will start with you, Slavomir," said Burislaf with a wry smile.

The older man grinned. "Aye! I will honor your words, lord. Christ as my witness."

Slavomir's reference to the Christ God startled me. If it rankled others, they did not show it. It spoke well for the future of the Christian faith in Wagria, which brought a frown to my face.

Burislaf nodded. "And you, Udo?"

Slavomir's son stepped from the shadows with his combed locks and clean tunic and bowed to his lord. "I will honor your word, lord. Christ as my witness." He then lifted the cross that hung from his neck and kissed it. It made me want to spit, but I held my tongue.

The ceremony went around the room until every nobleman, including Olaf, affirmed Burislaf's proclamations.

Burislaf then raised his goblet to the men. "So be it. As you have now sworn, I trust that every man present will take this ruling back to your people and spread the word. Now then, let us celebrate this new line of succession. Long live the Wagrian realm."

"Long live the Wagrians!" the men called in response and drank.

"What about him?"

All eyes turned to Udo, who had stepped once again from the shadows and was pointing at Olaf.

"What about me?" asked Olaf, his voice a low rumble. The hall fell silent.

"Udo," Slavomir grumbled. "Not now."

"No, now," Olaf interjected. "I would hear Udo's words. Please, continue."

Udo paused, his dark eyes shifting about him as the room tensed. On the throne, Burislaf frowned. My heart quickened. But Udo was committed now and so he straightened, set his jaw, and spoke.

"It is a question all of us have asked, yet it appears that only I am bold enough to speak it aloud. He," he pointed at Olaf, "rules Plune and the lands around it. But that fort and those lands do not belong in a Northman's hands."

"Says the man whose lands abut mine," called Olaf. "Tell me, Udo: is it all Northmen you disdain, or me in particular?"

Udo's cheeks reddened as his eyes shifted. He did not like being challenged so publicly. "All Northmen, but you in particular. We have all heard the tales of how you slept your way to the head of a princess's household in the Eastlands. And here you sit again." Udo raised his arms to indicate the hall and, I think, the kingdom. "Sleeping your way to a slice of Wagria's realm. It seems your snake has more skill than your sword."

We had checked our weapons at the door. Had I my axe to hand, I would have split that bastard's skull then and there for the insult. Olaf's hands went white as they gripped the arms of his chair, yet somehow, he restrained himself. "It is true. My prowess in bed is great. Alas, it is second only to my prowess on the field — the truth of which you have not experienced. I did not see you in the shield wall driving the Danes from your lands, like me and most men here. Like your father, even, though he is gray-haired. Mayhap you were too busy beating your wife instead, eh?"

The hall went still. But not Udo. He spat and cursed at Olaf, then stepped forward as if to challenge my friend. Between the two snapped a hearth fire. It was narrow enough to leap, but Udo held himself back. It was a shame — I would have enjoyed watching the whoreson burn.

Olaf did not bother to rise. Instead, he laughed and taunted Udo by raising his cup in a toast.

"Enough of this!" Burislaf bellowed. He was standing now, his gaunt face ablaze. "Udo, you will keep your lips tight. As will you, Olaf." He then reclaimed his seat and took his time organizing his finery. Reluctantly, Udo retreated.

"The lands that Olaf rules belonged to my daughter," Burislaf said with finality. "Through marriage, they now belong to Olaf. He might be a Northman, but he has earned his right to sit among you and to rule in my daughter's stead. And so he shall until I decide differently." His eyes moved to Udo. "Are my words clear?"

The council mumbled their consent. Udo gave a curt nod.

"Very well. We will adjourn until this evening and until our tempers settle." With that, Burislaf rose and in a sweep of his cloak, exited.

The governors stalked quietly from the hall. I noted that Slavomir had taken hold of his son's arm and was whispering emphatically to the young man as they exited. Olaf and I remained behind until the Slavs departed.

Together we reclaimed our weapons, then walked to the northern wall of Starigard. A light rain had dropped while we sat in Burislaf's hall, and this now splashed under our boots as we ascended the steps to the fighting platform above. As I stared out past the docks and dying landscape to the gloomy waters of the northern sea beyond, I felt the press of the graying world upon me. It felt devoid of life and warmth. Like a corpse, I thought.

Beside me, my friend rested his thick forearms on the parapet and sighed. A cloud of breath formed before his face, shrouding it. "Bleak," he said after a time.

I looked at him, expecting more. But when he did not speak, I pressed him gently. "Bleak?"

"Aye. This whole cursed place. It has suddenly turned so damned bleak. One moon ago, my heart was full. I had a wife I loved. A child close at hand. Mayhap even an heir to this kingdom. And now what? Jealous Wagrian nobles. Danes harassing us. Saxons who send priests to convert us." He spat over the wall to show his disgust.

I grunted. "Bleak. It is a fitting word," I offered with a nod. I hated Wagria. I had always hated Wagria. Had fate not landed us here summers ago, I might yet be married to Turid and raising my child in the North. Instead, I sat here biding my time, a vassal to both Olaf and Burislaf, wealthy but wifeless.

I shifted the subject to a more comfortable topic. "So what now?"

He sighed. "I know not, Torgil. Truly. I know only that my future is no longer here. I cannot live out my days as the unfavored former son-in-law of Burislaf, especially with the memory of Geira everywhere I turn and with the Wagrian lords always casting a wary glance in my direction. The kingdom is closed to me now, and I am stuck."

Long ago, Olaf had told me that he believed the weavers of men's fates — the Norns — had woven a path of fame for his life. And then, with Oskar, he had found a way to confer with the gods. Mayhap all of that was still true, but it seemed different now. As if with Geira's death and Oskar's mistaken prophecy, Olaf had lost the trail of his life. Or, mayhap more accurately, he had lost the belief that he was yet blessed by the gods and fate. I had never seen him so, and it alarmed me. Of course, I could not say such things to him now, with his heart still heavy from the loss of Geira, and so I pressed him more delicately. "What, then?"

"I know not. Truly."

We stood in silence a bit longer, and then my eyes locked on the warship tied to one of the docks below us. Though of medium length, it was a sturdy ship and capable of taking us across any sea. "We could take *Sea Wolf* and head somewhere more favorable."

Olaf grunted. "East? Vladimir is there, drumming up support among the Jomsvikings and Swedes to contest his brothers in Gardariki. I could beg forgiveness and see if he would take us in."

The words turned my stomach and, frankly, surprised me. Olaf had never begged anyone for anything. To go back to Vladimir now felt like a whipped hound returning to his master for food. Vladimir, I knew, would just kick Olaf again, or worse, take his head with a sword. As his protector, I could not let that happen.

"I would strongly urge a different course than seeking out Vladimir," I said.

Olaf studied me through his right eye. "Where, then? West?" he guessed.

"West was not on my mind," I responded. "I know little of those lands. What about the North?"

"The North? Why?"

His reaction was warranted. The North presented its own difficulties. Its rulers were vassals of the Dane king, Harald Bluetooth, and we were no friends to the Danes. But just how much influence the Danes had in the land of our birth was difficult to say. The simple fact was that we needed a friendly haven in which to collect ourselves and plan our next steps, if only for a short spell. Though I had no great desire to see my former wife or her husband again, the truth was that Turid and Sigurd were family, and right now, we needed that support.

"To rest," I answered simply. "With your uncle."

Whether Olaf understood what I said is hard to say. He merely grunted and turned his eyes back to the landscape, his face shrouded yet again in the warm mist of his breath. "This will be twice now that we've sought the refuge of my uncle. Once as children, and now as men."

I held my tongue, for it was painful for me to admit that he was right. As painful as it was for him, I am sure.

"Do you think *Sea Wolf* could make it to Sigurd's estate?" asked my friend after a time. "She has not been to sea in a moon's time or more."

"Aye," I responded. "She's sturdy enough." I cast my gaze at the gray skies. "I worry more about the weather and the seas. Winter's cold will come soon enough. We will be stuck here then."

He turned and nodded. "Aye. You are right."

I nodded, feeling the first tinges of excitement in my gut. "Then let us make haste. Winter is nearly upon us. I will send the wolves to Plune under Berse's command and tell them to return with all they can carry on their horses' backs. Weapons, wealth, everything. We'll have *Sea Wolf* ready to sail as soon as the councils end."

"It may be night," said Olaf.

"Aye," I confirmed.

Olaf smirked, though it was not quite the grin I was used to. "We will sail at night into a winter sea?"

I nodded. "It is a risk, but if done right, we will slip away without anyone the wiser. Until it is too late."

Mist shot from Olaf's nose as he snorted. "Alright, then."

"Alright," I responded, then went to find the lads.

5

So crowded was the feast that I could not see into Burislaf's hall. That was where the nobles and their families sat, including Olaf. We warriors sat outside in a yard crowded with lowlier guests, servants, and whores. Children darted between the tables. Hounds gnawed on discarded bones. Several bonfires crackled and spat their sparks into the darkness. I sat open-eyed and vigilant at our table along with Sveinn, Berse, Orm, and Ulf — the longest serving and most trusted members of Olaf's hird. The others were already on *Sea Wolf*, readying her for departure. No one drank, save for water.

I glanced at Dragomir, who stood in the shadows, keeping watch on the feasting lords in the hall where Olaf sat. I had not liked Olaf going alone, but Burislaf had commanded it.

"My arse is getting sore," grumbled Orm as he picked his nose and flicked his prize into the darkness.

His mood was sour, and he had reason to be. They all did. They had made friends here. Some had women, and all had left behind the wealth they could not carry in their travel sacks. But they were Olaf's men, like me, and oath-bound to serve him wherever he went. Bitter or not, it was their duty to follow him, as it was mine. And so we watched and idled away the night until Olaf felt the time was right to take his leave.

A staggering drunkard bumped my shoulder and brought me back to the present. He mumbled an apology and slipped into the crowd.

"Gods," Ulf growled at Orm. "Dig any deeper and you'll poke your brain."

"Too late for that," Sveinn chimed in without looking up from his whittling. "The poor man can't remember half of his words."

It was true that Orm was quiet, but not because he was dim-witted. He was, in fact, a clever and highly observant fellow. He just preferred to keep his words to himself.

"Ignore the lads, Orm," I offered. "You just keep eating the jewels you're picking. Your brain will be fine."

The men let out a collective groan. All but Orm, that is. He smiled.

"You all should eat, men," I taunted the group, motioning to their half-eaten bowls of stew. "You'll need your strength tonight."

Only Orm did as I suggested.

The night moved on, and the feast slowly dissolved into debauchery. Here, a man puked next to his bench. There, a couple groped, oblivious to the revelers against whom they knocked. Men snored. Couples argued. Two warriors competed in a drinking bout as their comrades cheered them on. Off in the distance, a table burst into song. I glanced at Berse, who had taken Dragomir's place on watch. Still nothing.

Tiring of conversation, the men moved to more productive pursuits. Dragomir turned his attention to his seax blade, which he sharpened on a whetstone. Beside him, Sveinn whittled happily on a piece of wood he'd found near *Sea Wolf*. Ulf adjusted the rings on his belt while Orm worked the dirt out from under his fingernails with the point of his eating knife. I reminded myself that these were men accustomed to training and fighting, or to drinking and carousing when inactive. Mindlessly sitting was not something that came naturally to them.

I glanced back at Berse just as he pulled the hood of his cloak over his head. The signal.

"Come," I said to the men as I stood.

So as not to rouse suspicions, we took different paths to Berse, carrying our cups and staggering slightly in mock inebriation. By now, most guests slept. Those still awake drank on, though they were too ale-afflicted to notice our departure — or so I hoped. Seeing us coming, Berse slipped out of a side gate before we reached him. One by one, we followed.

Olaf met us in the shadows beside the Slavic temple that stood just outside of Burislaf's yard. "Come," he whispered and began to walk in the direction of the inner town.

"The ship is that way," I argued under my breath.

He held his finger to his lips and pointed at two swaying forms in the darkness. They were making their way to the smithy, which was on the opposite side of the anterior yard from where we now stood. With hand signals, Olaf motioned for the men to wait in the shadows, then beckoned me to follow him. I gave the men a confused look, shrugged, and followed Olaf into the darkness.

Sticking to the shadows of the wall, we inched toward the smithy, into which the shapes had disappeared. As we drew nearer, I heard them giggling, then shifting about. What this was about, I knew not, but it was too late to turn back. We were at the wall of the smithy now. Within, the giggles deepened toward heavier breaths, then pants, then groans. A man and a woman. A coupling in the darkness.

I sensed malice in Olaf's scheme, and it ignited my senses. My heart began to thump. My limbs tingled.

Olaf tapped me, drawing my attention back to the task. His silhouetted hand lifted. Moonlight danced along the blade of his seax. He pulled my hand axe from my belt and handed it to me. Then he drew his finger along his neck to explain his intent. My heartbeat quickened.

Quick as a cat, he moved into the smithy. I came behind him, hand axe ready. There was no door to kick in. No great space to cross. Not three paces away was a man with his bare ass facing us and the shins of the woman into which he thrust.

Olaf drove his blade up into the man, just below his ribs. The man arched and squeaked as the breath shot from his lungs. The woman lay on a worktable and rose to her elbows just as her lover fell away. I swung the blunt end of my axe at her temple, but in the darkness, I could not say if I hit the mark. All I could see was her head spin sideways, then her body fall in a lump onto its side. I hoped I had not killed her.

"Your axe," Olaf commanded in a gruff whisper.

I did not realize what Olaf intended with my axe until he held the grisly head of Udo before me, and I faltered at the shock of it. Then, I smiled. I knew my friend would not let Udo's slight go unanswered.

"Come," he commanded and moved from the smithy.

I cast one more glance at the girl, then followed.

Returning to the shadows where the men waited, Olaf lowered Udo's head into a sack, then ordered us to pair off. Near the town's north gate, we broke into an old Norse ballad, arms entwined and legs unsteady. Several hounds awoke with our voices and barked. We barked back, then cursed at them in the Northern tongue. The guards heard us coming and walked from the guardhouse with their torches. Recognizing Olaf, they stopped. If they saw the blood spattered on my friend's tunic, they said not a word. Perchance, in the darkness, they thought it merely remnants of the feast.

The older guard nodded at Olaf. "Lord," he said. "You know the rules about leaving so late. I must ask your business."

"I know the rules, but the feast has ended and I wish to celebrate longer with my crewmates. We go to my ship."

The guard peered at us all. Seemingly satisfied that we meant no harm, he motioned at his comrade. "Open the gate for Lord Olaf," he called.

We lavished our thanks upon the small garrison, then strolled out into the night with the old Norse tune on our lips.

By the time the guards discovered Udo's head upon a stake outside Starigard's walls, we were well on our way to the East Sea in our ship, free of Wagria at last.

6

We reached Sigurd's lands on a cloudy afternoon. It had not been an easy journey. *Sea Wolf* had fifteen oars to a side and we were only eighteen men, so each of us pulled nearly twice our weight. To make matters worse, the cold winds blew against us for much of the voyage, churning the sea and pushing gray waves against our hull. There were days when all we could do was sit in the lee of the wind in some hidden cove, or huddle beneath the tent we formed from our sail and wait for the weather to subside.

If there was any comfort to it all, it was that we encountered no Vikings. The raiding season had already ended, and most fighting men were home in their halls, enjoying the fruits of their aggression and the warmth of their hearths and women. Even the traders had vanished. I suppose we were the only half-wits to brave such wind and weather.

And so it was with great relief that we pulled into the small bay beneath Sigurd's hall and out of the chill wind that had been our companion on the sea. The guards at Sigurd's docks were young and unfamiliar to us, though it had only been one turn of the sun since our ship had last graced Sigurd's shore. As *Sea Wolf* glided to a halt, they challenged us with weapons drawn and shields high. I did not blame them. Even a small group of warriors could do damage, though we did not look as if we were ready to fight. We were hungry and weather-worn and, more than anything, needed to rest our bones in the welcome hall of kin, all of which Olaf explained as he called to the warriors on the wharf.

"Who are you that calls himself kin to our lord?"

"My name is Olaf Tryggvason. He knows me well."

The young man nodded to his young comrade, who ran up the hill behind the strand. The man then pointed at the water. "Drop your mooring stone there. We will see how well Lord Sigurd knows you."

Olaf could have bristled at the reply. After all, Sigurd was his uncle. But he did not. Instead, he motioned to Berse, who tossed the stone into the harbor and let it sink to the seabed. Almost at once, the crew erupted in giddy anticipation of the warm food and tasty ale that would soon hit their bellies.

I, on the other hand, ignored their words, for my thoughts were on the meeting that would soon take place. As I've already said, Turid had been my wife and Sigurd my former lord, and the prospect of seeing them again unnerved me. So too did the idea of seeing my daughter, Sigrunn, whom I had only met on one other occasion. Perchance because of them, I worked my way to the mast and to the barrel of drinking water so I might rinse my face and hair.

"Remember, Torgil," said Sveinn to me as I dipped my cupped hands into the water. "She is no longer your wife. You impress no one with a clean face."

I threw a harsh gaze at his smiling face. He had meant his comment in jest, but it bit a little closely to the bone. The last time — the only time — we had visited, both Turid and Sigurd had been pleasant to me, but cold. And Sigrunn had not known that I was her father. Turid had kept that truth from her. I frowned at the difficult memory. "Mind your own business, eh?" I growled at him. "Or better yet, why don't you join me? You smell like a lamb's arse."

He chuckled. "That is your own stench that has stuck to me."

I splashed him and turned back to the water, but my thoughts were now in tumult. I know not why Turid had chosen to hold the truth about me from Sigrunn. Mayhap it was to free me from my responsibility as a father. Or mayhap to spare her child the pain of my absence and possible death. Perchance it was just easier this way, with them both living under the roof of Sigurd. Whatever the reason, I could not see my child without feeling the burden of my failed attempts to support them. And so I dipped my hands in the water and splashed it over my hair in a small attempt to appear as a man of dignity and wealth.

The sky darkened around us, and as it did, the men reclaimed their seats and relaxed beneath blankets and cloaks. Conversations gave way to the splash of fish in the harbor and the call of gulls overhead. Only Olaf stood, his broad shoulders motionless near the prow as he watched the land. He had not spoken since our arrival, which for him was strange. The man liked to talk. Something, I knew, was troubling him. My thoughts flew back to his comments in Wagria about seeking refuge with Sigurd for the second time. Mayhap he felt that being here was too akin to failure, and he would not be wrong. He had been so close to ruling Wagria, but that dream had disintegrated.

"Here they come!" he suddenly called as he turned to us. "Grab your gear. Berse, pull in the stone."

I stood and gazed inland, where a procession of people had appeared with several oxcarts in tow. The last time we had visited, Sigurd had occupied the hall we could see from the water, but this time, he came from farther afield at the head of a small group that included Turid and others. There was a young girl by their side whom I knew to be Sigrunn. The sight of them together was as thrilling as it was painful, and I exhaled audibly to calm my nerves.

"Easy, Torgil," Sveinn whispered.

From the grin on his face, I could see that Sveinn enjoyed tormenting me with his jests, but I was in no mood for his teasing. It made me feel weak, which I liked not at all. "Keep your mouth shut," I growled at him as I grabbed my oar and we pulled *Sea Wolf* toward the dock.

Olaf disembarked first, followed by his crew. I waited to muster my courage, then with yet another audible exhale, stepped onto the dock to greet them.

"Be welcome, friends," called Sigurd as his smile stretched his ochre beard. "It is good to see you all again."

He greeted each man with hugs and warmth, but then he came to me. I had served him well in Gardariki for many summers, which is why his theft of my wife was all the more painful. He had not meant to cross me, I knew. He had thought me dead, and so he had offered his hand to a young mother he knew and respected. On the face of it, I understood. But beneath that objective understanding was the open wound that had not yet scarred. I suppose at some level he knew that, which was why there was no hug or warrior's wrist-grabbing welcome for me. There was only a face-to-face nod, which I suppose was appropriate, but awkward all the same.

"Welcome, Torgil," he said, as smile lines creased the corners of his blue eyes. Summers ago, his had been a warrior's face, lean and firm and etched with the responsibilities of one accustomed to leading and losing men. Now it bore the gentle curves of a more peaceful man, albeit one with scars. His body, too, had thickened, though it was hard to tell just how much, given the fur cloak that wrapped it. "I suppose it pains you to be here, and so soon after your last visit, but you are welcome all the same."

"It does," I admitted, "even though it was my idea to come."

He flinched at my words, then recovered. "Well then. I suppose I have you to thank for this reunion."

"I suppose you do," I responded flatly.

He nodded, then turned to greet Sveinn, leaving me face to face with Turid. Some found her freckled face and flame-colored hair unattractive, but I loved it. Just as I loved her eyes, which always put me in mind of mountain pools. How often as a youth had I seen those eyes look upon me with pleasure? But no longer. Now there was a hardness to them as she lifted her chin and gazed at me. I interpreted it as haughtiness, and it angered me. "It is good to see you, Torgil," she said as the fur of her coat fluttered over the line of her chin.

"Is it?" I asked. I could not help myself — the words slipped from my mouth before I could think to stop them.

She sighed, then indicated the girl beside her as if to deflect the discomfort of the conversation. "You remember Sigrunn, do you not?"

I looked down at the girl, and my breath caught in my throat. With her raven hair — my hair — and the blue eyes she'd inherited from her mother, I found her utterly striking. The last time we met, she bore her mother's freckles, but they had receded somewhat into her fair skin. From her neck hung a silver coin attached to a leather band, and my heart soared at the sight of it. "How could I forget?" I asked as I knelt to her. "It has not been long since I saw you last, but you have grown. I see you're wearing the necklace I gave you at our last meeting."

She blushed as her fingers moved to the necklace. "That was you?"

I nodded. "Aye."

She knew not what to say to that, so she just nodded. I smiled knowingly at her loss for words.

"The last time we met, you hid behind your mother's dress," I teased her. "Now, you stand boldly. I am impressed."

Her blue eyes narrowed, as if trying to discern whether I was serious. I thought to tussle her hair to show I merely jested and then stopped myself. I did not know if she would like that. I rose to meet Turid's face once more. Her features had softened and her shoulders lowered.

It was as if my interaction with our daughter had somehow allowed her to lower her defenses.

"Be welcome, Torgil," Turid said, more warmly this time, then moved on to greet the others.

I nodded to her, then headed for more friendly faces: Ulrik, Sigurd's indestructible second-in-command, and Bolek, who had joined Sigurd's hird after the death of his former lord at the battle of Drastar. My relationship to both men had been prickly at first but had grown into a trusting camaraderie — a friendship, even — and I greeted them fondly.

"Damn. I'd hoped we'd seen the last of you," Ulrik said to me with a grand smile that stretched the many scars upon his grizzled face. His snow-blond hair was receding, revealing two wild eyebrows I had not noticed before. "Gods, you stink," he grunted as he bear-hugged me, then stepped back as if stricken. "Gods, Torgil, you smell worse than a pen full of pigs. What have you been rolling in?"

"I told you," Sveinn quipped behind me.

I blushed. "And here I thought that was you, Ulrik."

He laughed and looked at Sveinn as he jerked a thumb toward me. "It's a wonder you didn't toss him overboard."

"You Northmen have no manners. Is that any way to treat a weary traveler?" interjected Bolek, who forced his way into our group and hugged me. "Did you miss me so much, Torgil, that you had to come back so soon?"

"That is exactly the reason we are here," I said through my chortle.

Sveinn reached over and grabbed the man's beard. "What is this thing growing from your chin, eh?" Long before, Bolek had followed the style of all Slavs: shaved cheeks, thick mustache, long brown hair. Now a thick beard fell from his face and rested on his burly chest. Like his hair, it was streaked with silver strands.

He glanced down at his facial hair. "That's a fine beard. Ulrik made me grow it. Little did he know just how fine it would look. Now he's jealous, of course."

Ulrik snorted. "Jealous of that mangy gray tuft?"

"Gray!" Bolek feigned chagrin. "Are you calling me old?"

Ulrik smiled. "Take no offense, Bolek. Age catches us all."

And so it did. Like them, I was growing older. By my reckoning, I was now in my thirtieth year. Though I had no gray in my hair, I could feel my aging wounds.

Bolek turned back to me. "It is good to see you, old friend." He patted my shoulder.

"And you, Bolek."

After loading the carts with our goods and sea chests, Sigurd and Turid led us up the track to their estate. When we passed the hall where they had originally lived, Olaf inquired about it.

"My father has gone on to the next life," Sigurd responded. "As his eldest son, I have taken over his farm. This hall we keep as a barracks for the men watching the bay. My estate lies farther inland."

"I see," said Olaf.

"So tell me, Nephew," Sigurd said as we continued our walk. "Why have you come? You are always welcome, of course, but I did not expect you so soon. Has something happened in Wagria?"

It took Olaf a moment to answer. "Aye, Uncle. It is a long tale, but the simple version is that there is no longer a place for me in that land."

Sigurd glanced at Olaf. "But your wife? What of her?"

"She is dead," Olaf mumbled.

Turid gasped. "That is horrid news."

"Horrid news, indeed," Sigurd added with a sad shake of his head. "I am sorry."

Turid touched Olaf's arm but said no more. There was nothing to say.

It was early evening by the time we reached the high wooden walls that marked Sigurd's estate. It was not so much an estate as it was a fort. A borg. And a new one at that. Even in the growing gloam, I could see, and smell, that the walls were new. Within them, we found several guest halls, barracks, a larger feast hall, a smithy, and a large barn. Beside the barn was a massive pen in which sheep and chickens and a few cows roamed. There was also a practice field complete with an archery range and wooden replicas of men.

"Are you expecting a fight?" Olaf asked his uncle as we entered.

"These are uncertain times, Olaf," replied Sigurd.

"Oh?" asked Olaf. "How so?"

Sigurd glanced over his shoulder at his nephew. "It seems we both have much to discuss. Rest and bathe, then come to me and we will discuss how things lie." He indicated the door of the guest hall we had just reached. "Please, enter and rest. I will have my thralls bring you water for bathing. The gods know you need it." He winked. "There is also a bathhouse, should you prefer that. Be welcome."

And with those weighty words ringing in my ears, my one-time lord departed with my former wife and child in tow.

7

"Come, Torgil," Olaf called to me as he shimmied into his tunic. I gazed at him from my cot. "Come where?" I asked.

"Sigurd has asked us to join him. Do you not remember?"

I scoffed. "He asked you to join him. I am perfectly comfortable where I am." Which was true. My skin was still tingling from the heat of the bathwater and the scrubbing the thrall woman had given me. My hair was combed and braided, a luxury I had not enjoyed since living among the Rus with Turid. I wore unsoiled clothes and, for the first time in days, I relaxed. But more than comfort was on my mind. I had no wish to attend a meeting with Sigurd. Though it had been my recommendation to come to his estate, I still resented the man and wished to speak with him as little as possible.

The other men looked from me to Olaf, who was now frowning. "That is not a request," he said to me.

With a snort, I hauled myself from my cot, wrapped a cloak over my shoulders, and left with Olaf.

"This was your suggestion," Olaf said to me as we walked to Sigurd's hall.

"Aye, but he is your kin," I spat back. "I want little to do with the man."

"You will need to cast your anger aside," Olaf replied. "As you said, we need his help. Besides, we are here through Yule."

I grunted, then forced a grand smile to my face as we approached the man standing on the porch of his smaller, private hall. Sigurd hailed us with a wave and beckoned us to follow him into his quarters. I sighed and fell in behind Olaf, keeping my silence as Sigurd escorted us to his eating table. To my left crackled a small hearth fire. Its warmth eased my tension, though it did not touch my sour thoughts.

A thrall brought us a pitcher of ale and three cups. Only after we had poured ourselves a measure and toasted to each other's health did Sigurd speak. "Be welcome, my old friends. Your faces have been missed."

I studied Sigurd, wondering if he truly meant what he said or if his words were meant for Olaf alone. Surely he felt as awkward in my presence as I felt in his.

Olaf's gaze shifted from his uncle to his cup. "Thank you for welcoming us into your home, Uncle."

Sigurd brought his cup down to the table. His face softened with an almost paternal concern. "How did Geira die, if I might ask?"

It took a long moment for Olaf to speak. "She was wounded in a skirmish against a Danish raiding party. She didn't recover."

Sigurd grunted. "She fought alongside you?"

Olaf nodded. "She was bold. Much like Turid."

Sigurd glanced briefly at me, and I did my best to keep my expression still. Thankfully, he detected nothing. "But surely her death did not lead to your appearance here. Were you not close to her father?"

"Was, aye. But not to his governors, who had their own eyes on his seat."

Sigurd nodded his understanding. "I am sorry. That is a bitter draught."

The condolence left Olaf bereft of words, and Sigurd let him have his time. I shifted on my seat, made all the more uncomfortable by the stretching silence.

"You will stay with us through Yule then?" Sigurd prompted delicately.

"Aye." Olaf pinched his lips together. "If you will have us that long."

Sigurd smirked. "And where else would you go with winter upon us?" he asked.

Olaf shrugged.

The fire popped, and I took a sip of ale. Olaf remained uncharacteristically quiet, and I did not feel much like talking. Sigurd looked from his nephew to me and back again. Seeing he would get no more words from us, he sighed. "I see that I will be asking the questions this night. Very well, come the spring, where will you go?"

Olaf shrugged again. "I have not yet decided. Part of that depends on what I learn here, from you."

"And what do you wish to know?"

"Earlier, you mentioned that things here have changed. How? Why?" Olaf asked.

Sigurd grunted. "Aye. When I came back from Gardariki, I expected peace in the North, and there is, but it is tenuous. It is better here than Gardariki with its civil war, mind, but there is a growing problem. Before coming here, I knew nothing of how much control the Danes had over our lands and our people. It is not overt. They do not come to harry our shores as they used to, but they don't need to. Instead, they rule through their lapdogs: namely, Hakon Jarl, who we call Sigge, who rules in the west, and your cousin, Harald Grenske, who rules in the east. The Danes let them have their power, and in exchange, they pay the Danes tribute or support them in war."

"Not so unlike the Rus and the Slavs," Olaf commented.

Sigurd nodded. "Maybe not that brutally or directly, but aye, like the Rus controlled the Slavs."

I remembered how the Rus treated the Slavic tribes they ruled and how we, the warriors of the noble class of Rus, came each winter to take what little they had for taxes. And how, if they could not pay, we stripped their villages of food and livestock, and of women and children. It was a bad business, that. "Surely it cannot be so bad," I remarked.

"No, it is not. But many fear it is headed in that direction," Sigurd said. "I fear it." He took a few gulps from his ale and poured more into his cup. "Each year, our taxes rise a little higher to fund Bluetooth's projects and army in the Danelands. And each year, Sigge and Harald Grenske build more ships and amass more power here in the North. As a people, we are being split. There are those who support the Danes and their lapdogs, and those who do not."

"But I thought you supported them," Olaf said. "It is why we saw you in their army at the Danavirki."

Several summers before, Sigurd had fought with the Danes, who had invaded Wagria and the Saxlands. We had found ourselves in the Wagrian army then, owing to Olaf's budding relationship with Princess Geira. It had been a bitter fight from which, thank the gods, we at this table had walked away. Many were not so lucky.

"Aye," Sigurd confirmed. "It is why we were there." His face turned stony. "It is the price we all must pay. You either serve the local kings or you stand against them."

Olaf grunted.

"And now they bring their damned priests to our lands…" Sigurd offered this last bit almost as an afterthought, but it was an important piece of the tale. A piece we knew about all too well.

Olaf latched onto it quickly and looked up from his cup. "We saw this in Wagria also, though the priests came from the Saxons. So what will people do?" he asked. "Will they fight Grenske and Sigge?"

"No," Sigurd said. "Not yet. But if Grenske and Sigge keep raising the taxes and foisting the holy men upon us, that day will come." Sigurd swirled his cup mindlessly, then backhanded the air before him. "Enough of that. Let us talk of better things, eh? The spring and your adventures. Will you head west?"

Olaf shrugged. "Mayhap."

"I have heard tell that Frisland may hold some opportunity, but you may want to practice your seamanship. It is tricky water, that. One day there is a channel, and the next day you run aground on a sandbar in the same spot.

"If not Frisland, then Saxland, England, Irland — they all hold opportunities, though they have their challenges. As I have not raided in some time, perchance one of my Yule guests can offer more news of those places."

"We may also need a place from which to operate," I interjected. "Do you know what has become of Olaf's family estates? Or of my father's borg on Jel Island?"

Sigurd's face turned serious again. "Forget about those. Harald Grenske has taken them, or he has given them to his loyalists. You could try to take one back, but Harald may not tolerate that. You could, of course, go to him and ask. Since you are kin, Olaf, he might make an exception, though I doubt it. He is a greedy bastard." Sigurd sighed loudly. "If he does stand against you in your request, you are free to return here after your raids until you find a place of your own."

Olaf was about to speak, but Sigurd cut him off. "Which reminds me… while I feel sorrow for your loss, Nephew — and I mean that — I offer you a roof and food because you are kin. And you, Torgil, are a friend, though you may not think of me as the same. But my home will come at the price of silver and work. You are many new mouths to feed, which I had not planned for. So I expect you to pay with your silver and to work around the estate. I expect you to prepare for the spring, and then I expect you to depart with your men. If you brood and lie abed, Olaf, I will cast you out. If you or one of your men, including you, Torgil, breaks my trust or abuses my kindness or my people, I will toss the lot of you out, winter or not. Are we in agreement?"

Sigurd's sudden change in demeanor brought me back to the days of Gardariki when I served in his hird and he was my lord. My response was habitual. "Aye, lord."

"Aye," echoed Olaf.

"Good," said Sigurd definitively.

"There is one more thing, Uncle," said Olaf.

"Oh?"

"We will need more men when we set sail."

Sigurd smiled. "I figured that already. You and I can speak with families during the Yule and send out word when spring comes. I am certain there will be plenty of eager young warriors looking to escape."

"We are indebted to you, again," said Olaf softly. "Thank you."

Sigurd held his tongue but raised his cup. We returned the salute, then drank.

The sound of laughter and the smell of fish drew the men to the feast hall later that night. Again, I was reluctant to go, but Sveinn reminded me that it was poor form to upset our hosts. And so again I pushed myself from my cot and joined them.

Unlike Sigurd's private quarters, the feast hall was cavernous and gloomy, despite the large hearth fire crackling in the center of the space. A dais sat on the far side of the hall and a row of tables stretched down either side. On the walls over the tables hung shields and tapestries that added some color to the otherwise wood-lined place.

"Come, men." Sigurd ushered us into the hall. "Grab a seat where you can, and enjoy some ale and bread. And please, introduce yourselves to these men." He motioned to his hird, who sat at the tables closest to the dais. "They will not bite. Not all of them, anyway." He laughed, then turned to Turid and Sigrunn and herded them to the long table set upon the dais.

I found a seat with Olaf, Ulrik, Sveinn, and Dragomir at the front of the hall, tore myself a chunk of bread, and smeared soft cheese upon it. Its rich taste brought to mind the mountain cabin where we had hidden as children on our long flight from my father's home. Back when Olaf was a small boy and I was not much older. The cabin had belonged to Sigurd's father and Olaf's maternal grandfather, Erik. I had a vague recollection of the man — short and bald and sour of nature. Nothing like his children. I remembered that he had not liked Olaf for some reason. It is funny, what certain tastes and smells can conjure in a man's memory.

"Sigurd has done well for himself since returning from Gardariki," I commented as I chewed.

"That he has," responded Ulrik after sipping his ale. "He attacks sheep-farming like he attacks his enemies." He made a fist and brandished it, though there was a smile on his face. "With vigor."

Olaf cocked his head. "Sheep? So now he's a sheep farmer? He did not tell us that."

"Oh, aye. And a damned good one at that. He grew up sheep-farming alongside your mother, Olaf. It is what they did."

At the table next to us, Ulf roared in delight at something. He was already well into his cups, no doubt.

"So you've replaced your swords with shears?" Olaf asked with a grin. "It is hard to imagine that."

"I see you smiling, Olaf," added Ulrik. "You will not be when you're knee-deep in sheep shit and entrails during the slaughter. Though I am certain Sigurd will appreciate your help."

With winter approaching, I would have thought that the slaughter had already happened, but Ulrik's comment confirmed that it had not. Olaf's smile melted to a frown.

Ulrik laughed at Olaf's expression. "It is not so bad as that, Olaf. You'll be fine."

Sveinn changed the subject. "Olaf tells us you fight for Harald Grenske when he has a need?" We had told the men of our conversation with Sigurd and of how things lay in the North.

Ulrik shrugged. "He rules Vest- and Ostfold, which includes Vingulmark. So if he needs us, we come. But we also raid by ourselves. The men get bored, see." Ulrik smiled, then drank. "Besides," he added, waving his cup around, "the Danes need their tribute, so we keep the silver flowing and the men happy."

"Sigurd mentioned that Bluetooth has projects that need funding. What are those?" Olaf asked.

Ulrik scratched at his old beard. "Ah, aye. Bluetooth is an industrious prick. He does not want to fall prey to the Saxons again. So he builds his forts. He fortifies his Danavirki. He improves his roads and grows his army. But his projects come at a price, eh? So we pay." Ulrik shrugged his big shoulders. "It is his right, I suppose, though no one likes it." He took a sip from his cup again.

"It also funds the priests that come to your shores," Dragomir interjected.

Ulrik frowned at him. "How's that?"

"It's the price the Danes — and Wagrians — paid for the Saxon victory. The Danes control you, see, but the Saxons control them." His eyes were intent and his face red. "Those taxes you pay are not just for the Danes and Bluetooth's projects. Much of that silver goes to their Saxon overlords, who in turn send much of that silver to their damned holy men. The Saxons do the same in Wagria. You are funding your own conversion, as the Wagrians are. It is madness." I had not known Dragomir felt so passionately about the subject or that he had even thought of such things, but I knew now. And so too did the whole hall.

Olaf placed a calming hand on the young man, then turned back to Ulrik, whose face was now a mask of disgust, though I sensed his displeasure was not with Dragomir but rather at the truth of the lad's words.

Just then, the thralls placed bowls of fish stew before us, and I took that moment to steal a glance at the dais. My eyes fell on Turid, who had stood and was taking a baby from a woman's arms. "Who is that?" I asked with an edge in my voice.

"The baby? That's their new child," Ulrik said.

I turned and frowned at him. "Whose new child?"

"Sigurd's and Turid's new child," Ulrik replied, speaking to me as if I were a dolt. "Astrid is her name. After your mother, Olaf."

"That is kind," said Olaf in a rough voice.

I looked at him and he at me, and in his face I saw his pain. I too felt a stab of pain, though the cause of mine was twofold. Like us, Olaf's mother, Astrid, had disappeared into slavery during our attempt to reach Sigurd in Gardariki. We had vowed to save her, but our duties among the Rus, and then in Wagria, had hindered that effort. Oh, we had inquired among traders, but no one had seen her or knew of her. It was a poor excuse. In truth, her rescue, if indeed she was still alive, needed our full attention, and thus far we had failed to give it. But my guilt for our failings did not come close to the pain I felt at seeing Turid's new child. The memory of my former wife was still too fresh for me, though it had been four winters since we'd separated. Mayhap there was part of me that still hoped we might reunite with Sigrunn as our child. The new babe had trampled that longing.

I looked back at the dais, but Turid was gone. So too was Sigrunn. Sigurd was still there, and he was eyeing me over the rim of his cup. Was it satisfaction I saw in his eyes? Pity? Or mayhap a warning? Perchance it was all of those. Or none. I grunted and looked away and, from that moment on, spoke not another word.

It was going to be a long winter.

8

As Ulrik promised, the slaughter of winter livestock began soon after our arrival. It was grueling work, but I did not mind it — it gave me something to do and kept my thoughts from Turid and Sigrunn, at least during the shortening days of the encroaching winter.

The slaughter was an affair that required the entire farm. Sigurd and his shepherds sorted the sheep between those unlucky beasts that would feed us for the winter and coming year and those to be returned to the fields and forests that lay inland from his estate. Once they'd been separated, the slaughter began, and not an ounce of the animal was spared. Each was stripped of its wool and butchered. The wool was washed and hung to dry so that it could be woven into clothing, used for blankets and other items, or sold as raw material to Harald Grenske or traders. The meat was consumed that day, or smoked and salted, or boiled and preserved in vats of sour whey. Offal and suet were made into sausages and blood pudding or stuffed into the stomach lining and cooked. Sheep heads, rams' testicles, udders, and jelly from the feet were all stored for later use. Often I had been the beneficiary of slaughter month, but never had I been elbows deep in the midst of it, especially one on the scale of Sigurd's operation.

Of course, it was not all about the sheep. To accompany the vegetables that had already been harvested in the fall, we slaughtered several of the weaker cows and some of the chickens. We also hunted in the woods before the deer disappeared for the winter. Fish we caught in the streams and waterways using traps and nets until winter's bitter cold and snow descended upon us and Sigurd and his holy man declared an end to slaughter month and a start to the Yule season.

We returned to the ships then and spent two hard days cleaning *Sea Wolf*'s deck and hauling her into one of Sigurd's three boathouses, where she and her sails could dry for the winter. When the snow fell in earnest and the days shortened, I spent much time in the guest hall, mending clothes and tending to my equipment, whittling with Sveinn, and practicing the pan flute, an instrument I had learned from an old comrade named Halfdan in Gardariki. I rolled dice with Dragomir and the others or played Hnefatafl with Orm, a strategic game that suited his quieter, more thoughtful demeanor. On warmer days, I made the men practice with me in the training yard. They complained, but I ignored them. I did not want them to merely grow fat and lazy on food and ale until spring came again.

As the Yule celebrations neared, Sigurd invited guests from the neighboring farms. Some were kin, such as his brothers Jostein and Thorkell, who were farmers and raiders like him. Though while Sigurd had gone off to fight in Gardariki, they, it seemed, had spent more time and energy in bed, for Jostein had ten children and Thorkell had eight. Others were friends and supporters of Sigurd, minor landowners who depended on their lord as much as he depended on them. They kept coming, family after family, and I wondered where Sigurd might house them all. He, of course, seemed nonplussed by their appearance, for he had invited them in the first place.

A day before the official Yule celebration began, we gathered in the feast hall for an evening meal and to celebrate the introduction of Sigurd's winter ale. With much fanfare, Sigurd's hirdmen hefted a barrel onto the dais, careful not to spill a drop of the fine liquid. The ale master then dipped a fine drinking horn into the barrel and passed it to the holy man for a blessing. Once done, Sigurd took the horn and drank deeply. His guests, including me, watched in rapt silence. Though I did not drink as much as my comrades, I found myself entranced by the spectacle of it all — so much so that when Sigurd pronounced the ale excellent, I jostled others to get my cup and groaned with contentment at its rich, earthy taste.

"I thought you did not drink," came a familiar voice from my side.

I turned to see Turid, her eyes full of amusement.

I felt the warmth rising in my cheeks. "I do not, normally. But this is a special occasion, is it not?"

"That it is," she conceded and lifted her cup to me. "Sköl."

It felt like a small peace offering, though I knew not if that was what Turid intended.

I returned the gesture. "Sköl."

I was about to say more when the doors of the hall swung open and a blast of cold air rushed past us. A couple entered with three young children and a wolflike hound beside them. All were bundled in layers of clothing, which they began to peel from their heads as soon as they entered. I stood close to the door and gazed with interest at the newcomers, not only for the oddity of the sight but because they were somehow familiar to me. Both were of middling years, with hard faces and deeply grooved skin. The man was fair to the point of whiteness. Snow white hair. White complexion. Light blue eyes. And the woman, who seemed slightly older than he, was rounder than her partner and slightly hunched, but in no way soft. More like a sharp-edged runestone, I thought. Her braided hair was blond with few signs of gray, as if her body had aged faster than her locks.

The woman lifted her chin at the people inspecting her. There was pride in the backward tilt of her head that jarred my memory. I stepped toward her, not yet trusting my eyes or my thoughts.

"Lady Astrid?"

Her eyes settled on me and for a moment, she did not speak. Then a grin appeared, softening her etched face. "Torgil," she declared softly and stretched a hand out to me, though it looked more like a claw with its misshapen fingers. I went to her and took it in my own. It was cold and bony, but wonderful nonetheless.

"Mother?" Olaf called from behind me.

I moved aside to let Olaf see for himself who stood near me.

"Mother!" he called and, in four long strides, he arrived to envelop her in his long arms. I laughed involuntarily, and my sight grew blurry with tears.

I turned to her partner as his name suddenly leaped to my mind. "Lodin, is it not?"

"It is," he said simply and nodded.

I was not the hugging type, but the moment overwhelmed me and I threw my arms about the man. He laughed and hugged me back. "How could this be?" I asked as I gaped at them. "The two of you? Here?" I looked at Astrid, who was wiping tears from her cheeks, then I hugged her, too.

Sigurd joined us then, and he threw his arms over our shoulders with a laugh. "Surprised?"

Our mouths fell open, but it was Olaf who finally spoke. "You knew?" he asked.

He nodded. "Of course! It has nearly killed us to keep our lips tight!"

Behind us, the other guests laughed, as if they too were in on the secret.

I gazed back at Turid, who was approaching. She was wiping tears from her face. Sigrunn walked with her, her eyes moving from her parents to us to the newcomers and back again.

"Sköl!" Ulrik thundered, and the guests returned his call with a thunder of their own.

"Sköl!" the guests replied.

We sat at a quiet table on the far end of Sigurd's hall, away from most of the revelers. The guests left us alone. They sensed the importance of the moment and let us have our peace.

As we made ourselves comfortable, I noted the stiffness with which Astrid shed her travel cloak. Long ago, she had been my foster sister — a pimple-faced, carefree girl who had ultimately grown into the beauty that had married Olaf's father. But the loss of her husband, the fears endured in our flight from the North, and the torture of thralldom had beaten her down into the hunching, middle-aged woman who now sat before us. It was sad, and yet it dawned on me that mayhap all of us — Olaf, Sigurd, Lodin, Turid, and certainly me — had also hardened with time.

"Come, children," called Astrid to her younglings with a wave of her crooked hand. "I would like you to meet your brother."

Three children appeared at the end of the table. All were fair of skin and hair, though none as pale as Lodin. "Our brother?" asked the tallest of the three, a boy whose age I guessed at roughly twelve.

"Aye," said Astrid with a wide grin. "This is Olaf. And this here is his lifelong friend, Torgil." She motioned to me. "And this," Astrid motioned to her boy, "is Thorkell, and his sisters Ingerid, who's in the middle, and Ingegerd, the youngest. Please greet your kin, children."

Each mumbled a sheepish greeting. Then Thorkell asked, "Can we be excused now?"

I laughed aloud, though judging from Astrid's stern gaze, I suppose I shouldn't have.

"Aye, you may go," said Lodin gently. "Though do not leave the hall, and be sure to get some food in your bellies."

"We will, Father," said Thorkell, who then turned to his sisters. "Come on." And they bolted away.

I watched them go with a smile on my lips, but Olaf's next words sucked the pleasure from the moment.

"We never came to find you," he said to his mother, his voice dripping with remorse. "We promised ourselves, Torgil and I, but we…"

"Shhh," Astrid reproached him delicately, then gripped Lodin's arm. "Rid yourself of that shame, Olaf. I am here, thanks to Lodin, and all is well."

"And how is that so?" I asked, as much to salve my curiosity as to wipe away the heaviness of the moment.

"Lodin found me in a market in the Estlands, much like Sigurd found you. It seems the Norns saw fit to weave some goodness into our lives after all."

I turned to Lodin. "Were you looking for her?"

"No," he replied, "but I remembered her from our journey together. How could I forget?" He winked at her.

"And how did you find yourself in the Estlands?" I asked. "You were not a sea trader."

"When I was young, no. But I eventually made enough silver to buy a ship, which had been my dream. I have been trading ever since."

It had been many winters since I had last seen Lodin. And though my recollection of him was hazy, I did remember that he was a loner and a man of few words. It struck me now that his strange looks may have been the cause of that, but I did not recall thinking that then. He had been a man of the forest and had taught me much about the ways of nature and about the dangers of men. It struck me now, as I took in the bands on his wrists and the quality of his clothes, that those attributes had served him well in life.

"And he's a good one," added Astrid proudly.

"Well, we thank you for saving my mother," Olaf said. "If there is ever anything I can do for you in return, you need only ask."

Lodin nodded his thanks. "I will ask, though we want for nothing."

Astrid reached across the table to grab Olaf's hand. "We have everything we need, Olaf. A home. Children. And now you. I am happy. We are happy." She glanced at her man.

Olaf smiled. "Then I am happy."

"Do you live close?" I asked to end the sentimental moment. It made me uncomfortable.

"Close enough," responded Astrid. "After we'd been living farther south, my brothers were kind enough to provide us with a plot of land closer to them, on the coast. That was last spring. We pay for it, of course, and one day it will be ours outright. And then yours." She smiled at that, and I saw then how bent her teeth had become. Thralldom had changed her, as it had changed us all. "But enough about us. Tell us of yourselves. I would hear everything. Of your time in the Gardariki. Of your time in Vendland." Her words came at Olaf like a flight of arrows on a battlefield. "Sigurd tells me you are married to a princess there. It makes me proud to hear such things. You follow your father's path, as I knew you would."

The mention of Geira found its mark. Olaf's face hardened, and he turned his eyes to his cup.

Astrid's jaw stiffened. "Has something happened? I apologize if I have presumed too much."

Olaf gathered himself and sighed. "I was married, but my wife died along with my unborn child. It is newly happened so there was no way you could know. I left because there was no longer a place for me there. Her father might have granted me her lands, but as a Northman, I could not achieve more. His council would never permit it."

Astrid's brows bent lower, and she reached across the table to touch her son's hand. A gesture of sympathy. "So what will you do now?" she asked delicately.

Olaf took a drink, then sleeved the excess ale from his lips. "You and Father once said that greatness is in my future. I suppose I will go to seek it."

I detected a trace of pride on Astrid's face as she nodded. Lodin grinned. It was clear that they both liked what they heard. But I did not. I had been part of Olaf's fame-seeking ways for too long and understood well the sacrifices it demanded from me and from others. Those sacrifices did not merit a smile, but rather conjured memories I would just as soon forget. And now, with Olaf's feelings standing on uneven ground, it felt doubly hard to find pleasure in the plan.

"You will need men and ships, I presume?" asked Lodin.

"Aye," said Olaf. "I have spoken to Sigurd."

"And what about you, Torgil?" asked Astrid.

I shrugged. "I made an oath to your previous husband, to my father, and to you that I would protect your son. I have kept that oath. And I will continue to do so for as long as Crowbone here will have me as his man." I winked at Olaf, trying hard to keep the conversation light despite my misgivings.

Astrid's brows arched. "Crowbone?"

I waved the question aside, even as Olaf frowned at me. "It is nothing. A foolish byname."

Astrid glanced at her son, then moved to her original thought. "You are a true and honorable friend, Torgil. As your father was to Olaf's. I thank you for that."

"Or a fool," I deflected with a snort of mirth. "I am not sure which. Mayhap the gods will tell me in the end."

Astrid and Lodin chuckled. Olaf, I noticed, did not. "Then, to your success," Astrid toasted her son. "And to yours, Torgil. Sköl!"

"To success," we responded and drank.

The toast made me uneasy, as did the words leading to it. I had tried to move past my feelings with humor, but underneath simmered a stew of thoughts and memories driven by all the talk of loyalty and greatness and honor and dreams to be achieved. Words Olaf had been fed his entire life, but words that neglected the corpses over which Olaf had and would tread to achieve the triumph of which Astrid spoke. None of it squared in my mind, so much so that it drove me to my feet. I suppose my move to flee was a bit too abrupt, for the others gawked at me in surprise.

"You will not stay?" asked Astrid.

"I will return later if I can," I said with an awkward smile as I tried to escape her gaze. "In the meantime, I am certain you all have much to discuss. Please, do not let my absence stop you."

I patted Olaf's shoulder and fled.

The days that followed were bittersweet, at least for me. It was painful to live so close to Turid and Sigrunn and feel the distance that had grown between us. I took pains to avoid them so I would not upset Sigurd, which was easy enough with Turid. As the estate's lady, she saw to the day-to-day operation of all that went on and was frequently on the move. Besides, I was still angry with her and had little desire to stoke my vexation.

It was different with Sigrunn though. I yearned to speak with her and to know more about her, but I did not understand where the boundary with her lay. I decided to be prudent and keep my distance, but doing so grated on my nerves as badly as any good blade being dragged slowly and improperly across a whetstone. My relationship with her took the form of stolen glances and offhand comments, many of which she did not understand. When we gathered in the feast hall each night for Yule, I watched her play and giggle with her friends and kin, or only nibble at her food despite her maidservant's futile attempts to get her to eat. But I rarely approached her, and never did she seek me out.

On the morning of Yule's main feast, I hurried from the guest hall at the sound of shrieks and screams, only to find a large group of children throwing snowballs from the previous night's storm. And there I stood, captivated by the children and their innocence and joy. In their midst was Sigrunn, whose long body and quick moves, even in the knee-deep snow, reminded me so much of her mother. As I watched the fun, I sensed someone near and turned to see Turid in the distance, observing me. She grinned and walked on, and I turned back to the children. And that was when the snowball struck.

It hit me square in the nose and exploded across my face. I was so surprised, I knew not how to react. For an instant my anger flared, but I quickly remembered who had thrown the projectile, and my ire turned to laughter. Another snowball hit me, this one on my side. I quickly grabbed some snow, formed a ball, and tossed it at the first victim I saw: a young boy. It hit him on the shoulder, and he screeched with delight. My retaliation, of course, could only mean one thing to the children: it was me against all twenty of them, and I did not stand a chance.

"Shield wall!" I shouted and tossed another snowball as four more struck me.

Men piled from our guest hall with shields in hand, thinking my call was serious. But when they saw what was afoot, they dropped their protection and grabbed for the snow. Sveinn, Ulf, Orm, and Dragomir joined the fight with laughter on their lips and not a care for their lives. The battle for snowy heights had begun!

I will say this about the children — they understood the strategy of circumvention. Rather than stand shoulder-to-shoulder as we did and take the blows, they feinted at our front, then wheeled about our flanks and attacked us from behind. And they were quick. I cast a ball at Sigrunn. Seeing it coming, she dropped to the snow. My poor attempt flew over her body. She came up with her arms in motion. I ducked her first snowball, but the second hit me right in the ear.

I staggered and fell to my knees, groaning, tongue out, feigning a death dance. I expected mercy, but the children had none to give. While the others circled my men, keeping them busy, Sigrunn and Astrid's son, Thorkell, ran in and tossed their remaining snowballs at both sides of my chest. In a cloud of exploding snow, I fell to the pillowy power and twitched in my final moments. The children giggled and turned on my men, who, one by one, collapsed beside me. It was a slaughter.

That night, Sigurd hosted the main Yule feast. To celebrate the eventual return of the sun, he honored the god of Yule, Odin, with a ram sacrifice, then sprinkled the sacrificial blood upon our upturned faces. He cast the Yule log into the fire and invited guests to make their boasts as it burned. Intoxicated by the Yule ale and the good spirits, I joined in the toasts and the cheer and realized with a start that I could not remember ever feeling such lightness within me. Whether it was the shadow of my abusive father, the horror of slavery, the bloodshed of Gardariki, or the forced entanglements of Wagria, I had always worn a cloak of hardship on my shoulders. And now, with Sigrunn happy and hale, with my body feeling less pain than I could ever remember, with Astrid alive and out of harm's way, and aye, with the ale coursing through my veins, I could think only of how grateful I was for this time.

Things were not perfect, mind. Turid was with Sigurd, and I was now an interloper. And Sigrunn believed she was their child. It all hurt, but I came to believe during my stay there that there was a certain sense to it. An order. I would soon leave again and for how long this time, I knew not. Mayhap forever. Unless Turid cast aside her children for a spear or I foreswore my oath to Olaf — both of which would never happen — then it was all for the best. Turid needed a husband and Sigrunn a father who was near — or at least nearer than I could ever be. And that realization, though it had taken many winters to reach, was like a festering wound finally healing. It was tender, aye, but it was healing.

Overwhelmed by the emotions and drink within me, I pulled my pan flute from the pouch on my belt and began to play with some others in the hall who had their own instruments to hand. After several summers of toying with the instrument, I had become pretty good at coaxing a song from its pipes. It was unlike me to do such a thing, but that night, I felt compelled, as if led by an unknown source that I let guide me. The guests sat and listened to our moody melodies or clapped as the pace picked up. Several couples danced, as did the parents and children. Turid and Sigrunn were among them, and my heart soared to see them.

When the music finally ended, I returned to my comrades and drank deeply of the ale to wet my parched throat. I then hoisted my cup with a grand flourish. The men eyed me as if I were an amusing foreigner in their midst, and I suppose I was — most had not seen me drunk. I cared not a whit what they thought.

"To the future!" I hollered at them over the merriment of the hall.

"To the future!" they responded, laughing.

9

Yule passed, the days lengthened, and the guests returned to their homes. With each departure, Sigurd reminded the family of Olaf's impending adventure and of the opportunity that awaited them, should they decide to go. Some of the younger men committed to Olaf before they left and promised to return in spring with their gear. If they did not commit, they promised to spread the word to their neighbors, their kin, and their friends. It was an encouraging start.

The last to leave were Astrid, Lodin, and their children. It was more emotional than I imagined it would be. Life was hard and times uncertain, and so was our future. We knew not when we would return or when we would see Astrid again, and that truth was a weight that sat upon us all. After an extended exchange and multiple farewells, Lodin patted our shoulders a final time, then helped his children into the crowded bed of his oxcart.

After swiping at tears, Astrid finally lifted her chin and said, "It is time to go." With a grunt, she climbed up into the seat beside her husband and called down at me, "Keep my son safe, Torgil."

"You can see he is larger than me. Mayhap he should be keeping me safe."

She grinned at me. "He may be bigger, but you are wiser."

"Hey!" Olaf interjected with a laugh. "What words are those from my own mother?"

Her smile faded. "As a lad, you needed to be reminded that you are a king's son. Do you remember? I meant it to lift your spirits in that cesspool of Estland. Now I say the same, but for a different reason. Men get drunk on their stature. It blinds them and makes them do foolish things. Do not let it, Olaf. See that he doesn't, Torgil."

I am not sure what prompted Astrid's words, but they could not have been more well-placed. As I have said, Olaf believed himself destined for great things. Gods-touched, if you will. I glanced at my friend, knowing he would not appreciate the advice, even if it had come from his mother. The scowl on his face confirmed my suspicions.

"Until we meet again," Astrid called, then turned her eyes to the gate as the oxcart rolled away.

"Well, that was sobering," I said in an attempt to lighten the mood.

Olaf snorted and stalked away. I grinned at his back. He had needed someone to tell him that for years, and who better to deliver the message than his mother?

After Astrid's departure, we turned our attention to the work of the farm and the future. We helped Sigurd's men breed the ewes, and on quieter days, Olaf and I trained the men when the weather permitted. At night, or when the storm clouds brought rain, we remained indoors, honed our gear, and mended our clothes. And we discussed our plans.

Yule had provided us with much input from others. Mayhap too much. Irland, Hjaltland, the Orkneyjar, the Sudreyjar, Daneland, Frisland, Saxland, Valland. Even Engla-lond, which men were now calling England. All were possible targets. All had their benefits and their dangers, especially for one ship, experienced warriors though we were. In the end, we settled for the west coast of Daneland, the northern portions of Saxland, and the northern islands of Frisland. We could expand from there, of course, but it seemed the best place to start. We could sail in and strike, then quickly make for the sea. Frisland also offered its maze of islands in which to shelter and hide. If we took on trade goods, Ribe was close. If we needed larger ports in which to harbor, Jorvik in England and Kaupang here in the Vik were options. As was Sigurd's estate, though I sensed Olaf wanted to taste success before he presented himself to Sigurd again. It was a conservative plan, which made it less appealing to Olaf, but the one most favored by the crew.

Our new recruits began to appear three full moons after Yule, and by the fourth moon, we had twenty-three. Many were as wide-eyed as the new lambs being born — the second and third sons of landholders who had few possibilities here in the North. Most knew us from Yule and came with friends they trusted and who could join them in this grand adventure.

The very first to arrive were two young lads. One was tall and lean, with long, straight hair the color of wheat pulled back into a ponytail. He reminded me of a young Sveinn. The other was a giant of a lad whose light, fluffy beard and soft body made him look like an over-grown pup. I recognized them from the Yule as the sons of Sigurd's brother Jostein.

"Gods," Dragomir grunted as he looked up from mending a missing link in his byrnie. "Is Crowbone taking on babes now?"

"Crowbone?" asked the lad.

"Olaf," Dragomir clarified.

"Ah. Well, he's twice the size of you," replied the lean lad as he jerked a thumb at the giant. "And my guess is, twice as strong."

"Oh, the boy has a tongue on him," laughed Ulf.

Dragomir grinned wolfishly. "We will see about that, boy."

"I am Finn," said the lad. "This is my brother Hauk." He nodded toward the lumbering giant, who lifted his big palm in greeting.

"We know," I said as I looked up from donning my boots. "You're Jostein's boys."

"Aye," responded Finn.

"Good to have you," I replied. "Find an empty cot, though I'll warn you now to stay clear of that fellow." I jerked my head at Orm. "He stinks up the place, especially at night."

"Can't help myself," said Orm. "It's all the good eating."

"Oh," I added, "and that bastard snores." I pointed at Berse, who glared back at me. I ignored him.

"Thanks for the advice," Finn said as he led his brother to some cots farther back in the hall.

Some saltier hands who had heard of our adventure also joined us — men who had been to sea a time or two but had no lord to serve at the moment. All were Northerners from Vingulmark, and all were in their prime, save for the last man to arrive, who was older than the rest. His arrival captured all of our attention — not for anything he said or did, but merely because of the gray in his brown beard, the long scar upon his cheek, and the nice sword strapped to his back.

We had been training with the new recruits in Sigurd's yard when the man walked through the gate. "What are you all gaping at?" he asked.

I stepped toward him. "You," I answered. "Are you here to join Olaf?"

"Is that the name of the lord seeking men?" he asked. His voice sounded as if he had gravel in his throat.

"That is the name of our lord. And aye, he is seeking men."

"Then I am in the right place, I suppose," he said.

I studied him a spell longer. He looked capable enough. Still, I sensed something was not quite right about the man. "Are you trouble?" I knew not what prompted me to ask that.

"Only to myself." He grinned. Owing to his scar, it was a lopsided affair and full of brown teeth. "Not to others. But I can fight, and I heard tell from one of your neighbors that there is a lord seeking men. And so I came."

"Fair enough," I said. "You can drop your sword and gear there." I gestured to the fence he had just come through. "What is your name and from where do you hail?" I asked when he had set his knapsack aside.

"My name is Ottar," he called, "and I hail from everywhere. Most recently Kaupang, but I ran into a little trouble there with Harald Grenske's men."

I cocked my head at him. "Are you an outlaw?"

He shook his head. "Nah. Just made poor decisions. Where do you want me?"

"Grab a practice sword. You can fight Berse there."

I called to Berse, who had been coaching one of the younger lads, and asked him to evaluate the newcomer with a quick match. Truth be told, I wanted to see if my appraisal was correct. Of course, if Ottar bested him it would not only help me appraise the newcomer, but also provide some good fodder with which to tease the arse-licker Berse. And so I watched carefully as the two picked up their practice weapons and shields and readied themselves for combat.

It began tamely enough, with each man testing the other's skills and reactions. I understood then that Ottar knew his way around a sword. But rather than stop the match, I let it go. Seeking now to end it quickly, Berse sped up his pace and attacked with energy, but Ottar repelled the assaults deftly and danced away from Berse to give himself room.

"Who is that?" came Olaf's voice at my ear.

"Calls himself Ottar. He just arrived," I answered without turning my eyes from the fight.

"He can fight," said Olaf.

Ottar launched into a series of thrusts and hacks that, combined with the swipes of his shield edge, drove Berse backward. It was an impressive display that I would not have let end. But Olaf had another mind. It was a shame. I would have been pleased to see Berse bested.

"Well done," he called and clapped. "Well done."

The two men dropped their blades and looked at Olaf.

"I am Olaf," my friend called to Ottar, who was wiping the sweat from his brow. "And you are welcome to join us."

Ottar nodded to Olaf. "Thank you, lord."

"It is good that you are here because the time of our departure is near." Olaf raised his arms to quell the sudden hum of voices.

"Shut your mouths, lads!" growled Orm, who completed his rebuke by blowing his nose on the wet ground.

"On the morrow, we will pull *Sea Wolf* from the boathouse and get her ready to sail. We will work in shifts. While half of you train, the other half will prepare the ship. And then we'll switch. If the gods are kind and our work is fruitful, we will be ready to go by the next moon. Are my words clear?"

"Aye, lord," the men called.

And so we began.

After hauling *Sea Wolf* from storage, I took half the men and Olaf took the other. Each morning after breaking our fast, we trained with sword, seax, spear, and axe. We trained in single combat and together in a shield wall. We trained until the sweat drenched our hair and stung our eyes, though that may also have been the rain, for it fell often that spring. I scrutinized their every movement as my father had done to me and smacked the men with a stick if I saw a mistake. Not hard, mind, but enough to make my point. Then I ran them through the move again, breaking it down into its various parts before asking the men to repeat it.

It was not long into our training that one lad threw his spear into the mud after I corrected him. Anund was a pimple-faced boy whose cheeks flushed as red as his hair when he was tired or annoyed. "What do the sheep care if my wrist twists right or left?" he asked me.

I cocked my head at the boy. "Sheep? Is that who you think we will be fighting, Anund?"

"We go a-viking, do we not? We appear, we steal, and we leave."

"Is that why you joined us? For sheep? Mayhap a little silver, if you are lucky?"

He scratched his short beard, confused now. "Aye," he answered tentatively.

His response received a few chuckles from the older men and those who had been with us in Wagria. I did not laugh, for it concerned me.

I turned to the onlookers. "Who here is of Anund's mind? That the chance of fighting is slim?"

A few other boys timidly raised their hands.

"Ah, lads." I shook my head as I tried to think of words to say. "That is only part of the tale, eh? We may steal a sheep or two, but you will find no silver at a poor farmer's hovel. For that, you need a church or a town. And there you will find men with weapons who want to keep their silver and who do not like Northmen. They will fight, and some of them will fight well." I lifted Anund's spear and handed it back to him. "And the more silver you find, Anund, the more silver you will want. Because silver buys you better weapons, and prettier women, and land on which to raise a family. Besides, no one writes poems about a man who steals sheep. But a man who earns riches can pay his skalds to write many poems." I stopped and looked at all of the men. "So, if any among you want only to steal a few sheep and do not have the stomach to kill men for their silver, leave now. There's no shame in it." I pointed to the gate, where I saw Olaf and his group congregating. They, too, listened to me. "That goes for you men also!" I called to them.

Anund blinked and looked back at the others. One lad dropped his spear and walked away. No one else moved. Nor, to my relief, did they chide the boy for his departure. There was no need. His shame was written on his downturned face and in his sagging shoulders.

"Come," I said to the remaining men. "Let us return to this on the morrow after we have toiled on the ship."

Work on *Sea Wolf* offered little reprieve from the strain of training. While not as physically demanding, pounding new pegs into holes, replacing boards, and mixing new caulking under the watchful eye of Sigurd's local shipwright could be monotonous, sticky, and dirty work. But I did not mind it, for it was a curiosity to the children, who came each day to watch us when their own chores were done. Sigrunn was especially inquisitive, so I often invited her to help me.

"Why do you do this?" she asked as I pried at a barnacle with a knife.

I looked down at her and smiled. "Would you want a barnacle stuck to you?"

She giggled. "No!"

"Ships are the same. The barnacles hurt the wood. And they also slow ships down." I patted the hull. "These ships are fast, and they don't like to be slowed down."

"What is Sveinn doing?" She pointed at my friend, who sat on a stump nearby, patiently carving pegs to replace those that had warped or been damaged. He had fashioned a wooden "hand" with an attached blade for carving. The blades could be replaced depending on the need, but it had still taken him many months to get used to it. By now, though, he was good at it.

"He is making pegs to replace those that are damaged. We take out the bad ones and put in the new."

"And what are they doing?"

"You ask many questions," I teased her as I cast my eyes on the boys passing a hemp rope, ell by ell, through their hands. With each ell, they would pull and yank and test it for weakness.

She frowned.

"I jest," I said. "They are examining the rope. We do not want our lines to snap at sea. That is dangerous."

I turned back to my barnacles because I did not know what else to say to a girl of four winters. She must have tired of me, too, because she suddenly stood and skipped away without a word of farewell. I smiled at her departing form.

At night we gathered in Sigurd's hall with his men and their families. Some nights, it was tame and quiet. Others were more unruly, but always there was food to eat and ale to drink. I was glad Sigurd had asked us to pay him, for we had the silver from our exploits in and around Wagria and the meals, while not extravagant, could not have been easy on his stores, especially after all this time and with our growing crew.

On the eve of our departure, we gathered yet again in the feast hall, our spirits high with the adventure so close. The men boasted of the things they would do and the fame they would earn. Sigurd and Turid made their rounds, wishing each man well in his exploits.

I avoided the attention, choosing instead to play on my pan flute. It was my escape from worries and discomfort, especially when the men grew rowdy and I had little inclination to drink. That evening, I fell into a tune I had been working on through the winter and had almost mastered. It reminded me of looking out over the windy sea when I was a small lad. Before I had fled my home. So engrossed was I in the song, I did not notice Sigrunn sidle up next to me to listen. Nor did I notice others watching me. When I finally did, I blushed at the unwanted attention.

"What song is that?" Sigrunn asked.

I shrugged. "Just something I play from time to time."

She smiled. "I liked it."

My heart skipped a beat, for I saw so much of her mother in that look. "Thank you," I said when I had recovered myself. "Would you like to try?"

She hesitated.

"There is nothing to fear." I held it out to her, and she took it in her small hands. "Here, blow in these holes."

She blew, and the pan flute screeched. I am certain it sounded the same when I first tried.

"The different holes make different sounds," I explained. "And when you understand what sound comes from each hole, you can start to make music."

She looked at me, then tried again, this time running her lips over each hole.

"Aye, that's it," I encouraged her.

Her grin widened.

I wished the moment could have lasted longer, but Olaf's booming voice interrupted our exchange. He was standing on a tabletop with his arms raised for silence.

"Would you like to keep it?" I asked her in a whisper.

She nodded shyly.

"Then, it is yours. Though the next time we meet, I will expect you to play me a song." I winked at her, and she blushed.

"While I am known to speak mayhap too much," Olaf called to the now-hushed crowd, "I have no words for the kindness and hospitality of our hosts. So instead of words, I have decided to present Sigurd and Turid with a gift." He bent and lifted what looked to be a board. "To you, Sigurd, I give a Hnefatafl set with a board and pieces meticulously carved by the talented hands of Sveinn." He handed the set carefully to Berse, who walked it to the dais, where Sigurd accepted it.

"And to you, Lady Turid, I give a silver brooch crafted in the Wagrian style. May you wear it like the noble you are." I swallowed hard, for it pained me to see it. Not because it was going to Turid, but because Olaf had planned to give it to Geira after the birth of his child. Olaf stepped down from the table and handed it to Turid.

He then grabbed his cup from the table and lifted it to our hosts. "May the gods reward you tenfold for your hospitality to each and every one of us. Sköl!"

"Sköl!" we shouted and the lord and lady of the hall smiled with the recognition.

Our departure from Sigurd's estate was harder than I expected it to be. There was the usual chaos of loading the ship with goods and oars and weapons and sea chests. That part of it, I expected. What I did not expect was the sadness. It hit me like a blind strike from an unseen foe. I was not prepared for the misting in my eyes while hugging Ulrik and Bolek and, aye, even Sigurd. Nor the tightness in my throat when Turid planted a small kiss on my cheek. Looking back now, I suppose it was the dismay of deep connections once again being torn apart, though at that moment, I found it confusing and embarrassing.

"May the gods keep you and that thick-headed friend of yours," Turid said with a nod at Olaf, then winced when her babe Astrid grabbed a few strands of her red hair and pulled.

I grinned and nodded. "The gods always keep Olaf, remember?" It was a poor attempt at humor to shield me from my sadness.

Turid grinned. I averted my eyes from her captivating face and knelt before the black-haired creature at Turid's side. "Remember what I said about the gift I gave you. The next time we meet, I wish to hear a song from you."

She nodded timidly, as if she sensed some import to our arrangement but did not quite know what to make of it.

"Good," I said and stood, but the moisture in Turid's eyes turned me away.

I did not look back. Instead I turned my attention to the men loading the ship and yelled at the two lads who spilled some fresh water from one of the barrels.

Nearby stood Sveinn, grinning at me. "Not what you expected, was it Torgil?"

I smirked. "Life never is, eh, Sveinn Oakfist?"

He laughed and lifted his wooden right hand. "So true, Torgil. Let us make the most of it then."

I grabbed him behind his neck and shook him gently. By my reckoning, I was nearly thirty summers in age, but after this Yule, I felt half that. I was sorry to leave Sigurd's estate behind, but I was ready for whatever may come. *So let it come,* I told myself, *and let me face it boldly.*

PART II

"Thou art a God too,
O Galilean!
And thus single-handed
Unto the combat,
Gauntlet or Gospel,
Here I defy thee!"

The Saga of King Olaf
Henry Wadsworth Longfellow

10

Dyflin, Irland, Spring, AD 983

A light rain had come in from the sea during the night and now tapped on our hooded heads like impatient fingers. Or perchance it was my own eagerness that I felt. I stood at the steer board of *Sea Wolf*, cold and achy after spending days on our ship. We were close now, and I wanted nothing more than to rid myself of the confines of the oblong deck.

In the murky distance sat the silhouette of the town known to us Northmen as Dyflin, though I had heard others call it Dubh linn. Our four other ships rowed beside mine. Beyond them, to the north, a spear of light broke through the clouds, illuminating a grassy hill bright and light — it seemed the thing of dreams. To the east of it glowed part of a rainbow. Despite my impatience, I smiled. In the Northern belief, rainbows were the bridge between the worlds of gods and men, and I wondered briefly if it was a sign from the world beyond. At the very least, it was a good omen and somewhat eased my reservations about leaving Frisland behind and traveling to this far-flung place.

It was our sixth spring since leaving the North for our life of raiding. Six springs of bloodshed and plunder. Six springs of a life without rules save to serve our lord Olaf and to fight. I had lost count of the number of settlements that had fallen prey to our blades. Early on, most had been quick strikes on farms that had cost us little and earned us less. A few sheep here. A few coins there. But what they did offer was experience, especially for the new men in our crew. Through those brief encounters, they learned what it was like to truly fight. But more importantly, they learned how to kill. It was a knowledge that cannot be taught in a practice yard, for no man knows if he is capable of slaying another until the moment comes.

We were lucky. The gods aided our raids by sowing strife in the kingdoms we targeted. A war that broke out between the king of the Saxons, Otto II, and Lothair of the Franks diverted attention and warriors from the coasts of those realms for three summers. In England, a boy king named Ethelred took the throne. His accession and the chaos that followed invited new attacks upon his shores. We benefited mightily from it all, and the size of our targets grew. Rather than single estates, we attacked villages and churches and even a few towns, and we found within them more plunder to trade in the Northern markets. We built a fort in the maze of Frisland islands and more ships to support our growing army. We celebrated our victories and mourned our fallen.

But each season also brought new challenges. The political strife in Frankland, Saxland, and England brought new raiders to the North Sea. Competition for plunder stiffened and led to fights between sea kings. The war between Lothair and Otto also ended, as did the ineptitude of Ethelred's jarls. What had been easy for the taking had now become more treacherous. Though our following had grown, we were by no means a powerful army. We avoided pitched battles as much as possible, though we could not avoid the downward pressure in prices the glut of trade goods brought to the markets of Ribe and Jorvik.

It became increasingly clear that we needed more lucrative means of earning profit. Which meant only one thing: thralls. Having been one myself, I abhorred the idea. Olaf was more amenable to the notion, though he too had been enslaved as a boy. Unlike me, he could cast aside his values if it meant more profits and more men. And so, by the fourth season, we added people to our booty. I did not capture thralls, though it is true my actions led to their enslavement. Nor did I take part in selling them or using them for my pleasure. But I did not refuse the profit they earned me. It is a feeble and murky distinction, I realize, but the only one I could find to make slaving more palatable.

As distasteful as it was, it proved to be the right move. The silver flowed more freely, which in turn brought more men to Olaf's banner. Men, I might add, from all over the known world. Northmen, Danes, Frisians, Swedes, Vends, Finns, and many other tribes besides. They were pagans mostly, though a few Christ-followers also walked among us. It mattered not to Olaf, so long as they were willing to fight for him and obey his commands. The men learned quickly to abide by his rules, for there was not a man among us who could best him in a fight. And believe me, men tried. In return for our obedience, Olaf showered rings, silver, weapons, and ale upon our heads, as any good lord should. I must admit, besides the unsavory capture and sale of people, life in Olaf's army was good.

Those who came were mostly transients. Men seeking silver in the army of a lord with battle luck. Most did not stay long. Some perished, like poor Anund, who had thought we would terrorize sheep and farmers only. Others quickly got their fill of killing and slaving and returned to their homes with their new-won silver. It was understandable. A life of raiding and adventure was not for every man. But for some, there were no options. Our home was by Olaf's side, bound by oaths to protect him with our lives. These were Olaf's hirdmen, his trusted inner circle led by those who had known him longest: Berse, Sveinn, Dragomir, Ulf, Orm, and of course, me. To that nucleus we added others who had shown their skill and their loyalty, but who had not yet sworn their lives to our lord. Men like Ottar, Finn, and Hauk.

Beyond them were nearly two hundred others under his command. Men who followed Olaf as long as his luck held and their purses filled with silver.

Yet Olaf remained restless. He had earned wealth and grown a sizable army, but he wanted more. A realm of his own. Fame and glory. Skalds to sing his praises. Men to fear his name. But to get it, he needed more swords and spears to follow his banner. And that took silver. Which is why he had turned a blind eye to slaving, and why I now stood at the steer board of *Sea Wolf* and gazed at Dyflin in the early spring morning.

Here, according to many traders in the Northern markets, a new king named Iron Knee — one with the blood of Northmen in his veins — sat upon the Dyflin High Seat. His reign was new and tenuous and therefore, Olaf reasoned, vulnerable. Perchance, he exclaimed to us, the new king needed men. And if so, he might pay good silver to have them. I, of course, was not so optimistic. Long before, Olaf had listened to the divinations of his seid-man, Oskar, and that had led to tragedy. I knew not how the rumors of drunken traders in Jorvik could be any better. It all felt wrong and hasty.

As we drew closer, Dyflin took form before my eyes. The town rested on a bulb of land formed by the bay into which we sailed and a river that broke off to the south, on the eastern side of the walls. There was a large harbor before us, with a number of fishing skiffs and trading vessels bobbing beside the docks. Beyond a narrow beach rose a tall, sloping earthwork rampart with a wooden parapet set upon it. I could see little of the town itself save for myriad gray tendrils of smoke rising from countless smoke holes, but I guessed from those alone that the place must be large. Here on what to me seemed the edge of the known world, I had expected a small cesspool of a settlement, not a town nearly as large as Hedeby in the Danelands, and I gazed upon it in slacked-jawed surprise.

Near the mast, Ottar coughed beneath the furs we had laid upon him. I stared with pity upon the fellow. For several moons now, his body had withered and his stomach had grown. Not in the normal sense, mind, but in the way an animal's belly extends after eating too large a meal. His skin had taken on a sallow, waxy gleam and his lungs, a raspy cough. We had taken him to healers and all of them had said the same: he had the wasting disease, and there was nothing they could do for him save give him a bag of leaves to boil into a painkilling tea. But Ottar refused to lie down and die, and so he had come to Dyflin. We, of course, had obliged. In truth, I had expected the man to die on the sea, but the tough old bastard had proved me wrong.

A war horn blared its welcome as our small fleet slid into the harbor. A small troop of guards awaited us on a short dock. They were a wild-looking bunch. Some had long, disheveled hair matted by the rain. Others were bald. All wore mustaches of varying lengths. Woolen breeks covered some legs. Others wore no breeks at all. Some carried smaller, circular shields and long spears, but I saw, too, the larger shields of Northmen. Were it not for the long, patchworked tunics that each wore, I might have said the group consisted of many different peoples.

"Oars up!" I shouted at the crew.

Our ship glided to a halt beside the others. Only Olaf's ship rowed to the dock. There, after much talking and hand-waving at the warriors, he hailed us from his ship and we rowed to the wharf. The Dyflin guards departed.

"What now?" I asked Olaf as the helmsmen gathered at his ship.

"It seems the king is busy," Olaf explained to us. "So we wait."

"For how long?" grumbled Orm.

Olaf shrugged and examined the mold growing on a chunk of bread. "As long as it takes. He is a king." Olaf tossed the morsel into the harbor. "Let's use the time to find some fresh food and ale. Torgil, pick some men and come with me. The others will wait."

"Barrels of ale," called Ulf. "I have a mighty thirst."

Olaf patted his shoulder with a laugh. "Aye, Ulf. We cannot have you thirsty."

"What about Ottar?" I asked.

Olaf glanced past me to the deck of my ship, where the pale-faced old warrior shivered. "We will find him a healer, though I doubt there's much to be done."

Together with Sveinn, Dragomir, Finn, Hauk, and a few others, we headed for the gate providing entrance to the town. The familiar stench of fish and shit, mud and wood smoke greeted us as we wove through the dock workers and into the crowded streets. The townsfolk gawked at us and prattled behind our backs as we passed. I could not understand their words, for all spoke in a lilting language that I had never heard.

"Where are the Northmen?" asked Sveinn as he looked about him through the light rain. He was uneasy, and so was I. It seemed strange to see none of our people in this trading town.

Olaf shrugged. "Be easy. We have no cause for worry."

I spat at his comment. There was always cause for worry in new places.

As we neared the market square, peddlers called through the rain to us from their stalls, and we went to them. It took much gesturing and pointing, but eventually we managed to fill a cart with victuals to cook and a barrel of ale. Ulf would be disappointed we hadn't purchased more, but Olaf did not want him overly drunk in a new and foreign place. That handled, we sent Finn and Hauk with the cart back to the ships, then sat at a nearby inn to eat and discuss our next steps.

"There is something happening in the town," Dragomir mumbled as he gnawed on some flatbread. "Listen."

It had stopped raining as we ate, and through the sound of water dripping from the eaves, we heard some commotion in the distance.

"I cannot hear it over your chewing," I teased him. Dragomir had always been a noisy eater. All chomping and lip-smacking and burping. Like a pig at feeding time.

The others laughed.

"Cheering," Olaf commented as our laughter settled. "I hear it."

I confirmed his observation with a grunt and a nod. In truth, I was more interested in my fresh bread and slice of dried beef, which was a rare find.

"Come," Olaf said. "Let's see what it is about." He stood despite the grumbles and frowns of his men. They were not done with their meals, but Olaf had never been one to tarry when an opportunity arose.

We paid the innkeeper, then threaded our way through the busy wood-paved streets, following the noise until we reached a large yard that sat just below a wooden, banner-bedecked wall. There, a large group of men and women shouted and cheered and haggled. All faced inward, so we pressed into the throng until we could see what the uproar was about.

In the center of the circle, with a bloodied body at his feet, stood a man I would never forget.

11

His face was seared into my memory as if by a brand. So too was the spear he had used to topple the horse on which Geira had ridden into her final battle. It surprised me to see the man here in Dyflin, but I suppose it should not have. In Wagria he had been a raider. And like us, raiders traveled.

He was, in the simplest terms, a beast; a good head taller than most men, though I would not call him muscular. He stood now in the muddy circle in his breeks alone, his bare arms and dense chest mud-slimed and flabby, but underneath the filth and fat, I knew, was strength. I know not what sport they were undertaking, but I guessed it had something to do with fighting, for the man he'd defeated clutched his ribs as he rose. The beast kicked the poor fellow in the arse as he tried to stagger away, then he bellowed at the crowd like some primordial creature.

Behind him clapped a young lord with a band of gold resting just above his brow. From his clothing and ring-bedecked arms, I guessed he was the king we had come to meet. He was tall and lean and well-appointed, with a wavy mane of copper hair resting on his shoulders. Standing about him were other warriors with shields in hand and swords upon their hips. Like the king, they had the look of Vestmenn, which was our Northern word for Irland folk.

"Hurrah!" called the regal man to the beast. "Well done!" He spoke in the Northern tongue.

Another man stepped into the ring. He too was burly, though shorter than the beast by a head. His hair was also blond, with two long braids falling from his chin. I wondered if he had been the Dane leader on that fateful day so long ago, though it was difficult to say.

He called to the crowd in their tongue. Several men looked about while others murmured and mumbled, but no one moved. The fellow then spotted us. "Perchance one of you newcomers has the courage to test your skills against Styrr, eh?"

Before I could hold him back, Olaf stepped into the ring. "I will give it a go."

The man named Styrr stopped his bellowing and turned to his new challenger.

"Ah!" called the braided man with a clap of his hands. "A new rival. Do you know the rules of glima?"

My lord first offered his name. "Olaf. And aye. I know glima."

The sport of glima was familiar to all Northmen. It was a wrestling sport in which two combatants tried to throw each other. The first to do so and escape the grasp of his opponent unopposed was the winner. The combatants could not punch, kick, elbow, or knee their adversary. They could only grapple and throw. Though normally safe for the unskilled, it could be vicious for two experienced fighters. Olaf was large and dexterous, but I had not seen him wrestle in some time. To make matters worse, the mud was sucking. It would add an element of difficulty to the match that was hard to estimate.

"Olaf it is. I am Geirbjorn."

Olaf nodded to them both, then turned back to us and removed his cloak and tunic.

"What are you doing?" I asked my rash friend.

"I am fighting, Torgil," he responded as he handed his clothing to Dragomir. As he did, I marked the intensity on his face, and I wondered what that portended. For the briefest of moments I thought to press him and tell him he need not do this, but I could not. If I were in his boots, I would do the same. Any honorable man would. Styrr had killed his wife, and he deserved Olaf's vengeance, though I feared just what that punishment would be.

Olaf turned back to Styrr. The braided man said some words to the crowd, who cheered and began calling their bets to each other. Dragomir joined the shouting, using his fingers to call out his bets. Geirbjorn then stepped back to give the two wrestlers room. I glanced at the lord, who whispered something to one of his guards, a small, burly man with a broken nose and curly black hair. That man whispered back, and the king cocked his head, as if suddenly more interested.

In glima, there is no signal given to begin. The two opponents merely grasp wrists briefly, then launch into their bout. And so began this fight.

Styrr was quicker than I would have imagined. His left hand grabbed Olaf's right wrist, while his right hand slid into Olaf's armpit. The beast tried to heave, but Olaf's left elbow shot down to knock Styrr's arm away.

Styrr slammed his fist into Olaf's gut. An illegal move, but one the crowd appreciated by the sound of their cheers. The punch forced Olaf's left hand down so that Styrr could twist his body, grab Olaf's right arm with his left hand, and pull Olaf over his shoulder. He did it with such speed and deftness, it drew a grasp from the onlookers.

But Olaf did not panic. As his body flipped, he clung to Styrr's right arm so that, as he plummeted toward the ground, the giant could do nothing else but go with him. Styrr launched from his feet and spun over Olaf as Olaf himself rolled on his shoulder in the mud. The beast landed heavily on his back, the impact of which shot mud into the air and forced a grunt from his lungs.

Had Olaf merely spun away at that moment, he would have won the bout. But Olaf was not interested in winning — he wanted revenge. So rather than scoot away, he spun his body and locked his right forearm around Styrr's neck. Styrr tried to roll to his side, but Olaf put his weight into his hold so that Styrr could not get his shoulders over. More panicked now, Styrr grabbed a handful of Olaf's hair and pulled with all of his strength. Olaf roared in pain but refused to relinquish his grip.

Styrr's face was purple from lack of air. The crowd yelled and pointed, concern masking their faces. Still Geirbjorn did nothing, thinking mayhap his man could still find a way to best Olaf. But as Styrr's eyes began to roll in his head, Geirbjorn intervened. It took him and two others to pry Olaf's forearm from Styrr's neck, and even then, it was no easy task.

I ran to my friend and hauled him away before Geirbjorn retaliated or Olaf did worse damage.

"Are you mad, man?" Geirbjorn yelled at Olaf.

Olaf spat some filth and phlegm from his mouth, looking as if he were ready to take on the entire lot of Danes.

"Easy," I said to Olaf. "It is over."

Olaf squinted at me and took a deep breath to calm himself. Near us, the young lord clapped and whispered once again to his guard, who nodded. The braided man and his comrades saw to Styrr, who had not yet risen from the brown mire of the yard.

"That was a skillful display, Olaf," called the lord as the crowd began to settle.

Olaf swiped the mud and sweat from his brow, then acknowledged the lord's compliment with a nod.

"Though the point is to throw your opponent and escape from his grasp."

"I know the point, lord," Olaf responded in a dull voice.

"Yet you chose to ignore it?"

Olaf shrugged as if it was of little concern.

The lord lifted his chin. "Do you know who I am?"

Olaf shrugged again. "A lord."

"A king," the man corrected. "*King* Iron Knee. And you will respond when I query you."

Olaf nodded again. "Aye, King Iron Knee." There was little complaisance in his flat tone.

"You are newly arrived?"

"We are," confirmed Olaf.

"I understand you seek an audience with me. Is that so?"

"It is," Olaf replied.

The young king regarded Olaf for a long moment. "You do not make very good first impressions, Olaf. But you have me curious, so I will hear you out. On the morrow, I will send guards to the docks to fetch you. We will speak more then."

Olaf nodded his head in what might have been a bow.

The man turned with his guards and departed.

"We should leave before that beast regains his strength," I said in a weak attempt at levity.

Olaf glanced back at Styrr, who was being helped from the yard. "I should have killed the bastard," he said as he flung a chunk of mud onto the ground.

I grabbed Olaf's slimy arm and turned him away.

"Look here." A laughing Dragomir approached us with a small pile of silver in his cupped hands. "We should do this more often."

"Oh, aye," said Sveinn in mock delight. "I am sure they would love for you to stay." He jerked his thumb at the Danes, who were watching us depart with rage in their eyes.

Dragomir smirked. "Taking their silver makes this win all the more sweet," he said as he joined us in our retreat toward the market.

"That it does, Drag," I said. "That it does."

Guards escorted us to Iron Knee the morning after our arrival, which in hindsight was not such a bad thing. The wait gave us time to beach our ships upstream from the harbor, to bathe, and to erect a makeshift camp. But more, it gave us time to celebrate our arrival in Dyflin with a sacrifice to the gods as well as some warm food and good ale.

The guards led Olaf, Sveinn, Orm, and me through the town, past the wrestling yard, and into an estate, where we were directed to a large hall. Within its long, firelit space we found Iron Knee sitting on his dais on a capacious, throne-like seat. On his knee sat a young, dark-haired woman clothed only in a linen tunic that fell to her thighs, though with Iron Knee's hand up it, her arse cheek was plain for all to see. Neither the cooking servants, the warriors lining the walls, nor the priest who sat at a nearby table with his vellum and ink seemed bothered by their lord's indiscretion.

A guard with a broken nose cleared his throat to turn the king's attention away from the lass. "My lord," he added in his nasal tone. Based on where the man stood, he seemed to be the head of the king's guard.

With a perturbed sigh, Iron Knee glanced at us, then with a heavy sigh and a light pat on the girl's arse, he sent her away and turned his focus toward us. I suppose he would rather have been playing with his nymph.

"Who are you?" I had noticed the king's haughtiness the previous day, but here, in the confines of his hall, it dripped from his tongue and every feature.

Olaf straightened to his full height. "As I said yesterday, my name is Olaf. Olaf Tryggvason."

Iron Knee studied the nails on his bejeweled right hand. "I do not know that name. Should it mean something to me?" His bored eyes scanned Olaf, then shifted to me and my comrades. "You bring many men to my harbor. Are you a prince? Or are you a trader who has done well for yourself?"

"I am both of those things," Olaf answered. I could not see his face, but I knew he spoke through gritted teeth.

"I do not have the patience for riddles," said Iron Knee. "Are you a prince, or are you not?"

"I am a prince," Olaf answered vaguely. "My father ruled the fylke of Vingulmark."

"And you rule it now?" The man was baiting Olaf, testing his lineage and his patience.

"No. It was taken from me."

"So you are a prince without a kingdom," Iron Knee surmised. "And how does that benefit me?"

"You are a new king, and I command a fleet. I thought that you might have need of men, new to the High Seat as you are." Olaf was struggling to keep the derision from his tone, but I heard it there, slithering through his words. I wondered briefly if the king heard it too. "But if you have no need of them, I will take my warriors elsewhere." Olaf turned, and we started to follow.

"I have not given you permission to leave," called Iron Knee to Olaf's back.

We turned back, though Olaf held his tongue.

"What makes you think I have need of men?" The king had cocked his head slightly to the side.

Olaf smirked, though there was no mirth in it. "Kings always have need of men, and new kings especially so."

King Iron Knee shot forward. "Do you think I know not what I need?"

"I merely offer you assistance. That is all." Olaf kept his tone mild. Like me, he must have sensed that we stood on dangerous ground.

"And I merely wish to know who you are. You come to my shores from a place I do not know. You ignore the rules of glima and nearly kill one of my retainers. And now you stand before me, patronizing me. Do you know anything of me? Of this land? I sense not."

The young king snorted and fell back into his oversized throne. His fingers tapped on the chair's broad arm as his eyes scanned each of us yet again. "The land of the Éireannach is a tangled knot of alliances and marriages and kinships," he explained, using what I took to be the Irland word for the local people. "Your friend today is your enemy on the morrow. I ask questions because few can be trusted. I also ask questions because you are a Northman, and there are few of your ilk brave enough to visit Dyflin now that my father is gone. So either you are blind to what has happened here, or you are well aware and, therefore, a man to question."

"So what is it you would like to know?" Olaf offered into the silence that had fallen on the hall.

"I would like to know what I originally asked. Who are you?"

"I am a prince's son, driven from his homeland as a child, enslaved in Estland, and rescued by my uncle, who served the grand prince in Gardariki. There, I served for several summers and earned fame before the grand prince's son drove me from the land because of his jealousy. Luck took me to a kingdom called Wagria, where I earned the hand of a princess. But my luck turned against me when she died. Since then, I have raided the coasts of Saxland and Frankland and Frisland and England and, through those raids, built a fleet. Last summer, while in Jorvik, I learned of you, your rise to the Dyflin High Seat, and your possible need for men. That is why I am here. If I am mistaken in your need, I will take my leave."

Iron Knee continued to tap the arm of his chair. "Do you know the name Leinster?"

Olaf shook his head.

"Domnall mac Lorcain? Ivar of Waterford? Do those names mean anything to you?"

Again, Olaf shook his head.

Iron Knee grunted. "Do you always know so little of the places you go?"

"Do you always insult men who offer you aid?" responded Olaf.

Iron Knee snorted and sat up again. "Tell me, Olaf. Are you a Christian?"

"No."

"But you would offer aid to a Christian king?"

Olaf smirked. "Silver is silver. I care not if it comes from the hand of one who follows the Christ God or the old gods. So long as the lord I serve knows how to handle a blade."

"An opportunist then," remarked Iron Knee.

"Are we not all opportunists?" Olaf countered. "You have Danes in Dyflin. Are they not also here for opportunity?"

"Aye, but they are Christians. I worry more about pagans."

Olaf shrugged again. "Why? Do you think religion keeps one man from killing another? I have seen Christians kill plenty of other Christians. Likewise, pagans."

Iron Knee grunted, though I could not tell if it was in acceptance or denial of Olaf's remark. He reclined once again on his throne, and eventually, his gaze came to rest on me. "You have the look of a Vestmann about you. Who are you?"

"My name is Torgil. I serve Olaf and have done so since I was a lad. Where he has been, so too have I. The same can be said for my father and Olaf's father. Long ago, they raided these shores and my father captured the woman who was my mother. My father always said I have her look about me, though I barely knew her."

Iron Knee's features stiffened. "Long have the Northmen raided our shores and taken our women." He waved the comment aside, but his response troubled me as much as his questions to Olaf confused me. For the life of me, I could not decide where this man's allegiances lay. Perchance he himself did not know.

After another long moment, Iron Knee turned back to Olaf. "Very well. You and your men are welcome in Dyflin so long as you have silver to spend. I may indeed have use for you, but we will see how things go before I call upon your swords." He then waved us away. "You may go now."

We retrieved our weapons and strode silently from the yard.

"That is not what I would call a warm welcome," I grumbled when we were out of earshot of the king and his men.

Orm spat to show his displeasure, then looked back at the estate walls. "If he treats all Northmen so, it is little wonder we see so few walking the streets."

"Mayhap there is a reason for his attitude," Sveinn offered. "As much as I dislike it."

Olaf grunted. "Wise words, Sveinn. We will give it a little time, eh? Perchance we will learn more before casting our lots in with this king."

I liked the thread of Olaf's thinking. There was much to unravel from the king's words before we chose our path. At the heart of it were questions I could not release from my mind: was Irland really so coiled upon itself that a king could trust no one? Had Iron Knee chosen a side in this twisted place? If so, what side was that and what, then, did that mean for us? I was still chewing on these gristled thoughts when a jagged voice called out to us.

"You!"

The voice stopped me cold. Instinctively, I crouched and brought my hand to my axe. My eyes moved to the sound, expecting a man with a weapon but seeing only a gray-bearded priest standing upon a box with a bent but accusing finger pointed at Olaf. Those standing beneath him turned to us as we stopped.

"You!" he screeched again in the Northern tongue.

We stood transfixed by the man and his crow-like caw, the more so because he spoke in our language. Finally Olaf managed to shake his surprise and point to his chest.

"Aye, you. The man who has come to these shores seeking fame like so many before you."

I studied the man with his disheveled hair and deeply grooved skin, trying to decide if he was serious or whether this was some sort of ruse.

The cross dangling from his neck told me he was a priest, though I had never seen a priest standing on a crate in the street. Mayhap the church had cast him out. That, I decided, was not hard to believe.

"Who are you?" Olaf called to the man over the heads of the stunned crowd.

"It matters not who I am, Olaf," declared the old man.

I gaped at Olaf, whose head cocked at the mention of his name.

"How do you know my name?" Olaf challenged him.

"I have seen you in a dream," he called.

Olaf laughed. "Are you a sorcerer then?"

The man sneered. "I am a messenger."

"Ah," said Olaf, relaxing somewhat. "A messenger from whom?"

The deranged man turned his palms and eyes upward. "God."

I might have laughed had I not been so surprised.

Beside me, Olaf snorted. "God, you say. Do you mean the god of the Christians?"

"Is He not the only God?" challenged the man, pointing his finger again.

Olaf chuckled and crossed his arms. He seemed to think this was all some sort of hoax, and mayhap it was, but it still unnerved me.

"And what does your Christian god have to tell me?"

"Only this: Unlike the others who have come before you, you will become a renowned king and do celebrated deeds. Many men will you bring to the new faith through baptism."

So preposterous were the man's words, I could only laugh. So too did Olaf and the others.

"I have heard many words spoken about me, old man," Olaf called as he regained his composure, "but never that."

"Do not doubt the words of our Lord, Olaf."

"It is too late for that," Olaf said, and turned with us to leave.

"Then you are a fool!" cawed the wild man.

It was too much for Olaf. He spun around before we knew what was happening and forced his way into the crowd, which scattered before him. I did not blame him for his anger. An insult was an insult, and he could not let it stand. Still, I pursued to stop him from doing something as witless as killing a priest in a Christian land.

The priest stood his ground and leveled his finger at Olaf, his face red with emotion. "Kill me if you wish, young prince. But know this: you will receive great riches and land, but before you possess those riches, you will be wounded almost to death by your own men and carried upon a shield to safety."

His words rang like a curse in our ears and stopped me in my tracks. Olaf, too, faltered, his outstretched arm now hesitating. "What did you say?" he demanded.

"After seven days," the man continued as if deaf to Olaf's query, "you will be well of your wounds and you will believe."

Olaf gawked at the man.

The priest twisted the blade of words even further. "Let us rejoice in the words of the Lord." He pressed his hands together and cast his eyes skyward.

It was rare to see my friend so stunned. He seemed not to know what to make of the priest or his proclamation. He turned to me, and all I could do was shrug. The priest climbed from his crate and turned from Olaf, unfazed by the threat of my friend. He pressed into the silent crowd and disappeared down a side street.

I looked at Sveinn and Orm, and they at me. No one spoke.

Eventually Olaf came to us, and I nudged his shoulder. "Put the man from your mind," I counseled. "His are the words of a wild man. That is all."

"A madman," Orm snorted.

"Aye," added Sveinn.

Olaf grunted and walked on, but I knew his mind was troubled.

12

Later that day, we received an invitation to join Iron Knee in his hall that night for some sort of feast. The invitation came as a surprise, though not a welcome one for Olaf, who had been surly and reserved the entire day. The words of the crazed priest were lodged in his head and he could not shake them, or so it seemed. As for me, the morning's run-ins had sucked the energy from my veins and set me on my guard. I did not like the idea of the false allegiances to which Iron Knee alluded or the notion that Olaf would be attacked by his own men. I too disliked the words of the priest, which sat upon my mind like a curse. All of it spoke to an invisible, and uncontrolled, rot that roused within me a general sense of mistrust of that place and that king.

In the end, however, neither Olaf's concerns nor mine kept us from honoring Iron Knee's invitation. It would have been a mistake. A slight. And so we hauled ourselves into our fine tunics and cloaks, brushed our hair and beards, and marched silently, resolutely, to the feast with Sveinn, Dragomir, and Hauk in tow.

Save for the blend of languages and style of music, it might have been any feast in any hall in the Northern world. It was loud, smelly, and packed with people. Men caroused and laughed and surrendered their faculties to their ale. Couples groped. A skald sang to the tune of instruments that, save for the drum and flute, I did not recognize. I could make no sense of what the skald sang, though from the pleased smile on Iron Knee's face, it was either well-known to him or complimentary. We pushed our way into the mob and sidled up next to a group of men at a table within view of the dais. They seemed annoyed by our sudden appearance but otherwise ignored us. That is, until several pitchers of ale arrived and we offered one to our neighbors.

"Gura mie ayd!" called the man closest to us over the clamor in the hall. He was a wiry fellow with a ruddy complexion and a scraggly brown beard. "Shoh Slaynt!" the same man said, then raised his cup to us. His four comrades followed suit.

For all I knew, they were cursing us, but we lifted our cups all the same. "Sköl!"

"Nort'men?" asked the scraggly man, who sat just to my right. His accent was unfamiliar to me, but he seemed to speak our language well enough.

"Aye," I confirmed.

The man's eyes scanned us all, then settled back on my face. "Nort'men are a rare sight t'ese days." The man seemed to pronounce all of his t's and h's with a hard *t* sound, which sounded to my ears like tapping on metal. "We," he patted his chest, "come from an island close to here," he declared, though I had not asked. "Part of what you call t'e Sudreyjar. We know t'e island as Ellan Vannin."

The kingdom of Sudreyjar included many islands, but I had not heard of the place he named. The others in my group shrugged when I looked at them for answers. I glanced at Olaf, but he was distracted by something on the dais. I followed his gaze to a captivating young woman with golden hair who was seated beside King Iron Knee. His wife, I presumed. To either side of them sat several other men of distinction, one of whom was a priest, though I recognized none of them.

"Are you here to serve t'e king of Dyflin?" The man's question interrupted my appreciation of the young lady on the dais.

"Aye," I admitted.

The man smiled, showing me his jagged teeth. He indicated the rest of the men at his table. "We, too, have come at t'e king's call." Again, I had not asked.

I scanned the crowded room. "The king's call? Is there trouble?"

The man looked at his comrades, one of whom spoke before Scraggly. "T'ere is always trouble in Éireannach. 'Tis a regular t'ing here," he explained in our tongue, again with the same hard *t* in his words. "T'e clans fight for land and power and cattle. T'e Danes and Nort'men raid and clash over trade. The Éireannach fight back against the invaders. If you are looking to spill blood, you will find your chance here."

"I see," I answered, and took a sip of ale to settle my thoughts.

"What are they quarreling about now?" asked Olaf, who sat across from me. He too had pulled his eyes from the beauty on the dais.

The second man leaned in and closed an eye. "Who? T'e clans?"

"Why are you here?" I clarified.

The man looked at me as if I were witless. "We're here because Ímar of Port Láirge — you would call him Ivar of Waterford, I suppose — has taken exception to Iron Knee controlling Dubh linn instead of him. And t'at very same Ivar has allied himself wit' t'e king of Leinster, see?"

Suddenly some of Iron Knee's earlier queries clicked. Were these not the names that he had asked us about?

"So Ivar and this king of Leinster come for Dyflin?" clarified Sveinn, who sat to Olaf's right and was listening intently to the exchange.

Scraggly nodded. "Aye. Maolsheachlann and Ivar bot' want to control trade, and Dubh linn is t'e center of it. But Maolsheachlann does not like Nort'men, who have long ruled here. The first t'ing he did after driving away t'e last king of Dubh linn — who was his fat'er, by t'e way — and giving Dubh linn to his kinsman Iron Knee was to release all the t'ralls. He now fights to drive all t'e Nort'men away, which is why it is strange to see you here."

"Who is Maolshe...?" Olaf gave up on trying to say the man's name.

Again the men looked at us as if we were half-wits. "Why, he is t'e high king of Éireannach and t'e half-brot'er of Iron Knee. It was he who installed Iron Knee on his seat here."

"Is he coming to support his half-brother in this fight?" I asked.

"T'at is the word, aye," said Scraggly.

"Why doesn't he favor Northmen? Is he not half Northman himself, like Iron Knee?" This question came from Sveinn.

"It's his fait'. He's a Christian. Your kind is not. Point is, Maolsheach-lann wants to rid t'e land of Nort'men, see? He wants t'em gone."

"So does he want to end the slave trade, too?" I asked.

Scraggly snorted. "Against his people, aye. T'ough he cares not a lick for his enemies, see. He'd be happy to sell t'ose who attack him off as t'ralls."

Understanding began to dawn on me. It explained why I had seen so few Northmen in Dyflin. But it did not explain why we were there supporting Iron Knee. Based on what I had just heard, our loyalties seemed better placed with Ivar, who seemed more partial to men of our kind.

"What of Ivar's army?" Olaf asked. "Is it large? Is it on the move?"

Scraggly nodded. "Aye to bot'. Ivar and his army march wit' Domnall and t'e Leinstermen even now. And t'at is why we're here."

"Why does Domnall march with Ivar?" asked Sveinn. "Is not Domnall a Vestmann and Ivar a Northman?"

Scraggly snorted. "Why does any king fight wit' or against anot'er king? Power? Riches? Revenge? In t'is case, I t'ink it is riches. Trade, mostly. Ivar already controls Waterford. Add Dubh linn to it, and he controls a vast network of wealt'. I could see Ivar putting Domnall on t'e t'rone here to see to his interests."

Sveinn grunted. "Sounds like we've stepped in a hornet's nest. I hope Iron Knee is a fighter."

"Oh, he's a fighter and a mite bit better one t'an you, I'd say," responded the second man with a nod at Sveinn's wooden hand.

I frowned. So too did Sveinn. He was not the compulsive type, but an insult was an insult; he would be well within his rights to retaliate. Still, I wanted no trouble. Scraggly must have been of similar mind, for he scowled at the man and rattled off a salvo of unintelligible words. The man made a face and turned away from us.

"Forgive my brot'er," he apologized to Sveinn. "T'e better t'e ale, t'e looser his tongue."

"Another comment like that, and he will have no tongue," Sveinn grumbled to Scraggly.

Seeing that things were deteriorating, I hoisted my cup to my neighbor. "We'll leave you to your ale."

Olaf raised his hand to interrupt. "Who is that seated beside Iron Knee?"

"Ah," said Scraggly as he grinned. "T'at is Gytha. Iron Knee's younger sister. Beautiful, eh?"

Olaf grunted, and I smiled. It had been many summers since Olaf had chased a princess. After the loss of Geira, I thought he might never do so again. But this woman might be worth the chase. She was mayhap in her twentieth summer, with long waves of golden hair and a face so fair and fresh, it rivaled any queen I had seen.

"A shame t'at she is leaving. It will be painful not having her face around."

"Where does she go?" asked Olaf.

"To England," said Scraggly. "Iron Knee went and married her to an old jarl t'ere. A waste of all t'at beauty, if you ask me. But Iron Knee wanted her away from here before t'e battle wit' Ivar. And t'e jarl made a suitable offer."

"It *is* a shame," admitted Olaf.

I half expected my friend to rise and present himself to her as he often did to the women he chased. But he remained seated, which I found curious.

Scraggly raised his cup to Olaf. "A shame indeed."

"And the others? Who are those men?" asked Sveinn with a nod at the dais.

"To t'e left is Maccus. To t'e right is his younger brot'er, Godfraid. T'ey are t'e kings of t'e Sudreyjar. Our islands. I do not know t'e priest."

I turned back to our party, though my thoughts were on my neighbor's words. A lord and a king were marching on Dyflin. And an army was gathering to meet it. But whether Iron Knee was a capable leader was still an open question. And so too was his openness to accepting us in his ranks. It all left me unsettled.

I was about to take a sip of ale when I caught a commotion out of the corner of my left eye. I turned, and there I saw Styrr and the braid-bearded Geirbjorn forcing their way through the crowd. Styrr led the procession, moving people aside with all the subtlety of a boulder rolling down a mountain.

I turned back to my cup, hoping to avoid trouble, but peace was not our fate that night. Styrr noticed Olaf and stopped behind me. I could feel him looming over our table as he gazed down upon us.

"This is our table," the giant announced. Or was he a troll? I had not yet decided. "Move off."

I cast my eyes about the hall and noticed several other spots where Styrr could easily have sat. His demand for our table was purposeful, if ill-advised, though he did not know that yet. I shifted my gaze to Olaf, who flashed his mischievous grin. The others smirked wolfishly. I nodded in return, feeling my heart quicken.

"Are you sure there are no seats elsewhere?" called Olaf to the giant.

"Move off," the fellow demanded again.

I turned to our neighbors, the island men. They had scooted down their benches to make some room between us. To my left, Hauk remained seated. Across from me, Olaf and Sveinn started to rise. I could not see Dragomir around Hauk's bulk, but I guessed that he, too, was moving. I waited until Olaf's feet were firmly planted before pivoting on my own bench, ale in my left hand, and made as if to rise. Beside me, Hauk did the same.

As I turned, all I saw was Styrr's thick belly and heavy belt before me. I tossed my ale up into his face, then slammed my fist into his groin. To my right, Hauk launched his head into the chin of Geirbjorn. But I saw no more than that. Styrr had bent with the impact of my fist and now I, too, rose to my full height. Only instead of my head, I used my right elbow to connect with the Dane's jaw. I hit with as much force as I could muster in that small space and thought, as the giant spun away and collapsed, that I had killed the man.

I did not wait to find out. The next Dane was before me, and I struck with a backhanded fist to the lad's ear before he recovered from his shock. To my right, Hauk kicked the fallen Geirbjorn in his head. The man I had backhanded tumbled sideways, then fell over Geirbjorn's body. I pursued, grabbed the lad's collar, and punched his face until I was sure he would not rise to fight me.

Dragomir pulled me away. I stood, ready to fight him, then stopped myself.

"Time to go," he said to me and pulled on my cloak.

I looked about me. A small crowd gawked at us. Two more Danes raised their hands in surrender. I spat at their feet and stepped over the bodies of their comrades. Guards appeared then, but there was nothing for them to do — the fight was over, and we were leaving. They let us pass. Olaf nodded at them in thanks, and together we departed the feast.

As I stepped out into the damp air, I sleeved the sweat from my face and smiled. I had not brawled in some time, and it felt good. Though I knew it was a mere sip of what was coming.

13

"King Malachy has arrived," Olaf said with a nod toward the field below us. He used a name we had heard others use for the high king of Irland. It rolled easier from my tongue than Maolsheachlann.

It was several days after the altercation at the feast, and things had been quiet…until that morning when the horns blared and flags rose to announce something. We had gone to the town's western walls, where a crowd had gathered. By the time we arrived, hundreds of mounted warriors had spread across the meadow below the walls. A vast line of foot soldiers and wagons and camp followers snaked out behind them and into the distance.

"Two thousand men," I said. "Mayhap more."

Olaf grunted his agreement at my guess. "Archers. Horsemen. Spearmen. And all Vestmenn. It will be interesting to see how these men fight."

"All Vestmenn, except us," I corrected him with a raised brow. I still had my reservations about fighting for Iron Knee and this high king, and I had not been shy about sharing my thoughts.

"I've heard your concerns, Torgil. But unless Iron Knee reveals us to his king, Malachy will never know of us."

I accepted Olaf's words with a snort, though my concerns encompassed more than just Malachy. Though we had seen no smoke or campfires to the south, those escaping the enemy's path were beginning to arrive in Dyflin. And they carried with them tales of Ivar's army. It was huge, some said. So vast that it covered the earth as far as the eye could see, said others. *And filled with horrid giants and fire-snorting horses, no doubt,* I mused. The typical exaggerations of traumatized people. Still, within those tall tales was a sliver of truth, and that was what had me awake at night. At the very least, it was wise to be prepared for a challenge.

"We should leave a few men here with the ships in case things turn against us," I suggested.

Olaf nodded. "Aye."

"And speak to the men to prepare them," I added.

"Aye." Again, the clipped response.

In the past few days, I had noticed Olaf's mind wandering. He would frequently disengage from conversations or lose his train of thought. I had oft heard him ask his men to repeat themselves. As children, this had been a regular occurrence for him, but that tendency had dissipated over time. Now it had returned, and I knew not why.

"You are distracted. Are you thinking about the priest?"

Olaf snorted. "No. The man was a blabbering fool."

"I am glad you feel that way," I said, though I doubted my friend's bold words. "So if not the priest, then what has captured your thoughts?"

Olaf glanced at me, then sighed. "It is not the crazed priest I think about, but what he represents. No matter where we go or where we turn, this Christian faith confronts us. From kings on their thrones to lone priests in their hovels with not an ounce of silver to their names, we see it. We see it seeping into Wagria and now, the North. We run into it in the streets in Dyflin and the markets of Ribe, where they sell Thor's hammers alongside Christ's crosses. It makes no sense to me. Are the gods themselves engaged in some epic struggle? Are our gods losing ground to this…" he flipped his hands in a questioning motion "…this man-god? *This* is what plagues me."

I too had been frustrated and worried about the Christian faith and its spread, though I thought of it more as a disease than a thing of power, like that unseen illness that was conquering Ottar's body.

"Are we fighting on the wrong side of this battle, then?" I asked. "Should we not be fighting with the approaching Northmen and Ivar?" I could not help myself.

Olaf turned to me sharply. "Enough of your entreaties. I have chosen a side. Besides, being a Northman means nothing. There are many Northmen now who are Christians. As I said, the faith is everywhere. And that is what worries me. That, and the feeling that I am now marked."

My brows creased, for his words confused me. "So the priest's words do worry you?"

Olaf snorted and turned away.

I shut my mouth and turned my gaze back to the meadow, watching silently as the Vestmann army flowed in and my own emotions ebbed.

Eventually Olaf patted the top of the parapet beside me. "Enough of this. It matters not what side of this fight we choose — our fates are woven already, eh? Let us speak to the men."

We arrived back in camp to learn from a herald that Iron Knee and his half-brother Malachy were marching the following morning. It did not surprise me. I gathered Olaf's inner circle of men and brought them to his tent, where a small fire crackled. We sat on stumps and logs and waited for Olaf to speak.

After describing what he had seen out on the field, Olaf turned to his younger cousins. "Hauk and Finn. You lads will remain here with the ships," he commanded. In truth, they were no longer lads; they were warriors who had fought beside us these past six summers and proved themselves worthy of command.

"But —" Finn began.

Olaf held up his hand for silence. "I have made up my mind, Finn. I need capable men here in case things turn against us. Pick twenty men to remain with you."

"Go easy on the ladies in our absence, eh lads?" Ulf added to lighten the mood.

They did not laugh.

"Ottar. You will also remain," said Olaf. "You must rest."

The aging man sat on the ground with his back against a thick stump, his frail body covered in furs. "No," he responded simply. It was a response that brooked no argument, even from Olaf.

Olaf bit his lower lip and looked at me, then the others. Most of us shrugged. If Ottar wanted to fight, who were we to stop him? He was a dead man anyway. Better he die facing the enemies he could see than the invisible enemy within him.

"Can you walk to the battle?" Olaf asked. "It may be some distance, and we will have no steeds or carts to carry us."

Ottar's brows furrowed. "I will manage."

Olaf accepted that with a nod. "At the battle, we will divide ourselves by ship, same as always. Each of you will lead your crews, save Torgil and Sveinn, who will fight beside me. Dragomir, you will lead Torgil's crew. Is that clear?"

"Aye, lord," we responded.

"Now, go to your men and prepare them. We have much to do. I do not think Iron Knee or Malachy will share their food with us, so carry your own supplies." Olaf cast his eyes to the sky. "It rains here as much as it does in Frisland, so do your best to keep your gear sharp and dry."

As we rose from the war council, a horn called out above us. Several ships sailed from the harbor and out toward the sea. As they slipped by us, a horn responded from one of the ships on which royal banners flapped. I guessed it was the princess, heading off to marry her jarl. Giving it no more thought than that, I bent to help Ottar to his feet. He pushed my hand away. I grinned at the man's determination, then turned my eyes back to the ships.

Olaf, too, studied them for a moment longer, then turned to me with a shake of his head. "A shame, indeed."

I smirked. Not at the comment, mind, but at the thought that we had not yet seen the last of the princess.

We marched from Dyflin the following day.

Though we comprised a large contingent of Iron Knee's forces, he afforded us no special treatment. If anything, we were treated slightly better than the camp followers who marched just behind us. Olaf was not invited to the war council the night before the march, nor to the feast that followed. Nor did we receive any instruction on what to do or where to go, save to join the end of the line. The Danes, I noted with aggravation, marched just behind Iron Knee, far from the rabble of the supply wagons and horseshit. If there was any solace to that, it was that we had found a spot for Ottar in one of the wagon beds. At least he did not have to walk through the flies and festering piles of dung.

We followed the river that flowed southwest past Dyflin's walls, then forded it to join a wide track that wound out into lush grasslands threaded with streams and hedgerows and stone walls. The beauty of it all did little to ease my foul mood, or that of the men.

"Save it for the shield wall," I barked at two men who cursed at each other.

They scowled at me but bit their tongues.

"Shield wall?" Ulf laughed as he waved some flies from his face. "Two coins says we never get close to Ivar's men."

"I'll take that bet," Dragomir countered. "It's pretty clear Iron Knee cares not a snot about us. He'll stand us in the front row, like fodder."

"And reveal to Malachy that he's using Northmen?" I asked. "I'm with Ulf. He'll hide us away."

"If all we have to do is march through horse scat to win some silver, that sits well enough with me," Sveinn called to no one in particular.

Olaf laughed. "I can hear the songs of the skalds now. Oh, how the Northmen braved the stinking piles to get at Ivar's men."

"Well now, welcome to the march, Olaf," Orm said in his deadpan way. "Glad to have you along."

"Mind your tongue, Forest Nose," Berse interrupted.

I rolled my eyes.

"Calm yourself, Berse. The men merely jest."

If anyone still had an ounce of mirth in them after Berse's grating words, the sudden shower that fell upon us doused it. We pulled the hoods of our cloaks over our heads and turned our eyes once again to the road to avoid the dung over which we slogged.

By the afternoon, the sun had returned and we found ourselves on a small hill overlooking a vast expanse of varied landscapes. To our left, in the distance, twinkled an ocean shining silver in the sunlight. To our right, the rain-drenched country rolled away in waves of green that were beautiful to behold. South, the land rose to a ridge of mountains at the base of which was a sparse forest. And among bushy trees of green winked the glow of hundreds of campfires. Ivar's army. I walked to the hill's southern crest and peered at the fires. It was hard to discern just how large Ivar's army was, but I knew it was not small.

"If the weather holds," Olaf said as he came up beside me, "we'll fight on the morrow."

He need not have said it. I had been through countless battles before and knew well what we faced and when we might face it. "Well," I finally said. "I did not brave all of that horseshit for nothing."

Olaf chuckled. "I will try to speak with Iron Knee and see what he commands of us."

"He'll want us in support, no doubt," Orm mumbled from behind me as Olaf marched away.

I smacked him gently on the arm. "Better than guarding the camp, eh?"

Orm snorted.

The men made camp as Olaf went to speak with Iron Knee. There was little dry wood and no dry grass, so what fires we did manage to light were more smoke than flame. Having eaten a little bread and cheese, I lay back on the wet ground and shut my eyes, letting the sounds and smells of camp wash over me. It was the hum of activity that I loved. The chatter of men, the creak of leather, the ring of metal, the hammer of a nearby smith. All of it swirled about me in the evening air, and I welcomed it like the return of an old friend.

But I could not deny the part of me that was unsettled. On the morrow, we would fight an army of unknown strength and skill alongside warriors none of us knew. Warriors who welcomed our presence not at all. Mayhap even resented us. I knew not what that portended, but I found it hard to release the thought from my mind. Eventually I landed on the words of Olaf, which calmed me. Our fates were already woven. It mattered not what we did to try and change them.

Olaf returned as the last rays of sunlight bathed the camp. I looked up from my repose, trying to read his face through the smoke of the fire. He was unreadable. "Well?"

He took a seat on the log beside me. Sveinn and Orm sat across from us, watching. "The Vestmenn are confident," he said, then shrugged. "I suppose they should be. King Malachy has succeeded where many others have failed."

"But?" I asked.

"Their confidence makes them unimaginative," Olaf said.

"How so?" asked Sveinn.

He squinted across the fire's smoke at Sveinn. "We march to a field. We line up. We fight. Not much more to it than that."

"Do we use the cavalry?" I asked.

He took the piece of meat Sveinn offered him and shrugged again. "No mention of it."

Orm blew mucus from his left nostril, then looked at Olaf. "Where does Iron Knee want us?"

"Behind his men," Olaf said as he chewed the meat. "In support."

"Ulf was right," Orm said.

"Does he not trust us?" I asked.

"King Malachy does not trust us," Olaf corrected me. "It was he who decided our position."

Sveinn shrugged. "So be it."

Olaf nodded. "So be it."

I nodded as well, then closed my eyes. On the morrow, we would fight. That much was certain. The rest of it lay in the hands of the fate-weavers.

14

The camp stirred the following morning at dawn. There were no war horns or calls to rise. There was no need. Nerves woke most men, if they had slept at all. And once those men rose, the din of it woke the others.

I sat up and worked life into my cold limbs. A gray mist greeted me, hovering like tendrils of smoke upon the camp. Thick enough to be detected and to dampen my clothing, but transparent enough that I could still see our army milling about. I did not like it but reckoned the sun would burn it away, and so I put my worries aside.

Nearby, some robed bastards carrying wooden crosses "blessed" us with hand gestures and their Christian curses. Most men ignored them, lost as they were in their own preparations and fast-breaking. Some shouted at them to go away, thinking them a bad omen before a battle. I too thought to chase them away, but the few Christians among us beat me to it. They escorted the priests a safe distance from Olaf's camp, then the fools knelt at the feet of the holy men to receive their blessing.

"To me!" Olaf called from the top of a large rock, his arms outstretched to draw us in. In his polished byrnie, with his two swords crisscrossed on his back and his auburn beard combed and braided on his chest, he looked for all the world like a lord ready for battle. He had always been tall and broad-shouldered, but six cycles of the sun had shorn him of the roundness he had acquired in the courts of Wagria and had transformed him into a lean, muscular fighter.

"Do not fret over the Christians in our midst, or the Christ God to whom they pray," Olaf called to us as he waved his hand in the general direction of the praying warriors. "If their god gives them hope and strength, then let them have their belief."

It was well-worded, for I had seen the Christian Saxons and Christian Greeks fight, and I knew their strength. For many summers, I had tried to reconcile in my thoughts how the gods decided who won which contest. After all, man, not the gods, grappled in the mud among the blades and shields. Summers before, I had realized that it came down to belief, as Olaf had just said. The belief that your god or gods would lend power to your strike, skill to your fight, and aye, luck to your day. The belief that, should death find you, your deity would celebrate your courage, for only with courage could one survive in this world of struggle.

Olaf's words interrupted my thoughts. "Think instead of the gods of our ancestors, and how they and your forebears watch you this day. You may not have rich gifts to offer them in sacrifice, but they will hear your words, they will see you fight, and they will envy you the havoc you wreak upon your enemy!" He brandished his fist at his men. We, in turn, roared our approval until Olaf held up his hands for silence. "So think nothing of that which you see from the Vestmenn. Do your duty, fight for your fame and your friend, and let the Norns see to your fate!"

I could not recall a more inspiring speech from Olaf. His words stoked a fire in our hearts that carried us forward in armor and shield, weapons-rich, into the men amassing to march toward battle. I found us close to the Sudreyjarmen, who sang and laughed as they ambled. They, like the Vestmenn, were a motley but high-spirited tangle of farmers and warriors, young and old, armored and unarmored. I hoped their liveliness would make up for their wretched equipment.

We strode down the hillside into a tree-lined gulley and out onto a broad, grassy field that sloped ever so slightly downward from the line on which we stopped. The mist here was thicker. Too thick for my liking. It could not hide the front line of shouting Northmen and Vestmenn who gathered three hundred paces before us, but what lay farther beyond that line was more obscured. Whether five hundred Northmen gathered against us or five thousand, I could not say, and that troubled me greatly.

"Ah, splendid," Orm grumbled as he stepped onto the field. "Might as well fight with one eye closed."

"Did you expect the Vestmenn to make it easier for you, Orm?" responded Ulf.

Olaf squinted at the sky. "It will burn away."

"Aye. It always does," added Berse.

I spat. The weather was just one more reason we should not be there. We had already scratched our wealth from the tribes of the North Sea and did not need to feed from the hands of these kings who cared nothing for us or our contributions to their cause. We were fools, and so were the Vestmenn. Had we any sense at all, we'd march from the field to higher ground, where we had an advantage and could see those we fought. But the Norns had not woven it so. Or mayhap it was more accurate to say that Olaf's will had placed us on this battlefield. Either way, we were here and Ivar's army was facing us, ready for a fight.

Around us, the units began to form. We stood by like dullards, waiting for instructions. Eventually one of Iron Knee's lords marshaled us to our position in the rear, behind Iron Knee's household guard and the Danish mercenaries. I noticed Styrr off to the left with his fork-bearded friend Geirbjorn by his side. Before them stood the men of Dyflin and the island men from Sudreyjar. Together we formed the left flank of King Malachy's army.

Two long lines of archers stood to our right, their bows unstrung to protect the bowstrings from the moist mist. We would see just how fast they could string them when Ivar's Danes and the Leinstermen came. Behind them sat Malachy on his horse with his lords and his bannermen gathered about him. With them sat the priests I had seen that morning, though instead of crosses, they now carried clubs and maces. It surprised me to see them there.

As I turned my gaze back to the field, a thumping of shields started up. Yells and curses soon followed. War drums pulsed. Birds screeched from their perches and disappeared into the murk. Horses whinnied, and war horns blew. I closed my eyes and took a deep breath, drinking in the cacophony, the camaraderie, the thrill, the churn in my belly that flowed to my limbs. Thor only knew how much I had missed it.

Olaf stood to my right, his eyes focused ahead, though there was nothing to see save the indistinct outline of Ivar's army. I had grown used to his habit of grinning before a fight, but I saw no grin now.

"What is the matter?" I asked him, thinking that the priest's words had once again burrowed into his thoughts. "Is this not what you enjoy?" My question was sincere, but once spoken, it hung like a reproach in the air between us.

He regarded me with steady eyes and sniffed.

To his right, Sveinn drew a wooden figurine from his purse and held it before him. He had whittled the wooden warrior with his own hand. He bent and stood it in the grass at his feet. I grinned at the small cere-mony, for it was one Sveinn had started during our time together in Bolgaraland. He called the figures tokens of remembrance with the hope that one day someone might find them and know that a clash of arms had happened on that spot.

Nearby, Ulf took a swig from his waterskin, which was undoubtedly not water at all, but ale. Dragomir and Orm checked their gear, then that of Ottar, who stood between them. The older man had planted his spear in the turf for support and shooed his friends away as if they were pesky flies. I strode to the ailing man and stared into his feverish eyes.

"You need not do this," I said to him. "No one will think the lesser of you."

He squinted at me, his face sweating and rigid. "The gods will think the lesser of me, and that is what matters most."

I nodded and took a long look at his face, searing it into my memory. "Stay close to Orm. He will see you through."

"I will look after myself."

I patted his shoulder, nodded at my other comrades, then returned to my place in the line. As I did, a cheer rent the air, and I looked about. Malachy had ridden forth and was pounding down the line on his horse, his sword drawn and twirling over his head, the fog swirling about him as he rode.

"For God!" he yelled to the cheer of his men. "For God!"

He cut an inspiring figure, I will grant him that. Even if his words made me want to vomit. Near me, Sveinn hawked and spat.

Olaf roared into the growing din, "Remember my earlier words, and let the gods see you this day, my wolves!"

The enemy charged as soon as the words left Olaf's lips, as if he alone had summoned them to the fray. Because I was standing behind several rows of men with the fog swirling about, my vision was obscured, but I did not need to see them to know they came — their pounding feet and high-pitched screams told me all.

To my right, the archers scrabbled to string their bows, then lifted their weapons to the sky and loosed. Their missiles vanished into the gray, though in the distance, I heard the screams of men. At the same time, arrows streaked down upon the front line of our army. Stricken men spun or simply collapsed. Warriors shrieked in pain and rage.

"Ottar! No!" yelled Orm.

But the old fool ignored Orm's call and charged past Iron Knee's men, vanishing into a small gap between the Dyfliners and Malachy's forces. Just as he disappeared, the army of Ivar and Domnall arrived in a frothing, angry wave, like a storm swell rolling out of a fog-covered sea. The streak of blades and bulk of shields rippled across the field. Screams tore at the thick air. Spears flew. And in the heavens, our gods laughed. Yet we, Olaf's men, stood by, waiting, shouting, itching to fight, like the giant wolf Fenrir yanking at his chains before Ragnarok.

The mist, I noted, had thickened, not burned away. Lines blurred. Bodies blended, and colors dimmed. In the brume, it was impossible to say who held the advantage, or where the battle line was. But that mattered not anymore. The battle was raging, and there was no stopping it.

"We're giving way," Olaf hollered.

Only then did I realize that Iron Knee's troops were backstepping. To our right, the center held firm. I glanced at Malachy. He pointed at our lines, and one of his banners waved, though I know not what effect it had on the mass of brawling bodies that filled the gloomy field before us.

At that very moment, Iron Knee drew his sword and shouted at his Danes to advance. They pushed ahead, with Styrr and Geirbjorn at their center. Only instead of strengthening the line, the bastards did something so unexpected, it took me a long moment to interpret it.

"Traitors!" Olaf yelled.

Instead of pressing into the front line to fight the enemy, the Danes hacked their blades into the backs of the unsuspecting Dyfliners. In short order, they split the Dyflin forces in two and created a channel through which our foe could fight.

"Protect Iron Knee!" Olaf roared and rushed forward into the swarm of bodies.

"Stay together!" I shouted at our men as we pressed past Iron Knee's bodyguards and into the fray. "Keep Iron Knee's banner behind you!"

Battles take many forms. Some are slogs where one shield wall moves step by step against another, grimly hacking and stabbing its way to victory or defeat. Others are small skirmishes or sudden raids where the fighting is fierce and open, but brief. But this was different. This was open and chaotic, immense and demanding, where friend and foe blended in a whirlpool of gray mist and blood and mire.

A warrior rushed at me and swung his axe hard at my head. I blocked the swing high with my shield and drove my own axe into the man's forehead before he could defend himself. Another came at me with his spear. I turned it aside with my shield, spun inside the man's weapon, and hacked my axe into his neck. Another swung his sword. I ducked and took his leg off below the knee. As he fell, a Vestmann rushed forward to get to Sveinn. I knew not if he was a friend or foe, but I thrust my shield into his side and knocked him from his feet. Sveinn kicked him hard in the face and knocked him unconscious.

Still more came. One after the other, and sometimes in twos. This was not the celebrated work of sagas and poems. It was the ugly, violent toil of killing and maiming, hacking and slicing, punching and kicking — whatever I could do to stem the tide that came against me. All this I did while trying to keep Iron Knee's banner to my rear and my comrades close. For I knew as soon as that position shifted, more of Iron Knee's men would see me — would see us — and think of us, with our Northern appearance, as the enemy.

Ivar's Northmen and Domnall's Leinstermen kept coming. We, Olaf's men, now held the center of Iron Knee's line. The perfidious Styrr and Geirbjorn were farther down to the right of us. I could see the giant's massive form from the corner of my eye. The Dyfliners and Sudrey-jarmen fought with us, but many had died and more had been wounded. I am certain I had killed a few on that field, such was the chaos of the fight. Behind us were Iron Knee and his bodyguard. I knew not where Malachy's Vestmenn were or how his lines held. Frankly, I cared not a whit, so intent was I on staying alive. My shield was cracked. My armor was nicked. My head rang from the screams and from a blade that had struck my helmet. Below my feet, the grass was slick with the blood and entrails of corpses.

To my left, Sveinn took a man's head with his sword. To my right, Olaf knocked a man's spear aside, then drove his blade into the same man's gut. Two more men came at him then, and he urged them on, smiling now. He parried the strike of one, then stepped back to avoid the swing of another. But in doing so, he tripped and fell from my vision.

A man who falls in a fight such as this is usually as good as dead. And so I turned in that instant, desperate to help my friend rise. I swung my axe into the enemy's neck as he stepped in to finish Olaf, then blocked the strike of another man who came from my left. As I turned back to help Olaf, I saw a sight I never thought I would see — one that would haunt me forever.

15

Olaf lay on his side with a spear protruding from the rings of his byrnie. The spear looked to be lodged in his upper side, though in the tangle and confusion, I could not be sure. The man who held it was one of Iron Knee's bodyguards, who must have mistaken him for one of Ivar's Northmen. I stared at the man for a second after he yanked his weapon free, and as understanding donned on his face, I saw his remorse.

"Bastard!" Olaf cried.

"Sveinn!" I yelled.

He glanced at me, and seeing the issue, stepped in front of me to offer himself as my shield, giving me a moment to grab Olaf's byrnie at his collar and yank him to his feet. Olaf yelled at the pain of it.

"We need to get you away from here," I shouted at him over the din. I knew not how serious his wound was, but I did know it would slow him, and as his oath-sword protector, I could not risk having him injured again, or worse, killed.

"No!" Olaf growled and pushed past me.

I thought to protest, but what could I do? Olaf had always done what he wanted and now was not the time to argue. Besides, it was happening too fast and the enemy was still coming at us.

Another Northman jabbed at me with his seax. I knocked the thrust away, then twisted my wrist and spun my battered shield rim into the man's face. He collapsed into the man behind him.

"Iron Knee!" The call came from my right; I glanced in that direction.

Styrr was closer now. Beside him was Geirbjorn, his braided beard dripping with the blood of his victims.

"You are a nithing, Styrr. A nothing!" called Iron Knee.

A few Vestmenn were all that separated them from each other. Styrr bludgeoned one aside with his shield. Geirbjorn made quick work of another. Dragomir, who stood closest to Styrr, shifted in that direction with Orm and Ulf by his side, but they found their path blocked by several Danes.

"Take him!" Olaf yelled to me in reference to the man he fought, then stepped from the line and pressed his way to Iron Knee's side just as Styrr reached him.

I parried a blow, then kicked the leg of the man who had been fighting Olaf. The man's knee gave, and he collapsed. I killed him as he fell, then glanced back at Olaf and Iron Knee.

The king came at Styrr's head with a powerful slash of his sword. The giant met the blow high and counter-attacked with his battle axe. The blade met the king's shield, knocking the younger, smaller man to his right and into Geirbjorn's path. Off-balance, the king could do little to defend himself as he stumbled. Styrr shifted his weight and lifted his blade to strike.

Olaf ducked the swing of another Dane and ripped his blade through the flesh and bone of Styrr's right leg. I do not think Styrr knew he had fallen until Olaf's blade hacked into his head.

Geirbjorn saw his comrade fall just as a cheer rose in the distance. The Dyfliners had broken the center and right flank of the line and now moved to roll up the enemy who faced us. Seeing their peril, Ivar's army blew their horns and disengaged. Geirbjorn and those of his men still alive broke off the fight with shouted curses and vanished with the retreating army. The survivors of Iron Knee's men could do little but watch them go. We were too exhausted to do much else. Besides, Olaf was now swaying on his feet and needed help.

I moved to my friend's side and ran my eyes over the blood seeping through the chains on his byrnie to run down his right leg. "Orm! Help me!" I commanded.

I pulled Olaf's left arm over my shoulder. Orm took the other. Olaf hollered a curse at that simple movement. "Put me down, damn you."

"No," I responded. "You need help. Not rest."

But as we tried to walk with Olaf, we found he could barely put one foot before the other, let alone avoid the corpses and detritus of war strewn on the ground beneath us.

"Put him on a shield," called Sveinn as he cleared a spot on the ground and placed two shields before us. "We will carry him."

"How is he?" asked Iron Knee as we gently lowered Olaf onto his makeshift stretcher.

"He needs help, quickly," I responded without looking up. I did not try to mask the concern in my voice. Olaf was more than just my lord and friend. We were like brothers, and the thought of losing him terrified me.

"Padraic," the king called to the head of his guard. "Lead them to my camp and find my healer. Go!"

Berse, Orm, Ulf, and Dragomir clutched the rims of the overlapping shields once Olaf lay upon them. I lifted Olaf's feet so that they would not pull against his abdomen, a movement that made him curse me all the more. Raising the shields gently, we hauled him, hunched and grunting, over the littered field. Sveinn and the man named Padraic went before us, clearing corpses and discarded gear that lay in our way until we reached a cart that carried equipment. We hauled Olaf into it despite his muffled cries of pain, then jogged with the horses back to the camp and to a clearing that served as a space for the wounded. Olaf was the first to lie on that ground.

"Lay him here," Padraic commanded in a broken version of our tongue as he pointed to a spot near a crackling fire. A woman stood nearby, watching us. Padraic spoke quickly to her, then retreated in the direction of the battlefield.

We found a discarded cloak and lay Olaf on it after stripping him of his byrnie. Olaf barely noticed. He was groaning now, his eyes shut, his skin a sickening shade of gray and white, his tunic a mess of crimson.

I know not why, but I expected the woman to go in search of an old healer or perchance a priest. Instead, she dropped a basket of rags beside Olaf's body, knelt, and pulled the tunic up and away from Olaf's side. The spear had ripped a groove across his pectoral muscle and to the center of his torso. In it, I thought I saw the white of his chest bone, though I could not be sure.

Upon seeing the bloody wound, the woman turned and pointed to a small pot that lay on stones near the fire. "Bring that here," she commanded in our tongue. Another surprise.

Berse brought the pot to the healer as I looked on in disbelief. My feet would not move, nor would my mind command them to. I had not expected to see a wound so deep and long, nor Olaf's blood flowing so freely from his body, and that vision held me captive. I suppose it was the same for the others, for they, like me, stood there dumbfounded.

The healer shoved a rag into the boiling water and rung it out before balling it and pressing it onto Olaf's gash. "You. Press here and hold. The rest of you leave."

I welcomed the distraction and moved to do the healer's bidding. The others shuffled away.

"Harder," she commanded. I pushed on the now-crimson rag, and Olaf groaned.

"Good," she said. "Hold it there."

She dipped a fresh rag into the steaming pot, wrung the moisture out, and pressed it on another section of the gash.

"Take it," she commanded. Then she lifted Olaf's tunic to her eyes and examined the tear where the blade had traveled.

"What are you doing?" I asked, as much from curiosity as to get my mind off of the ghastly shade of Olaf's skin.

"The cloth of his tunic is soiled. If there are bits of it in his wound, the wound could rot."

I had seen men die because of it, though it was hard for me to grasp that such a thing might befall Olaf. He was too strong, was he not? Too gods-blessed? Surely the Norns would not cut his life string because of fever?

She moved my hands aside and delicately pulled the wound open to examine it further. It *had* been bone I'd seen. His rib, I surmised grimly, and closed my eyes to it.

"Go to your friends," she suggested delicately.

The face that looked back at me was middle-aged and hardened from the stress of her task. Still, beneath the concern and blood streaks and coils of chestnut hair was a handsome face, with caring brown eyes and a dimple on her left cheek that somehow balanced a long scar that ran the length of her right. I must have stared at it a bit too long, for she turned her head away from my gaze.

"Will he live?"

"Go," she said again, more quietly this time.

And I left.

The men's eyes met mine as I found them in our camp. They sat at a firepit, though no fire burned within it. Some washed their weapons and their skin of the day's gore. Others ate.

"How does he fare?" Berse asked.

I shrugged. How was I to know the weave of the Norns' thread or whether this was where that weave ended? I also did not trust myself to answer, for I liked not what I'd seen.

"Come," Sveinn said as he rose. "Let us return to the field and make ourselves useful. There is no sense in sitting here and worrying."

He was right, of course. Olaf was in the hands of a healer. We could do nothing more. Still, I was loath to leave. I knew I could not sway what fate had in store for my friend, but leaving him felt like abandoning him, and I could not bring myself to do that.

"You go," I said to the men. "I will stay in case I am needed. Berse, see to the men and those who need help. And make sure the Vestmenn do not take the spoils that are rightfully ours."

I sat as they departed and, using my water skin, scrubbed the grime from my arms and face. It fell from me like crimson rain, as if I, too, bled.

Around me, the camp roused to the aftermath of battle. A few horses whinnied. Carts appeared carrying the first wounded. Behind them limped the injured, emerging from the billowing mist in the valley. They appeared in camp like draugr, those undead beings who crawl from their graves. Some moaned, others stared silently as they sought friends or places to rest. Camp followers went to their aid, or else wailed when they learned the fate of a loved one. I turned my eyes from it, though I could not shut my ears from the sound.

The sight of it all led my mind's eye down darker paths. And try as I might, I could not keep my thoughts from following. What if Olaf were to die? What would I do? I could not imagine the depths of my grief, or how my failure to protect him might cripple me. And if I were to recover from that, what then? Would I take over his army? Would there be an army to lead? Or would I return to the North and my daughter? Or mayhap to a shack where I could hide in shame? More likely, I would wander, for the only home I had truly known in my life had been impermanent. Transitory. Fluid. Home to me was a war camp, a ship upon the sea, and a group of hardened men to whom I entrusted my life. There was my daughter, of course, though I had not seen her in many summers. Besides, she thought of another man as her father, so I could not count her as belonging to me.

Unable to rid my mind of my dark thoughts or think of anything else to do, I returned to the spot where I had left the healer. She cared for another man now but looked at me when I arrived and wiped some errant curls from her eyes, leaving a swath of blood across her forehead. Her brows were angled down toward her nose, pulled perchance by the deep groove that sat between them.

"I have cleaned and bandaged his wound," she said with a jerk of her head toward Olaf's sleeping figure. "The blood has slowed. I will return later to check on him."

As I gazed upon Olaf's resting form, my thoughts flew to the strange priest in Dyflin. What was it the man had said? That Olaf would be grievously wounded by his own man? Did the spear of Iron Knee's guard count as that? I pushed the thought away.

"What can I do to aid him?" I called to her.

"You can let him sleep," she replied and turned her attention back to the wounded man she now tended.

Olaf's warriors staggered into the camp soon after. They came in ones and twos, some hale, others wounded and supported by their comrades. I greeted them as they passed, offering words of encouragement to those I knew. Most looked from me to Olaf, and though they held their tongues, I not only saw their bitterness but felt it upon me. Our lord had fallen, and we — his hird — had failed to protect him.

"How is he?"

I turned to Berse. "His wound is cleansed, but he rests."

Behind Berse stood Ulf and Orm and Dragomir and Sveinn.

"Ottar?" I asked, though I knew the answer already.

Berse shook his head and spat. "Gone."

I nodded. "He died nobly," I said as I pictured him feasting with his friends in Odin's hall. It brought a small bit of cheer to my sadness. "And the men? How many did we lose?"

Berse grimaced. "It was a hard day. Best we can tell, nearly half of our men were slain or wounded. And of the wounded, half again won't survive the night. I know naught of the entire army."

The words hit me like a kick to the groin. "Gods," I huffed.

"There is talk of raiding," Sveinn said, interrupting my thoughts.

"When?"

He shrugged. "Soon, I imagine. Iron Knee and Malachy wish to repay the Leinstermen for their arrogance."

"Go with them," I commanded Berse, "and take the men that are willing. Grab what wealth you can. We need to take something of value from this woeful affair."

Berse just nodded and walked away. The others glanced at me but said not a word. They too felt the weight of Olaf's wound. I could see it in their eyes.

I returned to my vigil by Olaf's side, trying my best to shield my mind from the sounds of weeping and the call of hungry ravens in the distance. At some point Sveinn brought me a bowl of stew, but I could not eat. My stomach was twisted, and my thoughts were more so. We had been through much, Olaf and I. Our escape through the forest of the Svear. Brutal thralldom in Estland. Vicious battles in Gardariki and Wagria. Summers of raiding and trading. And never once had Olaf been wounded. But now we had come to this random place on Olaf's whim, and a Vestmann had laid him low. It was hard to understand, but then, a man never knew what his fate held.

Daylight faded beneath a layer of clouds that rolled overhead. I sensed rain and covered Olaf with a blanket, then coaxed flames from kindling and started a small fire.

"How is he?"

I turned to the unfamiliar voice and rose to greet King Iron Knee. Warriors flanked the young king, who had shed his armor and donned an unblemished tunic and cloak. His hair was wet and pulled back into a ponytail, and his skin was cleansed of the day's grit and blood.

"He rests," I responded simply.

The king regarded Olaf for a moment, then turned back to me. "He saved my life today. All of you men saved us. I will not forget that."

I nodded but was unsure of just what to say. I had saved many men that day, just as men had saved me. It was the nature of the spear storm.

My eyes traveled to Padraic, who stood to the left of the king. Had he not been so careless with his spear, Olaf would not be lying behind me or fighting for his life. I thought to rebuke him but held my tongue. My stern gaze was enough to communicate what I felt. The young warrior lowered his head and eyed the ground at his feet.

"Keep me apprised of his condition," Iron Knee said, then walked away.

16

Olaf's condition did not improve that day or the next. I should know — I rarely left his side. Mostly he slept, and while he did, I whittled or sharpened my axe or ate — anything to keep my mind from the thought of his loss. When sweat beaded on his brow, I removed his cloak and mopped his forehead with a rag. When he shivered, I covered him. I heard his moans and watched as his head shifted from side to side. His body was fighting, but there was little more I could do to aid him.

The healer returned the first evening and placed her hand on his forehead, then lowered her ear to his mouth. She lifted his tunic and examined his bandage. It was dark with his blood. Gently, she peeled it away and sniffed the leaking wound. She washed it again, then reached into a purse that hung from her hip and withdrew a small bundle of sticky material that she rolled into an oblong ball. This she pressed into the wound.

"What is that?" I asked.

"Spiderwebs with a bit of honey added," she responded as she placed a clean bandage over the gash. "It will bond the wound and help with the bleeding."

I frowned but held my tongue. I had never heard of such a thing, but then, I had not been around many healers or spoken to them about their methods.

She glanced at me as she rose. "He is fighting. It is good that he is strong."

"Aye," I confirmed.

She frowned, though I know not why, then turned and left.

Later that night, she returned again to check on Olaf. She carried a small pot, which she laid on the stones by the fire. After checking my friend's forehead, she sniffed again at the wound. Apparently satisfied, she reached into the pot, extracted a ladle, and brought it to me.

"Sip," she instructed as she held it out to me.

I gazed up at her shadowed face. "What is it?"

"Tea. It will help you sleep."

"I do not wish to sleep," I replied.

She knelt and looked earnestly into my face. "You cannot help your friend if you are too tired. Besides, we have done what we can for today. It is up to his body now. Drink."

I took the ladle and sipped. The tea was bitter, but its warmth in my throat soothed me.

"How is it you know my language?" I was not sure I wanted to know the answer, especially if it was related to the scar on her face, but my curiosity had taken hold of me and my weariness had softened my hesitation to ask.

She sighed and I braced myself, thinking I had driven her away with my query. "You need not respond. I am only curious," I added hastily.

"No, it is alright. Drink more, and I will tell you."

I nodded. "A fair bargain." I grabbed the ladle and sucked the tea into my mouth, more as a peace offering than to do her bidding.

She sat before me and crossed her legs like a young child. "I am from a village not far from here. Several summers ago, a rival clan raided it. They killed my parents, my husband, and my child and took the survivors as slaves." Her eyes turned down. "But I was not very obedient, which is how I received this scar." She ran a long finger over it, then returned her eyes to me. They were moist. "I suppose my master did not like having a flawed woman in his home," she sneered, "so he sold me in Dyflin, where a Northman purchased me. He taught me the language."

As she told her story, the words of the Sudreyjarmen came back to me. *The clans fight for land and power and cattle.* I had not known that they took thralls as well, though I suppose it should not have surprised me. The slave trade was everywhere and always had been.

"You are free now?" I asked delicately.

"Aye," she confirmed. "When Malachy defeated the Northmen, my owner fled and Malachy released me from captivity along with all of the other Éireannach in Dyflin owned by Northmen."

It was what the Sudreyjar man had said. "That was good of him."

"Aye." She offered me the ladle, and I sipped obediently.

"How did you learn to be a healer?"

"That was my mother's doing. She was the midwife of our village and often took me with her on her rounds when I was a child. I worked by her side until the clan came and took her life."

Her troubled face made me uncomfortable, so I tried to turn her mind to other things. "And now you are Iron Knee's healer?"

She snorted and smirked. "It is like him to think so. No. I help in his household when he has a need for care. But I live not on his grounds and am only beholden to him when he calls on me."

"But you came with his army. It is a risk, is it not?"

She shrugged. "He summoned me, and he is my king."

As she spoke, my eyelids grew heavier. I rocked my legs fitfully, struggling to remain awake.

"And you?" she asked. "How is it that you and your lord are here?"

I sensed myself slipping and shifted my body to a more comfortable position. "I am just a warrior." I smiled. "I do what I am told."

Her chuckle sounded distant in my ears. "I doubt that," she said, and then I heard no more.

I awoke the following day to find a camp in motion. Normally when I slept, I awoke at the first sounds of movement. It was a defensive behavior that I had developed when fleeing my home as a lad. But this day, it took the nudge of Sveinn's boot to rouse me. I shot upright and peered around me, startled not only by the light of the morning but also by the commotion. Horses whinnied, and men moved about me. A smithy hammered in the distance. Someone shouted. I shook my head and wondered how I had slept through it all.

"Are you hale?" Sveinn gazed down at me.

I rubbed my face, but it did nothing to remove the fog muddling my thoughts. "What is happening?"

"Malachy has called men to arms. We go to take our revenge on Leinster. Do you still wish to stay?"

I nodded and glanced over at Olaf. It was hard to tell whether his sleep was temporary or permanent.

Sveinn must have seen my sudden concern. "Fear not, Torgil. He sleeps."

Only then did my eyes come to rest on something that lay on my friend's chest. I focused my eyes upon it, then stood quickly, if a little stiffly, and marched to Olaf's side. "Who put that there?" I growled at Sveinn, my finger pointing at the cross on Olaf's chest.

Sveinn raised his good hand to calm me. "Not I." He suddenly grinned. "Mayhap he asked for it."

I glowered at him and peered at the wounded man nearest Olaf. No cross lay on his chest, nor on the next man closest to him. Nor on the third man or the fourth. I bent and grabbed the charm, then tossed it as far away as I could. It spun over the top of several tents before vanishing into the camp.

"Damn Christians!" I spat and marched back to Sveinn, who was now squinting at me as if I had lost my mind. I calmed myself enough to remember that he was leaving with the others, though my anger still smoldered. "Be careful," I warned him. "And if wealth is to be had, take as much as you can carry."

"I will," he confirmed, then switched the subject. "You should check on the other men. In the absence of Crowbone, they look to you. It will lift their spirits."

I snorted, thinking he jested. "I am not one to lift spirits."

"Still," he said, "it will do them good." He nodded and left to join the other men assembling at the edge of camp.

"Why do you not join them?" a woman's voice asked from behind me.

I turned to see the healer. She had pulled her chestnut ringlets into a loose ponytail, though a few errant curls hung about her ears. She had also cleansed her skin of blood, though there was no hiding the dark rings under her bloodshot eyes. Seen in the morning light, I noticed just how attractive she truly was. Not in a young, seductive way that was devoid of blemishes and wrinkles, but in a mature, handsome way, as if life's sorrows had not yet extinguished the light and vitality within her.

"I remain here to aid my lord if he needs it," I finally responded.

"Then you have failed in your task, Torgil," she reprimanded me with a grin.

I cocked my head. "How so? And how do you know my name? I have not told it to you."

"No, you have not, but some of your men have. And you have failed because your lord has soiled himself."

I sniffed the air and found within it the faint aroma of urine. It had been masked by the smoke of cooking fires and horse dung and body odor and the myriad other smells that hung over our army. I cursed.

She chuckled. "Come. Remove his breeks, and cover him with a cloak. I won't look."

I peered at my lord's sleeping body and cursed again. He was a large man. It would not be simple to pull his thick legs free of his wet breeks without hurting him.

The healer cleared her throat and motioned to Olaf. "Well?"

I sighed and moved to his body. The healer left to check on other men and returned after I laid a cloak across my friend's exposed legs and groin.

"You have not told me your name," I said to her as she knelt by Olaf and lifted his tunic.

"It is Deidre," she responded, then sniffed the bandage. Ever so gently, she undid the ties that held the bandages in place and peeled the material from his wound. The crusted blood cracked as the bandage pulled away, and fresh blood oozed. Olaf moaned and opened his eyes for a moment before drifting back to sleep. I might have been alarmed, had Deidre not been humming a melody, completely at ease. She wiped the blood away with a fresh rag and moved closer to the wound and the bruised skin beside the gash. She then gazed at the sky.

"It is warm today," she remarked. "We will leave the bandages off and let air in."

"What if dirt gets into it?"

She glanced at me. "That is why you are here."

She unfolded a clean, dry rag and laid it over the wound. "Keep the rag on it, but don't press down. The goal is to let air in but not dirt. Do you understand?"

"I understand," I said.

She winked at me and rose. "How did you sleep last night?"

"I do not remember ever sleeping so well," I admitted.

She grinned. "That is good. You needed it." She turned to leave.

"There was a charm on Olaf when I awoke this morning," I called to her. "Did you put it there last night?"

Her brows bent at the question. "What sort of charm?"

I feared she would hear the accusation in my voice and get defensive, but there was no anger in her response, only curiosity. I shook my head. "It was nothing."

She regarded me a moment longer, shrugged, then strode away with her basket of rags and pot of steaming water.

That afternoon, I did as Sveinn suggested and walked among our wounded. The area where the wounded lay was on the other side of the supply tents, far removed from the Vestmenn, as befit our status as Northmen in Iron Knee's army. In truth, I smelled the area long before I reached it, though the gathering ravens waiting for their pickings told me as much as the stench.

I stopped as I neared and stared at the sprawling men. For six summers we had enjoyed a life of sudden raids and very few losses, but here outside Dyflin, the scales had evened and the gods had taken their tribute. I stepped carefully through the place and did my best to acknowledge each man with a few short words or, at the very least, a nod. Gods, was it hard for me to see so many in their condition, and harder still knowing that they had not received the care that Olaf enjoyed. Judging from the blood-soaked rags covering their wounds and the way in which the wounded men assisted each other, I doubted any healer had walked among them at all. The guilt of that knowledge hung on me, and I silently vowed to speak with Deidre about it, though I knew not what she could do.

She listened earnestly to my entreaties later that afternoon and when I was through, she sighed. "The priests tried to help your men, Torgil. But your men chased them away."

"Perchance if you went to them?"

She shook her head. "I have not the supplies or the people," she said with a vague wave at the camp. "I am sorry."

I accepted her news with a nod and turned away. It was a painful draught to swallow, but I reminded myself that it was no different than any other battle I had survived in the past. Rarely had we had healers to help us. The men, including Olaf, were in the hands of the Norns, as they always had been.

On the third day of Olaf's convalescence, we moved those of the wounded who couldn't walk to carts and returned to Dyflin, for the clouds had begun to spit their moisture down upon us again and it would do little good to have the injured lying in the gathering puddles. Despite their protests, Deidre had convinced the priests and camp followers to take the Northmen as well. I am certain it saved the lives of more than a few.

I thanked her for that small kindness.

"There is no need for thanks," she replied. "Did they not fight against the Leinstermen too?" She answered her question before I could reply. "It is the least I can do."

I climbed into the cart beside my friend. Behind us gathered those Dyfliners and Sudreyjarmen and Northmen who could still walk. I marked the two men I'd sat beside at the feast table. A bandage wrapped the head of Scraggly. His brother wore his arm in a bloody sling. Still, it was good to see them alive.

The cart lurched forward, and Olaf winced, then opened his red-rimmed eyes a slit and shifted his gaze to me.

"Is it as bad as it feels?" he croaked. His voice was a whisper.

My heart soared, though it did not alleviate my concern. "Aye. It is bad," I told him, then cursed as the cart suddenly jolted again.

Olaf gritted his teeth against the pain and scowled at me.

I shrugged. "It was either this or leave you to lie in the mud. Which would you have preferred?"

The cart rocked again. "The mud," he hissed.

I smiled. It was good to see him awake, if only slightly. "Where is the fun in that, Crowbone?"

He closed his eyes. "Damn you," he mumbled.

"You have been through worse," I reminded him. It was an attempt to lift his spirits, but it was not true. He had never been so injured in his life.

When we arrived in Dyflin, those of our party who had remained at the ships organized a group to help transfer the wounded to tents in our camp. I did not tell them of Olaf. I did not wish to alarm them so soon. Thankfully, I had no need to. Iron Knee had commanded Deidre to watch Olaf until he was on his feet or he was dead, and so she took him to her dwelling, where she kept more herbs and healing supplies.

Deidre's place was nothing more than a single room with two cots. There was a table holding various jars, spoons, knives, and other utensils. Dried herbs hung from the beams above it. Across the room was a small firepit surrounded by stones and pots. There was not much else, and it somehow saddened me. To my mind, a woman of such value should have more, but perchance she preferred it so.

Day after day I checked on Olaf, and never did I see him awake, which troubled me.

"He wakes from time to time," Deidre assured me, "though he does so on his body's time, not ours."

Then one day I knocked on her door and she opened it with a smile. I looked from her to Olaf's bed, where my friend rested with his eyes open. Even in the gloom of her dwelling, I could see the color in his face. I looked once again at her smiling face, then went to Olaf's cot.

"It is good to see you awake," I said as I placed my hand on his shoulder.

Olaf smiled. "It is good to be awake," he replied groggily. "What day is it?"

I shrugged. "Torsdag, I believe."

His jaw fell open, and he blinked. "Seven days," he muttered.

"Huh?"

"Seven days," he replied, his voice more pensive.

"What are you telling me?" I asked, not understanding.

"The priest. His warning. Seven days, Torgil." He stared at me. "It has come to pass."

17

The men returned from ravaging Leinster with silver in their purses and souvenirs on their belts. I was glad to see them happy and hale, though a little surprised that most of the silver had come from a monastery. I had not known that the Vestmenn would attack their own holy places. Nor had I expected to see priests among the thralls and cattle and wagons of loot that they paraded into Dyflin. Deidre had alerted me to the dangers of rival clans and counties, but to enslave holy men was something altogether different. Perchance they did not fear their God's wrath. Still, it seemed strange to me.

We honored the return of our men with a raucous, days-long feast that washed up from our riverside camp and spilled into the streets of Dyflin, where Iron Knee held his own victory celebration. I worried that our men might not mingle well with the Vestmenn, but my worry vanished when the men greeted each other with hugs and backslapping and pitchers of ale. It seemed the fighting had woven the men more tightly together. Rarely did I allow myself to drink overmuch, but it was hard to contain my own elation at having survived and, more importantly, at Olaf's survival and recovery. And so I drank with

Olaf's merry wolves around me, though I tasked Sveinn with containing me, should I go too far.

I remember not which day it was, but Olaf did appear at one point. Many of the men were away at the ale houses, or sleeping off their headaches. I remember the cheers that rose as he stepped into our camp with his hair combed and a new tunic draped over his thinner frame. Sadly, what pierces my memory most was not the elation of his appearance, but the cross that twinkled in the midday sun from his neck. Mind you, it hung beside the amulet of Odin, but I did not see that, of course. I saw only the cross and, as was my wont when drinking, I lost control of my emotions.

"So you are a Christian now?" I said as I stood.

"Torgil, don't." Sveinn placed his good hand on my forearm.

Olaf scowled. "Say no more, Torgil. You are drinking and forget yourself. King Iron Knee gave me this as thanks for saving him." He plucked the cross from his chest and lifted it to us. "I go to see him next. Am I not supposed to wear it?"

"So King Iron Knee would have you converted?" I raised my arm to indicate the others. "And us? Would he like to convert us, too?"

Deep lines formed between Olaf's brows, but rather than speak, he turned and strode away.

I spat and reclaimed my seat.

"He is only doing what he must," Berse said as Olaf disappeared into the throng of revelers.

I glared at the man. "Pull your head from Olaf's arse." I motioned at Olaf's retreating figure. "Old Crowbone risks the wrath of our gods, Berse, and I have no desire to be on the receiving end of that anger."

"Gods, Torgil," said Sveinn. "You are wound tighter than a tangled spool. Be at ease."

Across the fire, Ulf jangled his silver-filled purse and hefted his ale cup. "If this is suffering, I am glad for it." He turned his face to the sky. "More suffering, gods! Do you hear me?" He howled at the sky.

He roared at his joke, and the men howled with him. I did not join them.

Eventually the priests grew tired of our debauchery and demanded the feasting come to an end. Malachy returned to his stronghold, the Sudreyjarmen returned to their islands, and life settled back into its mundane rhythms.

Olaf rejoined our camp just after the feasting ended. I kept my distance from him, though I did keep an eye on his health and on the cross at his neck. He did not yet train with us, though I often saw him work his shoulder as if to loosen the muscles in his chest, which was the only indication he gave us that his health was returning. I noted, too, that he only wore the cross when interacting with Iron Knee and his lords. Both were good signs.

I had seen Deidre often as Olaf healed, but sadly, his return to our camp meant that I saw her only on rare occasions. It was usually on Dyflin's streets and always from a distance, but it built within me a desire to see her again. And so, not long after Olaf returned to our camp, I went to her dwelling with my hair combed and my stomach fluttering. Of course she was not there. I did not let that stop me. Again and again I tried, and again and again her absence thwarted me until, at some point in the fall, I finally gave up.

It was well into winter before Olaf's wound scarred over and the threat of tearing had passed. Not that an earlier recovery would have mattered. Iron Knee forbade us from raiding the lands around Dyflin. Nor would he permit us going farther afield in Irland. We could have departed and set our own course, but winter was upon us and the weather was unfavorable for raiding. At least that is the excuse Olaf gave to the men. To my mind, it was a weak justification. Yes, it showered daily, but settlements were less suspecting of trouble when rain was hammering down.

I began to think that there was another reason for remaining in Dyflin. Though I shared it with no man, I am certain the priest's vision played on Olaf's thoughts, especially after his recovery. It was just like Olaf to latch onto a fiction if wealth and renown might lie at the end of it. Iron Knee, of course, played a part in that. He obviously favored putting his trust in a *Christian* Northman. Knowing my friend, Olaf smelled that opportunity and hunted it. Of course he knew not where it might lead, but that mattered little so long as it built his riches and his fame and kept his men loyal. And so we sat and waited.

I must admit, Dyflin's soggy weather often drove men indoors and the temptations for warm fires and good ale were great. I, of course, was not fool enough to let the men sit idly, for idle men turn to foolish distractions. Thankfully, there was still much to do. Gathering wood; tending fires; keeping men fed; repairing the ships, weapons, and armor; training — the list of tasks was endless. And though mundane, they were necessary, for they kept us busy and fit and away from trouble.

In the spring, Iron Knee held a feast, to which he invited Olaf and me. I took Sveinn and Dragomir with me, though Olaf also took Hauk and Finn so he could teach them the ways of statesmanship. They were his kin, after all. King Iron Knee had not told us why he was holding a feast, though we could hear from camp the church bells and the residents of Dyflin singing and dancing. I figured it had something to do with one of their dead holy men, who they called saints. It seemed they celebrated one of the bastards every week, though I wondered if it was just a reason to drink more ale. I was not wrong in either thought.

"It would be a fine day to sack this place," I whispered to Dragomir as we headed through the gates and into the celebration. "Even the guards on the walls are drinking."

He snorted. "Imagine the loot we could take."

"It would sink our ships," I guessed.

"A good problem to have," Sveinn observed.

As we snaked our way through the crowd, I noted all of the greenery. Dyflin was awash in it. Green cloaks. Green tunics. Green shamrocks woven into women's hair. Green leaves hung from necklaces and lines that dangled from doorways. I looked at the others for an explanation, but they could only shrug.

We entered the open doors of Iron Knee's estate, which was a surprise unto itself. I had never seen the estate unbarred to the people of Dyflin, though I suppose it needed to be to accommodate the throng of people within the royal yard. Revelers stood everywhere that there was not a long table at which to sit. People young and old laughed and drank and ate. Some hoisted their cups and sang along with musicians. Even the dour priests had ale cups in their hands. I marveled at the scene, unable to keep the smile from my face.

The hall was no less festive. Iron Knee's royal guests stood or sat in every crevice of the place so that we had to physically force our way into the crowd. Wool dyed green and shaped into shamrocks draped the walls where shields used to hang. On the dais, a giant green banner hung from the rafters behind Iron Knee's High Seat. From his boots to his neck, he also wore the color, while two similarly outfitted young women sat on his lap.

We stopped before the king, though in the clamorous hall, Olaf had to call to the young monarch to tear his attention away from the ladies.

Upon seeing us, the corners of his lips turned up in a grin. "Ah, Olaf. Welcome!"

"King Iron Knee," Olaf acknowledged.

"Come. I have news for you, and an offer that I must make before these two fairies take me away."

"What is this feast?" Olaf called to him as the king ushered the young women aside.

"It is the feast of Saint Patrick, who is one of our most revered saints. He who converted Irland to Christianity."

"And the green?" Olaf asked as the king stepped down from the dais before him.

The king smiled. "It is said that Saint Patrick used the three leaves of the shamrock to explain the Holy Trinity to his converts." He must have seen our puzzled faces, for he waved his hand at us in dismissal. "It is a lesson for another day. Padraic," the king called to his guard.

Padraic, who had been sitting at the table beneath Iron Knee's throne, stood and joined us. With him were two others I recognized from the battle but had not seen since. Together we walked into an antechamber containing another table and benches.

The king motioned to us. "Sit."

Olaf sat with Hauk and Finn. Sveinn, Dragomir, and I did not. I know not about the others, but I did not trust the guards standing near the walls. The king eyed us curiously, then shrugged. Padraic filled each man's cup, then sat near his king with his two comrades.

"I trust your wound is healing?" Iron Knee asked.

"It is, thanks to you and Deidre," said Olaf with a gracious bow of his head.

Iron Knee looked pleased. "You saved me from those traitors. It was the least I could do for you."

I almost laughed. The king forgot to mention that none of this would have happened had not his frightened guard thrust his spear so hastily.

"But that is not why I called you here," the king continued, as his face turned serious. "It seems we have received some unfortunate missives from my sister. Her new husband is dead."

"So soon?" Olaf asked.

"Aye," said Iron Knee. "Though he was old, it was still unexpected. It is unfortunate because it throws many plans into disarray." He tapped on the rim of his cup. "I had hoped to forge a stronger relationship with that region of northern England. But that is now in question."

"I see," Olaf said as his eyes shifted from Iron Knee to Padraic and back again.

Iron Knee studied Olaf a moment longer. "There may be a means to remedy this sudden change, and it involves you. I have instructed my sister to hold a thing and choose a new husband, and I want you to attend."

Olaf cocked his head. "That sounds like a command rather than an offer."

The king smirked. "Perchance it is. Regardless, if you would like the chance of becoming a jarl in England, I am giving it to you."

It is one of the few times I have seen my friend speechless. "You are offering me a jarldom?"

The king grinned but raised a finger. "If you can win the hand of my sister."

Even Olaf, who loved bold plans, was stunned. "I lack words," he said hesitantly. "I am humbled by your generosity. Truly, I am. Still, I would know more. Where is this jarldom?"

"The locals call it Amounderness. It lies on the northwest coast of England and abuts the jarldom of Jorvik. Jarl Thored's land."

"And Jarl Thored serves King Ethelred of England. Will not Ethelred look ill on a Northman controlling it? Will not Thored in Jorvik?"

Iron Knee smiled ruefully. "I imagine they will not. It is far too distant from either man for them to cause you any trouble."

Olaf grunted. "But they could."

Iron Knee conceded the point with a shrug. "They could." He then smiled. "It is an ambitious plan, I admit, but you are an ambitious man, are you not? That is why you are here, eh?"

Olaf smiled, though I could tell it was merely to shield the thoughts that must have been storming through his mind. "Will you also attend this thing?" he finally asked.

"Me? No. I must remain here. I will send Padraic," he motioned at his man, "and provide my blessing, should she ask for it."

I must admit, if Iron Knee's goal was to find a suitable ally among the northern English, it was a clever plan. And a generous offer to Olaf. But to Olaf's point, a risky one as well.

"Why me?" Olaf finally asked. "You must have kin, or men closer to you," he motioned at Padraic, "who are as capable as me. Mayhap even friends in England?"

"Why not you?" the king retorted with a grin. "You saved my life. I have grown to trust you. You know how to trade and fight. You are a lord of warriors and of noble stock. All you need is a kingdom. You have said as much to me before. Now I am putting that before you. All you need to do is convince my sister, which should not be hard."

"And convince Thored and Ethelred," Olaf reminded him. "And even if I succeed at that, which will not be easy, I then must control a land of which I know little, and fight off the forces who would seek it back, which could be many." Olaf paused to scratch his jaw. "And what do you ask in return for this gracious gift?"

The king's smile stretched. "Ah. I knew you would come to that. My father dreamed of a more direct route to Jorvik that he would control completely — one that circumvented the wild northern seas and your silver-starved kin in the Orkneyjar. That is why he ruled Jorvik twice, though matters in Dubh linn drew him back. I would see his dream become a reality. *You,*" he pointed at Olaf, "could make that dream possible."

Olaf scratched his strawberry blond beard. "A trade route to Jorvik? From the west coast to the east? There must be much land to cover. Many tribes and clans in the way. And if I do achieve this, what are the terms?"

Iron Knee waved the question aside. "We can discuss those details. I am certain we will land on an amount that is satisfactory. But know this — you will have help. I will send men. My sister has men too. You will not be on your own."

Olaf nodded, though his face told me he was unconvinced. As a younger man, Olaf would have leaped at an opportunity such as this. But now he seemed to see the potential problems in the distance. He was wise to be cautious, mind. There was still much to be answered.

"Well? What say you?" Impatience tinged the king's voice, and I wondered briefly if he was wanting to return to his two "fairies."

Olaf took a sip of his ale and sleeved the residue from his lips. "It is a generous offer, and I appreciate the faith you put in me, King Iron Knee. I will need to think on it."

The king's eyes hardened. "Of course. A man must consider his steps in life carefully, especially those with the greatest risks and the greatest rewards, eh?" He lifted his cup to Olaf, who returned the gesture. "My wish is that you decide in two days' time. If you reject the offer, I will have to make other plans."

I liked not the tone of his last comment, though whether Olaf heard an implied threat, I could not say. "You shall have it then," he replied.

We moved from the antechamber back into the crowded hall. Finding no place to sit, we entered the yard and headed for a half-empty table there. I, for one, was anxious to tell Olaf what I thought of the king's plan, but before I could reach the table, someone stepped in my path.

My heart skipped in my chest. "Deidre?"

Sveinn winked at me and moved on to the table with the others, leaving us to our sudden encounter.

Like the other women in the courtyard, she wore a green dress, which accented her chestnut curls. For the event, she had pulled them back into a loose bun and laced them with green shamrocks. "My neighbors told me of a Northman — handsome and black-haired — who came often to my door in the fall." Crow's-feet etched the corners of her brown eyes as she narrowed them playfully. "Was that you?"

I grinned. "It could not have been me — I am not handsome."

She grinned back but shrugged all the same. "That is a shame," she said, then walked away.

"Why is that a shame?" I called to her quickly, for I had not expected our encounter to be so brief. I had wanted it to last; at least longer than it had.

She turned back with a grin. "Because I would have liked for it to have been you."

"Then I shall come again," I said as the heat flooded my cheeks. "I just need to know when."

She barked a laugh. "On the morrow. Early is better." Then she spun and vanished into the crowd.

"That was quick," Sveinn said as I sat down at the table.

"Gods, man," Dragomir chimed in. "What did you say to the poor woman?"

I ignored them and turned to Olaf. "So? Are we headed to England?" In truth I dreaded the answer, but I had no wish to prolong the suspense.

Olaf looked at me, and that old mischievous smile broke over his face. "Of course we will go to England. I just wanted to see Iron Knee squirm a little. Mayhap it'll lead to more favorable terms."

The men grinned, but I did not. It is true that I had expected the answer — gods, how well I knew my friend — despite my hope for a different one. Once again, Olaf had changed the course of our lives with nary a thought. And just as Deidre had invited me to her door...

18

Dyflin was just beginning to awaken when I knocked on the door to Deidre's dwelling. My stomach fluttered as I rehearsed the words I would say to her. Gods, was I pathetic. Practicing words like I was a child.

I was mid-sentence in my mind when the door creaked open and Deidre stood before me, smiling. I noted a few things instantly. First was the genuine delight on her clean face. It was at once open and settling, and it banished any self-doubt that plagued my thoughts. The second was the wet curls that fell in chaotic ringlets beyond the shoulders of her simple brown dress. She had bathed, which surprised me. I had heard that Christians thought the chill of water invited sickness.

I too had bathed and donned a clean tunic. In my hand I carried a warm loaf of bread and some cheese, which I presented to her. "I thought we might break our fast together," I said.

"I would like that. Please," she stepped back and motioned inside her dwelling, "come in."

"You are a hard person to catch," I said to her as I stepped into her firelit room. The smell of dried herbs hanging from her rafters was strong.

"I am sorry. The needs of Dyflin's sick are constant," she said. "My days are often filled." She motioned to the bed where Olaf had convalesced. "Please, sit." There was a bench beside her table, but clay pots and baskets covered it.

"I am surprised that people do not go to the priests for their needs."

She grabbed the handle of her kettle and filled two cups, then passed one to me. "Tea?"

I sniffed at it. It smelled floral, though I could not identify the flower. "This is not one of your sleeping potions, is it?"

She laughed. "No."

I sipped at the hot liquid, which had a slightly bitter taste. She reached for a small pot and came to me. "It is better with a little honey. Would you like some?"

I nodded, and she spooned some into my cup. I sipped again and smiled. "Better." I realized that she had not answered my earlier question, and so I asked again.

She shrugged. "Some do. Though some feel more comfortable with…" she thought for a moment "…older ways."

She moved to the worktable as I grunted in understanding. "So you do not place crosses on men's chests in the hopes that it will heal them?" I said it lightly and with a smile so as not to offend her.

She looked over her shoulder at me and smiled, then turned her attention to cutting the bread and cheese. "I cannot spend my time whittling crosses when there are more effective means of curing wounds and sicknesses." She handed me a piece of bread with cheese on top. "Though I will admit, I do pray if someone is beyond my abilities to help." She sat on her stool across from me and shrugged again. "I know not if it works, but it is better than doing nothing."

This I accepted with a nod as she bit into the bread.

"This tastes wonderful," she said around her mouthful. "Thank you."

"It is nothing. Just a simple gift to thank you for inviting me here," I said.

She grinned. "A lack of invitation did not stop you from coming before. Did you come with warm bread and cheese on those days?"

I laughed as the blood flooded my face. "Mayhap."

She laughed too. "Then I owe you for a lot of wasted bread and cheese."

"It did not go uneaten. My comrades thank you."

She took the last bite of her bread and set her teacup aside, then stood and came to me. I looked up into her smiling face and felt the first stirring in my groin as she adjusted her dress and straddled my legs. I ran my hands up her thighs, feeling their firmness and strength. She moved some strands of hair from my forehead.

"So what was it you came to tell me on all of those visits, Torgil?"

I shook my head. "I did not have words in my thoughts. I knew only that I wanted to see you again."

Her smile stretched, and she bent her head to kiss me gently. It was light and quick. Exploratory. Still, my breath caught in my throat. It had been many seasons since I had felt the lips of a woman I cared for. She bent to me again. The kiss was longer this time. Hungrier. My hand slipped farther up her dress to her bare hip. Our tongues searched. Our breath rushed.

And then it ceased, for a heavy knock on her door ended our passion as quickly as it had begun.

She withdrew and huffed. "I am sorry," she whispered to me, then went to the door and cracked it open. After a brief discussion in her language, she closed it again and came back to me.

She sighed and rested her hands on my thighs. Disappointment pulled her features into a frown. "It seems your bread and cheese will need to feed your comrades again. I must go."

"Now?" I asked.

She pursed her lips. "Aye. There is a boy…" She stopped. "It doesn't matter. Will I see you again?"

"I hope so," I said as I stood.

She grabbed my hips and moved in to kiss me again. "I hope so too."

"I leave soon, Deidre," I blurted.

Her brows bent. "When?"

I shrugged. "I do not know exactly, but it will not be long."

"Do you leave forever?"

I shrugged. "It doesn't sound so, but I know not for certain."

"I see." She turned and moved to her worktable.

"I am sorry," I said, though the words felt grossly inadequate. I tried to think of something else to say, but my mind was empty save for the bitterness in my thoughts. I stepped to the door and reached for the lever.

"Tonight," she called to me. "Meet me here just after the sun sets, if you can."

I smiled at her, nodded, and left.

∽

Back in camp, I found Olaf's hird gathered around a small fire in front of his tent. He sat with the men. It was a cold day, the gray clouds threatening rain yet again. I was getting sick of the wetness.

"You are back soon," Berse commented when I approached.

"She kicked him out," Orm stated in his deadpan way, though he did not look at me. He was preoccupied with something in his teeth.

Sveinn smiled. "Torgil does not waste his time. He is an efficient man."

I reached the fire and found a spot to sit. "Enough jesting," I grumbled. "She is a busy woman."

Olaf was rubbing his chest and shoulder. "And a fine one," he added. "Better than the flea-ridden whores you all are chasing."

"At least they spend more time with us," Ulf blurted and laughed.

I tossed a pebble at him. "And that is only because you pay them to." I turned to Olaf as the men chuckled. "Did you tell Iron Knee you accept?"

Olaf nodded. "This morning. He was delighted, of course."

"And did you get what you wanted?"

"Enough," he responded cryptically but definitively. It was an answer that brooked no reply.

I grunted. "So when do we leave?"

"We were just discussing that," he responded as he scratched at his beard. His fingers landed on something, which he withdrew from his hair and studied. Whatever it was, he tossed it into the fire. "The thing will take place at the next moon, which gives us a little less than thirty days to prepare."

My thoughts raced, taking stock of the men, our equipment, and our ships. The men and equipment would be ready, and with a little extra work, so too would the ships.

"Where is this place, exactly?" I asked.

"Iron Knee has described it as being on the coast, straight east across the sea. Mayhap two days' sail. Perchance less with good currents and weather."

I looked at the sky. "Currents, mayhap. Weather?" I shrugged. "With a little help from the gods, I suppose. Still, it does not sound too burdensome."

"We felt the same," Olaf said, meaning the others at the fire.

I looked at them and nodded, then turned back to Olaf. "Have you wondered why he made this offer to you?" I did not mind saying this before the men. I wanted their input.

"Why would Iron Knee not? Olaf is a grand choice for his sister," responded Berse indignantly. "Do you feel otherwise?"

I scowled at him.

Olaf held up his hand to stop Berse, then turned to me. "It is not complicated, I think. He needs to be rid of us. However much we helped him against Ivar and Domnall, Northmen are not wanted here. It is clear, eh?" He shrugged his big shoulders and motioned toward the wall of Dyflin — a wall that still, after many turns of the moon, divided us from them. "Mayhap Malachy told him to be rid of us. Mayhap he, too, wants us gone. Whatever the case, we still offer him an advantage in an overland route to Jorvik, so he was wise to offer us something in return for our departure." He shrugged again. "If we fail, then it is no loss to him. He will look for another to open the route to Jorvik. Or, at worst, continue sending ships around the northern coast. But if we succeed, we have much to gain, and so does he."

"What Olaf is saying is that we are expendable." Dragomir smirked.

I snorted.

"Only this time," Olaf cut in, "the profit is greater. Still, we are nothing to him if I do not secure Gytha's hand. But that, too, matters little. If I fail at that, we will go our way and find silver elsewhere."

"Or let Torgil try his luck," Ulf interrupted to the delight of the others. "It's clear he has a way with women!" He laughed, and the others chortled with him. I tossed another pebble at the man.

"But again, if I succeed?" Olaf cut through the laughter. "If *we* succeed?" He smiled, and the laughter ceased as he left the question unanswered, for we all knew what he meant.

Just then, the clouds opened up, and the rain fell upon us. Our fire sizzled, and across the camp, a collective groan rumbled.

Sveinn looked at the sky. "Thor, at least, approves."

I returned to Deidre's abode after sunset, as she had asked. After a quick knock, she opened the door and yanked me inside into the darkness. I tensed, thinking only of trouble, but just as quickly, I relaxed.

"Shhh," she whispered and closed the door gently.

I stood like a fool, seeing only the indistinct outlines of her and her furniture as gentle light seeped in around the doorframe. "Why are we standing in the dark, whispering?" I asked.

"I do not want the townsfolk to know I am here," she explained as she clicked the door latch into place.

I smiled, but my face quickly fell as the greater meaning of her words struck me. This is what she had to do to find a bit of peace. She moved closer, and the gentle scent of flowers washed the sorry thought away.

"We will have a hard time eating in the dark," I joked in a whisper.

Her hands moved to my hips, then slipped along my belt to the buckle, unfastening it and guiding it quietly to the floor. "I am not hungry," she whispered. She moved to the strings of my breeks and deftly loosened the laces. They slipped from me. I shrugged from my cloak, yanked my tunic over my head, and stood before her, nude save for my boots. She was now naked too, and I found myself desperate for her. Boots or not, I wanted to pull her slender body to the bed and devour her.

But she was more patient than me. She eased me to the bed and knelt to remove my boots, and only then was I glad that I had obeyed. Her hands slid up my legs to my groin, lingered there, and then moved up my chest. I groaned in delight.

"Shhhh," she teased as she stood again and climbed onto my lap.

Then she slid herself upon me.

I know not how long we made love. I only know that I was lost in it. Twice someone knocked on the door. At least that is what Deidre told me. I did not hear a thing. Not that it would have mattered, mind. I would not have stopped. Nor, I think, would she.

In the calmer moments, we whispered, telling each other about our upbringing and our lives. The words flowed freely for us both, as if we had recently reconnected after a long absence from each other. She had a gift for speaking and toying with me, of drawing information from the recesses of my memory that I normally did not share. Activities and memories I had not thought of in many moons — some light, some heavier — drifted from my mouth with ease. I inquired about things in her life I had never asked others, and she shared with me freely. That is, until I asked about her home and the family she had lost.

"I am sorry. That is a memory I am not yet ready to share." She tapped my nose playfully to lighten her response.

I envisioned my own daughter's beautiful blue eyes staring up at me, lifeless. Gods, it was heart-wrenching to even think of such things. I could not imagine the pain and guilt and fury Deidre must have felt in that moment, or how it must still haunt her thoughts. I stroked the curls on her head. "There is no need to apologize. I too have seen my share of hardship and loss, and it is not easy to speak of."

"Your father whipped you," she guessed.

I grunted, knowing now that she had felt the scars upon my back. They were impossible to avoid. "My father liked to beat me, especially when he drank. But no, he never whipped me. Like you, I was a thrall. Olaf and I."

She rolled onto her elbow and looked at me. I did not look back. My vision had floated to the horrid farm and the bog Olaf and I had worked each day, searching for iron ore with the other thralls. I remembered, too, how Turid had been taken and made a plaything of the master's son and his men. I had tried to save her but had been whipped almost to death for my defiance. "Like you, I was not very obedient."

"I am sorry," she whispered in my ear as her hand glided over my chest.

"It seems our lives have held similar hardships," I mused as I turned my eyes to her.

"It is hard to speak of these things," Deidre said. Her voice was as soft as a breath. "Tell me of your home, then."

I chuckled. What home? "I have lived in many places, but my childhood home brings back my fondest thoughts, I suppose," I said. "My father was a lord and had a great borg on an island. The island had farms and beaches and a small harbor. Each spring after the planting, the king — Olaf's father — would come, and we would feast and the children would play. There was a cliff from which we could dive into the sea. I remember one year — my last in that home — diving with Olaf." It sounded lovely to tell it, but in truth, it had been a disaster that had almost resulted in Olaf's drowning. That was a tale for a different day, for I was loath to spoil the fondness of the memory.

"It sounds wonderful. And your mother? What of her?"

I shrugged. "I do not remember much of my mother. She died when I was small. She hailed from your island, though. My father used to say it is why I look as I do."

Deidre kissed my cheek again. "Aye. It is why you are so handsome. We are beautiful people." She tickled my ribs to let me know she teased.

I chuckled softly and rolled toward her.

In the morning I left with a promise to return another night, though I knew not when that would be. I hoped soon, for I had not experienced such warm feelings in many seasons. Not since Turid, really. Deidre had a peace about her that offered ease and contentment — feelings I had rarely experienced in the presence of another.

I realized as I walked back to camp that she offered a haven from the sense of foreboding that had recently settled on my shoulders. Part of that was England and the unknown that it presented. Just what we might encounter, I knew not, though I did know it would not be easy. Deidre only added to my reluctance. In truth, I did not want to leave her behind. At least, not yet. But no, there was something more. Something about Olaf I could not quite place. He had changed. Or perchance my perception of him had. Was it his fall in battle? The swirl of Christianity that clung to him? Or was it something more? Whatever it was, my worries nagged.

But there was nothing for it. A man needed to face his future, and so, as I stepped into the camp, I faced mine.

19

I t was sunny when our ships anchored at the thing site. We dared not land, for the small, rocky beach might damage our hulls. Besides, I liked not the look of the guards who lined the small rise just inland from the shore. To the east of us, a decrepit stone wall surrounded a town that lay close to the water. It looked like it might have held some importance when the Romans ruled this land.

Our journey to this spot had been as Iron Knee said — a roughly straight voyage across the sea to this coast. I was glad we had sacrificed to Njord before we left, for He had delivered fair winds and decent, if slightly gray, weather for our journey. And I was glad, too, for Padraic, for without him, we might never have seen the river's mouth, which sat in a silty estuary between two low-lying, marshy beaches. A short row upriver had brought us to the narrow, rock-strewn beach beside which our ships now lay — a beach, I realized, that was devoid of other ships. We, it seemed, were the only foreigners at the assembly.

"What is that place?" I asked Padraic with a nod at the stone-encircled town.

"The town is called Presota-Tun in the local language. It means the town of the priests."

"Gods." I spat over the gunwale as Olaf came up beside me. With his chest still sore from his wound, he had ridden on *Sea Wolf* with me.

Before us, the English guards assembled on the beach, their spear tips glinting in the sunlight. "Who are you?" called one of them.

"My name is Padraic Ó Congalaig, emissary of Princess Gytha's brother, the king of Dyflin. The princess has summoned us to her thing, and so we have come."

The guards conferred with another man, who called back to Padraic, "You are late to the gathering, Padraic Ó Congalaig. But come ashore if you'd like. The others must stay on their ships until the princess confirms your identity."

"And am I ensured of your goodwill?" he called back.

"You have my word," called the man.

Padraic turned to Olaf. "I will return."

He climbed over the gunwale, lowered himself into the shallows, and waded over the slimy rocks to shore, where the leader and another man escorted him inland. As they disappeared, more warriors gathered on the rise above the river. They were taking no chances, and I did not blame them. Olaf had come with all of his men and ships. He had wanted Gytha and others to see that he was a lord. And he had wanted protection, should hostilities arise from his presence. After all, he was a Northman and it was English soil onto which we would tread.

"When Padraic returns, we will leave most of the men here," Olaf instructed. "I do not want to make the guards any more nervous than they already are."

I glanced again at the guards, then called Olaf's message over to Berse's ship. "Hauk and Finn, Sveinn and Dragomir, Ulf and Orm — ready yourselves," I hollered to the others.

Padraic returned not long after and motioned for us to come ashore. Seeing that we came in peace, the guards let us approach, then escorted us through a sea of tents pitched by those who had come to court Princess Gytha. As we walked, I noted the curious eyes that shifted to us. It was hard to say from where they hailed by their clothing alone, though I heard a mix of languages among their hushed talk.

"If you come for the thing, lord, you might be wasting your time."

Olaf turned to the man who had called to him. A Northman by his speech. "Why is that?"

The man smiled. "It began yestermorn." The men around him chuckled. "The princess is already due to choose."

If the news deflated Olaf, he did not show it. Instead, he smiled back. "Well, I suppose there is still time to change her thinking, then." He winked at the fellow and moved on.

"Confident arse, ain't he?" the man muttered as I walked past.

We arrived at the assembly field not long after. It was cordoned off by a rope lined with guards. In the midst of the grounds stood an ancient oak, around which the lords and their men gathered. We gave up our weapons to the guards, as was the custom with assemblies, and then entered the thing site. I scanned the faces as we worked our way into the crowd and was relieved to see that we knew no one. Joining such affairs without ingrained and familiar animosity was always easier.

"It might have been wise to wear your finery," Padraic whispered to Olaf as we stood in the crowd.

Which was true. The lords in our midst, and even some of their men, had bedecked themselves in silver and gold, rich pelts and cloaks, and clean clothing. Most had even combed their hair. We, on the other hand, had just stepped from our ships in our soiled travel garb. Disheveled and stinking, we stood out like a clump of mushrooms in a field of flowers.

"Had we more time," Olaf responded, "I might have."

Still, he reached into his purse, extracted his comb, and worked it through his hair and beard. He then adjusted his sleeves to display his silver bracelets. As he did, a horn called us to attention and turned our eyes to the beauty who stepped before us.

We had seen her the previous year, but only briefly and only from across a crowded, murky feast hall. Even then, her radiance had caught our eyes. But now she stood in all of her splendor, clean and fresh, her honey-gold hair dotted with small white flowers and falling in waves upon a blue dress that accentuated the length and curves of her young body. Save for the silver cross dangling from her throat, she might have been perfect. I glanced at my friend, who, with his slack jaw and obvious stare, was not shy about his interest.

Behind Gytha stood a dark-haired lord, who stepped forward. "Would the suitors come forward?"

After some jostling, nine men came and stood within the circle we created. Olaf made the tenth. As expected, his appearance caused a stir among the assembly and drew the attention of both the princess and her guardian, who frowned at him. Behind them, the princess's maid-servants prattled.

"You are the Northern prince about which Padraic spoke?" Gytha's guardian demanded. He spoke in the English tongue, which we knew from our trading in Jorvik.

Olaf bowed briefly. "I am. My name is Olaf Tryggvason."

"You come to seek the hand of the princess. Yet you dress in soiled clothes, looking as if you've just risen from a night of feasting. Not only that, but you arrive a day after the thing began. You make poor impressions for a suitor."

"Cast him out," called a young lord who stood near us.

Olaf ignored the angry man. "I do not mean to," he exclaimed to the guardian. "My men and I heard late of the unfortunate demise of Amounderness's jarl and came as soon as we were able, for I have heard much of the young princess and her beauty."

The princess blushed, which forced another reaction from the young lord. "Come, Godric," he fumed at the guardian. "You cannot let this man just upturn the thing. We have already negotiated and settled our terms." He motioned to the other lords. "It is time for an answer."

The guardian's frown remained. "It is as Alfvin states. You are too late, Prince Olaf. The princess has already chosen, so please step back."

Gytha's gaze shifted from Olaf to Padraic and back again. She stepped toward Olaf and held up her hand to silence her guardian. "Tell me, Olaf," she said in the English tongue, though her speech was laced with the lilt of her Irland roots. "From what land do you hail in the North?"

Olaf's mischievous grin appeared. "I am a prince of men. A warrior and an adventurer who has seen much in my young life. Though I have never before seen a woman whose radiance could rival the fairest of goddesses, Freyja."

Gytha blushed again. The other lords groaned, and young Alfvin rolled his eyes.

"So you are a heathen," she surmised. There was no malice in her proclamation.

"I have recently been shown the power of the Christian god," Olaf retorted. "Though, admittedly, I know more of the Northern gods."

"Stop this, Godric," Alfvin protested.

Godric cleared his throat loudly to distract the princess from Olaf. "Come, my lady. It is time to announce your decision. Prince Olaf, I mean no offense, but it is too late."

Olaf did as he was told and stepped back into the crowd, though it took a long moment for Gytha to draw her gaze from him.

Finally she scanned the other lords and straightened her dress with the palms of her hands. "I have decided…" She stopped to glance at Olaf. "I have decided to hear Olaf's offer before making my final decision."

"My lady —" Godric blustered, but his words were lost amid the boisterous uproar. Lord Alfvin cursed aloud, as did a few of the others. Several threw their hands in the air. An older lord turned on his heel, gathered his men, and marched away. I know not if he planned to return, though judging from the cherry-red hue of his cheeks, I doubted it. Those who remained stabbed their fingers at Godric, their arguments blending in a cacophony of curses and accusations. On the opposite side of them, Gytha retreated into the safety of her guards and ladies, then slipped from the grounds, leaving poor Godric to manage the hostile men.

"This is a shock to me as well," he hurried to explain. "I knew nothing of this man. No, he is not known to me. I beg of you a bit more patience," he shouted at them with his hands raised in surrender. "Please, my lords."

"Step aside," Olaf instructed us, "and keep your lips tight. The last thing we need is to insult these lords further."

"A pity," Ulf mumbled as we shuffled out of the commotion and off to the side.

"Silence," Olaf growled at him.

It took some time, but eventually the other lords dispersed along with their men, most casting malignant glances in our direction as they withdrew.

Godric turned to us, looking haggard after the heated exchanges. "Come." He beckoned to us, scowling. "Let us be about this."

We retrieved our weapons and followed Godric to Gytha's tent with its standards flapping lazily and its guards at the ready. They stepped aside when they saw Gytha's guardian.

Olaf turned to me. "Padraic will join me. Stay here with the men," he said and entered the tent.

Godric followed him, and I frowned. There was no telling what lay inside, and it troubled me that Olaf and Padraic went alone. Because of that, I stayed close to the tent's entrance. The others seemed less bothered and sat on the grass nearby.

The meeting was much shorter than I expected. Before my back and knees even felt the pain of standing, Olaf emerged and cast a sly smirk at me. Padraic did not appear so pleased, but mayhap that was just his nature.

"Come," Olaf said, waving to me and the others.

We retraced our steps to the ships, where the Englishmen continued to watch us. Because of them and their suspicious stares, Berse had told the men to lay our sails across the decks to create tents. There would be no dry camping tonight.

"Well?" I asked as we neared the camp. "Do you plan to tell me about your council with Gytha and Godric?"

He glanced at me and shrugged his big shoulders. "There is not much to tell, Torgil. She is beautiful and intelligent. I have offered her what I can. Wealth. Protection. A kingdom. Though I am sure the others have offered her the same. Let us hope that a better connection to her brother in Dyflin is enough, for we spoke much of that and of a passage to Jorvik."

"When will she decide?" I asked.

He shrugged again. "Whenever she calls us all back."

As it happened, Godric sent word to the lords to gather the following morning. It was gray and drizzly, though a thin break in the clouds off to the west allowed a few rays of sunlight to shine through. I barely noticed. My thoughts were on the other lords and what they might do if Gytha chose Olaf as her husband.

The evening before, Padraic had explained who each was. Most were local lords who owned land in Amounderness. They did not trouble me. But three others did. The first was the lord of Lonsdale, a large section of land that lay to our north, just beyond Amounderness's border. The second was the lord of Blackburn, which lay to our east. And the third was the lord of Leyland to our south. All three men wished to extend their own land by possessing Amounderness and its wealth, though of the three, the lord of Blackburn, Alfvin, seemed the strongest contender. Not only had he the best chance of winning Gytha's heart with his looks and his age, but he also had the most to gain from the betrothal. As it stood, he currently had to sail through Amounderness on the River Rippel to reach the sea. Amounderness, of course, taxed his ships as they came through. Possessing Gytha's land would alleviate that problem.

This time, Olaf had girded himself appropriately for the thing. He had now bathed and combed his amber hair. He wore his best breeks and tunic and donned a cloak lined with sable, an animal not well known to the English. A polished brooch of copper held his cloak to his broad shoulders. Silver and gold bands flashed on his wrists. Half a head taller than any of the other lords, he cut a fine figure in their midst. They, of course, scowled and whispered with each other as we gave up our weapons and stepped into the thing site.

Gytha was already standing before us, and so too was Godric. They nodded to Olaf as we took our place among the others.

"Step forward, my lords," instructed Godric when all lords had gathered.

Gytha stepped up to Godric's side and scanned the lords before her. "First, I would like to say that I value the offers of all of you and appreciate the effort you have made to come here and present yourselves to me. I also beg your forgiveness for the delay in my decision. As I am certain you know, this matter demanded as much thought as prayer. Over the past few days, my mind has been astir with you all and your generous proposals. So to that end, and with God's guidance, I have finally chosen to put the decision in His hands."

Grumbles and protests erupted, for Gytha's words confused us all.

"Please," she said as she raised her delicate hands to silence the lords. "Please."

The lords calmed themselves.

"Let me explain. It has come down to two men, between whom I cannot decide: Alfvin of Blackburn and Prince Olaf, the Northman."

Olaf, of course, smiled, but Alfvin frowned and glared at my friend. The other lords accepted Gytha's words with varying reactions. Some cursed or spat in the grass before storming away. Others accepted Gytha's words with gracious bows and retreated.

"How is it that your God will decide, Princess Gytha?" Olaf called above the tumult.

"I believe your people call it a holmgang, yes?" Gytha replied.

Alfvin looked from her to Olaf and back again. "What is this? What is a holmgang?"

"It is a duel, Lord Alfvin," she explained. "A duel between you and Lord Olaf."

Alfvin's jaw fell open. "Do you jest?"

Gytha cocked her head. "Do I appear to be jesting, Lord Alfvin?"

He shut his mouth.

"Each of you," she continued, "will choose ten of your best men. The format will be a battle, of sorts. But there will be no killing."

"I do not understand. Why?" Alfvin demanded. His cheeks were red and he was frowning. "Surely I can match whatever this man has offered you." He indicated Olaf.

"It is about more than wealth, Lord Alfvin. Each of you has offered me riches and fine things. But you also have spoken to me of your ability to protect me and this land. Now I wish for you to prove it. Is that so strange?"

"It is a fine idea," said Olaf with a chuckle. "When shall we hold this holmgang?"

"This afternoon."

I almost laughed at the savviness of Gytha's plan. Lord Alfvin could not argue against the decision. He had been given a chance, and Gytha had put him in charge of taking it. He could reject it, of course, but to do so was to admit defeat and show his cowardice.

And so a fight it would be.

20

Naturally, Olaf chose his hird to fight. Berse, Ulf, Orm, Dragomir, Sveinn, Hauk, Finn, and me. With us were Padraic and one of his Vestmenn, who had insisted on helping.

I liked not having the Vestmenn with us, but Olaf said in the Northern tongue, "They insisted." He shrugged as we walked to the thing site. "So let us see what they can do."

I slowed my pace so that I walked beside Padraic. "Do not err," I said to him. "Olaf does not tolerate mistakes in his shield wall. Nor do I."

"Mind your business," Padraic said to me, "and we'll mind ours, eh?"

We arrived at the old oak, where the thing site had been converted into a rectangular dueling ground. Gytha's warriors supplied us with wooden practice swords for the match and took our weapons in exchange. Around us, a crowd had gathered, and I noticed the other lords within it. They had come, I assumed, to see Olaf fight and perchance to gauge his abilities, should they have to face him on the field in the future. Though I also think they were curious to see who Gytha would marry. Either way, it was wise of them to be there.

Across from us, Alfvin paraded before his men, clucking at them like a chicken. He spoke in a tongue I could barely understand, though I need not have comprehended it to know he was worried. I did not fault him for that. He had much to lose if he failed. A beautiful spouse. A large extra swath of arable land that provided access to the sea. Not to mention his reputation. Besides, Olaf had the look of a fighter. He, on the other hand, with his tall, thin frame, did not.

Standing in front of the oak were Gytha and her guardian, Godric. I gazed upon her with newfound respect. She was ravishing, aye. But beneath that beauty was a guile I had not expected. It was a dangerous combination but a necessary one in the world of power.

"Should I be jealous?" murmured Olaf in my ear.

I turned to him and smirked. "She is not my type."

"Good," he said. "So let us be about this, eh?" His old grin stretched across his face. Unlike us, he wore no armor and carried no shield. He rarely did when he dueled. It was a sign of confidence in his skills, which in turn intimidated his opponents. In either hand was a wooden sword.

"No foolishness from you, eh?" I reminded him. "Let us finish this quickly."

His grin stretched wider. "I have an idea."

I rolled my eyes. "Of course you do."

Olaf gathered his men to him and told us his plan. The men chuckled at it, but I did not. It seemed an unnecessary risk. Still, I kept my lips tight. After all, the fight was not to the death, and if Olaf wanted to risk his reputation on a harebrained scheme, so be it.

Per the plan, I positioned myself in the center of the line, with the remaining men stretched out to either side of me. We did not need to speak to know where each man stood and how best to cross our shield rims. Olaf stood silently behind us, waving his swords in circles to test their weight and balance. Across from us, the Englishmen also formed, though it was clear from the gaps in their line that they had less experience in a shield wall. Alfvin berated them for their carelessness and urged them to form a tighter line as he joined their ranks. It did not help.

"This should be fun," Ulf called to us from his spot, then spat into the dirt.

To my left, Dragomir stretched his neck and loosened his shoulders. To my right, Orm started to beat his sword upon his shield rim. I joined him, letting the rhythm arouse my anticipation. I breathed deeply and sent a silent prayer to Thor as I released my breath into the cold air. For Olaf's sake, I wanted to win this, and I sensed, as the men took up Orm's beat and Ulf let fly an animal howl, that the men did too.

Godric stepped forward and held up his arms for silence. We complied, though it was difficult, for we itched to fight.

"Men of Blackburn. Olaf. This is a duel for the hand of Princess Gytha. I remind each of you that no man is to be killed." He paused to scan both lines, letting his words sink into our thoughts. "Victory is earned by the defeat of every man in the opposite group, whether that defeat comes by surrender or by force. Are my words clear?"

"Aye!" we shouted.

"Very well," he said and took a few steps back.

I turned my eyes to the enemy, waiting for Godric's command, my heart thumping with the excitement of it all.

"Fight!" he roared.

As one, we rushed forth. We had done this so often in battle and in training that it came as second nature. The Englishmen had not expected such a rapid advance, and the shock put them on the defensive. Nearby, I heard Alfvin shout a command, but the words did not register in my thoughts. I was too busy assaulting the man who faced me. He lifted his shield to defend himself from the first poke of my sword, but in doing so, raised it too high. It was a common mistake and left the fellow's thigh exposed. I wasted no time in striking it hard with my weapon. In a battle, the man would have fallen, his leg a bloody mess, but here, with our wooden blades, he only yelped and stumbled backward. He was lucky I had not chosen to hit his knee.

I pressed forward into the gap, backhanding my weapon into the head of the man who fought Orm. The man's helmet flew, and he dropped to the ground, though I had not realized I'd hit him so hard.

"Bastard!" Orm yelled at me. "He was mine."

Just then, Olaf called the signal, and I dropped to my knee. Orm stepped in front of me to protect me in my vulnerable position. I braced for the weight, which hit me soon enough. Olaf bounded forward and planted his foot on my shoulder, using it as a stepping stone to hurdle the English line. Pain shot through my arm and down my back, for Olaf was a large man and his weight really crushed me. But it passed as quickly as it struck, and I stood to join Orm once again.

Olaf landed behind the English lines, rolled deftly, and rose. His maneuver distracted the English, who either turned to the new threat or lost their attention just long enough to feel the sting of our wood. In the corner of my eye, an Englishman jerked his head and dropped at Dragomir's feet, his face a wreck of blood. In two vicious strikes, Olaf dropped the man whose leg I had struck. He then cracked his blade across the back of another man's knees. Several more Englishmen fell in quick succession.

In a short time, only Alfvin stood, fighting for his pride against Finn. Their swords cracked. Their feet shifted. Their grunts rumbled. Occasionally, one of them eked out a strike against the other, but not hard enough to slow his opponent. We urged Finn on with our calls, just as the Englishmen cheered on their lord.

"Finish him, Finn," I mumbled under my breath.

And then it happened. Seeing a chance, Alfvin lunged for Finn's stomach. Finn leaped back, swinging down with his blade as he did. It was meant to parry Alfvin's strike, but it caught Alfvin so hard across his wrist that he yelled and dropped his blade. Around us, the crowd groaned. Alfvin lunged for another sword that had dropped upon the ground, but Finn blocked his path.

"Yield!" Finn said.

Alfvin stood, though there was no defeat in his eyes. Instead he turned to Olaf and spat on the ground at my friend's feet, then stormed from the dueling ground.

Olaf ignored the slight. Instead he wrapped his younger cousin in his big arms as Finn grinned buoyantly. "Well done, Finn. Well done."

"Olaf," called Godric across the field.

Olaf released his nephew and turned to Gytha's guardian.

"God has chosen, and you are the victor. Come, my lord, and be recognized as Gytha's betrothed."

Olaf went to Gytha, who stepped forward with a smile on her blushing face and grabbed Olaf's hands in her own. It was at once tender and frightful, for while I was happy for my friend, I could not help but wonder what this might mean for our future. The gods alone knew how torn I was.

"So," I said to Olaf later that evening after he had returned from Gytha's tent, where he had finalized the wedding arrangements. "What is the plan?"

Per his request, we sat alone on *Sea Wolf,* he with a cup of celebratory ale in his hands, me with water. Above us, the sky had turned to slate gray, threatening rain, though off to the west, the belly of the clouds shone a vibrant orange and pink from the setting sun.

"We have agreed to marry on the summer solstice," he said distantly. "Though there is something you should know."

My eyes had been on the sunset, but now they shifted to Olaf's profile. "What should I know?"

"To win Gytha's hand, I vowed to make her richer than the other lords could."

It did not seem so outlandish. If we managed to secure a trade route to Jorvik, wealth could easily follow. This I said to Olaf.

"A route to Jorvik, aye. But she wants more than Amounderness. She wants this entire area. Blackburn. Lonsdale. Leyland. So do I."

I felt my anger spark. "We have not the men for that."

Olaf held up his hand. "Peace, Torgil. Think about it for a moment. Amounderness can only provide limited wealth. But all of these areas together? That is worth something, eh? As for the men, we will get some from Gytha's brother in Dyflin and, mayhap, some from Sudreyjar."

I grunted. There was reason in his words that I could not deny. "Have you a plan for conquering these places?" I asked, though in my gut I knew the answer.

He smirked. "It is coming together."

I rolled my eyes at the expected answer. "If that was in Gytha's mind all along, we should have killed Alfvin when we had the chance."

Olaf nodded. "I said the same to Gytha, but her reasoning was sound. Had we done so, it would have put the other lords on guard and made our task harder."

I snorted. "Gytha surprises me."

He smiled. "Aye, she is a Viking to the bone. It is why I like her." Just as quickly as his face had brightened, it stiffened.

"What else?" I asked him.

Olaf sighed. "Gytha asked for more."

I frowned. "By the gods, she is bold."

"Aye," Olaf said, though this time his face had soured even more. "She would not accept the proposal unless I, and all of my men, vowed to be baptized."

I flinched as if slapped. "And you promised?"

"I had no choice."

I stared at Olaf, and he stared back. "You had a choice," I seethed. "And your choice was to abandon our gods for the sake of a woman."

"We add a god to those we worship," he hissed back. "And not for a woman — for a kingdom. And if the gods will it, a son, too."

I glared at Olaf. "We?" I growled. "It is you who stands to gain."

He scowled. "We all stand to benefit from this."

"If the gods don't punish us first," I replied. "How could you do this without conferring with us? The old gods have given us everything we have."

His scowl deepened. "Everything is not five ships and some silver, Torgil. That is scraps in comparison to what could be ours. As for the gods, we are not abandoning them. We are adding this Christ God, who, I might remind you, predicted all this."

My fury flamed. "You've seen the corrosiveness of the Christ God. The priests who spread across Wagria and turn its people from the old ways, just as they preach their lies among our people in the North. Today you will add this Christ to the gods you worship. Tomorrow, their churchmen will tempt you with their gold and silver, but the price for that wealth will be the sacrifice of our gods."

"I will never abandon our gods," Olaf said.

"Is that an oath?" I replied.

He hesitated.

"Are you making an oath not to abandon the old gods?" I repeated more forcefully.

He leaned forward and rested his elbows on his thighs, his eyes focused on the deck near his boots.

I cursed and turned my head from him. "I know you like I know myself, Olaf," I managed to say into the stretching silence. "And I know you will do whatever you can for power. I understand. You are a prince who wants to be a king. It is your lot in life. But I," I tapped my chest, "I am not a prince. Nor do I aspire to be one. I wish only to fulfill my oath to my father and to your parents. But that," I added, "is now in peril, for I cannot turn my back on my gods."

He looked back at me. "What are you saying?"

I sighed. "I feel in my gut that the gods have preserved me. That Thor has preserved me. There are many times I should have perished. Estland. Konugard. Drastar. Wagria. The Danavirki. Thor has seen me through. Becoming a Christian is a slight to Him. And I know in here," I tapped my chest, "it is not right. So follow this new god if you dare, but please, do not drag me or others into it."

I realized then that this should not have been a surprise. Since the encounter in Dyflin with that absurd priest, Olaf had not been himself. In the back of his thoughts, he had believed the priest. Not because the man had made sense, mind, but because the priest had presented him with a path to power. And now that the power was within sight, he could find no fault in the Christian ways. All it would take was a simple dunk in the water and, in his view, adding a god to his pantheon. But it would not stop there. Not until we, too, had followed him down this path of folly and the old gods were forsaken, because that was the price of Christian power. That is why the Christ church had spread like a fungus.

"To abandon me is to break your oath," he reminded me.

His words were like a sword thrust to my heart, and I hated him for that. An oath-breaker was the worst kind of person. A nithing. A man whose words meant nothing. I hated him because I had given so much and still he wanted more. More of my joy. More of my sacrifice. More of my blood…

"I swore an oath to your parents and my father, never to you," I muttered.

"What of my mother?" He looked back at me. Was it shock I saw in his eyes, or anger?

I sighed heavily and stood. "What of my gods?"

As I climbed from the ship, the clouds turned a fiery red. A warning perchance? But from whom?

21

The lords departed the following day with their men, leaving us alone with the townsfolk of Presota-Tun and the farmers whose steadings dotted the area around it.

We hauled our ships from the river and set to work on a more permanent camp under the dubious eyes of Godric and his men. I could not fault the man for his concern. He was a local who had originally served the former lord of Amounderness but, by way of the man's untimely death, had inherited this new burden from Gytha. His forces were a mix of Gytha's Vestmenn and the Northmen and Englishmen who had settled in the region and made peace. But they were few and scattered throughout the land and their homes. Should it come to a fight with us, it would not go well. Perchance because of this, and because of Gytha's choice of Olaf, Godric bit his tongue and served Gytha faithfully. He knew that to cross her was folly. In truth, I liked the man. He was attentive to Gytha and to us, but not overly obsequious, and he proved to be a good source of knowledge about the region and its people.

I could not say the same for Presota-Tun's other inhabitants, who seemed to view us as hostiles in their town. Mayhap they had seen too many Northmen come already to their shores and take what was theirs. Or mayhap they did not like our Northern ways. Whatever the case, they kept clear of us. This was especially true of the priests, who were numerous in that place, though I am certain that our jeers and sneers at them helped reinforce their hostility. Only the innkeepers were of a different mind. So long as we had silver to spend and bellies to fill, they were happy to see us.

Of Presota-Tun there is not much to say, save that it might have been something once but was no more. Godric told us it was an old Roman town on a Roman trade route, and as most Roman towns were, it had once been made fully of stone. But many of its stone walls and buildings had crumbled under the weight of age. The townsfolk had tried to repair the circular wall surrounding the town, but their skill could not match that of the old masters. By the looks of it, sections of the barricade had fallen more than once. The same could be said for the ancient streets, which now lay beneath layers of dirt and grass and only peeked through in spots. Wood beams and thatch filled empty sections of homes and halls and barns, making the place a strange blend of old and new. Similarly, the stone bridge that crossed the Rippel outside the town's gates retained its stone sections on the shore, but the middle had long since been replaced by timber. It was serviceable enough, allowing traffic from neighboring Leyland and towns farther south to cross with their goods.

Though I had not yet seen it, Godric described Amounderness as a long, gentle slope that started in the hills to the east and spilled down onto a plain marked by woods and farmland, then out toward the sparsely populated moors along the coast. The people of the area generally populated distinct places, with the Northern settlers in the west, the English mainly in the center, and the old inhabitants of the land, whom Godric called "Bryttas," in the hilly east. Of course, with time, the population had blended and the lines had blurred between the people.

In the many places I had lived, the area no longer resembled the features and characteristics that had given it its original name, but that did not hold true in Presota-Tun. In the town was a church, whose bell echoed off the Roman stones multiple times a day. Stretching northward from the town's gate was a large swath of land owned by the priests. As if grown like wheat from the very land they tilled, robed holy men surrounded us, and more important, Olaf. It seemed that no matter where we went or what event we attended, the priests were there. It made my head hurt and pushed me to the camp, where I found more comfort in the men, my weapons, and my old ways. I suppose I should have kept Olaf closer to me to counter the allure of the religion, but my irritation with him prevented me from such wisdom.

A week after the thing concluded, Olaf gathered his most trusted men to him in the town's royal hall. Godric, too, was present, though Gytha was not. We sat at a long table with Olaf at its head and Berse to his right. Godric sat to Olaf's left. While I feigned indifference, I could not help but think that the seating was intentional — a warning, perchance, of shifting loyalties — and it vexed me considerably. I suppose I deserved it for my comments to Olaf, but I had thought he might understand my position with time. It seemed that I was mistaken.

He waited until the ale, bread, and soft cheese had been served, and the servants had departed, before lifting his cup to us. We returned the gesture with a hearty "Sköl," though I am certain mine lacked the exuberance of the others.

"Please, men," said Olaf, "eat. Drink. There is plenty to be had."

"What news, Olaf?" We were all curious to know why Olaf had convened this meeting, but it was Berse who asked.

Olaf smiled. "I see you men are hungrier for news than for warm bread and ale. Very well…"

Just then, Ulf belched, then blushed. "Sorry, Olaf." He alone had partaken of the ale.

Olaf chuckled at the interruption. "Many things have changed in the passing of a moon. But you, Ulf, have not. Nor do I think you ever will."

The men laughed.

"Right." Olaf clapped his hands to calm the mirth. "To business. I have news to share. Gytha and I are to be married at midsummer."

"Hey!" the men shouted and raised their cups.

"That is good news, indeed," Berse called into the shouted cheers.

Olaf's eyes traveled to me, and I offered my friend a small, well-wishing smile. Knowing what terms had been struck, it was hard to offer more. He turned away.

"I have sent messengers to the lords of our neighboring lands to invite them to the feast, and Padraic," he motioned to the Vestmann, "will go to Iron Knee once the ceremony concludes to inform him of the betrothal. In the meantime, I will travel the land and offer peace to the people as their new lord."

"And what of the trade route to Jorvik?" asked Sveinn.

Olaf held up his hand. "I am coming to that, Sveinn. Godric here," he placed a hand on the man's shoulder, "has offered to provide what knowledge and men he can. I am certain his help will be invaluable to us. However, it will not happen immediately. Much needs to be done here in Amounderness before we start traveling eastward."

"There are many obstacles in the way, not the least of which is the land of Blackburn, which is ruled by Alfvin," added Godric.

Olaf nodded. "Alfvin is not a man I fear. But your point is taken, Godric."

Olaf scanned the faces of those who sat around him. Not one of us smiled back. We knew what an obstacle like Alfvin meant. He might

188 ERIC SCHUMACHER

have shown weakness at the thing, but who knew what forces he could conjure to prevent us from our goal?

"Good," said Olaf, raising his cup. "Then let us start planning, eh? Sköl!"

"Sköl!" the men echoed.

But I did not lend my voice to their cheer. I had other things on my mind. "Are you not forgetting something?" I called to Olaf.

The men swiveled from Olaf to me, then back again.

"Here is your chance, Olaf, to tell the men." My heart thundered as I called these words, for I did not like to embarrass my friend, nor pit him against the others. But they had a right to know.

"Aye, well. I was coming to that," said Olaf as he cleared his throat. "Torgil is correct. There is another part of the deal that I struck with Gytha. It requires a compromise of sorts from all of us."

"Which is?" I prodded. It was, I knew, like prodding a hive of bees.

"Gytha has asked for our acceptance of the Christian God. My acceptance and yours."

The men looked from Olaf to each other to me. There were some in our army who had already accepted the Christian God. But to those like me and the men at the table who were more stalwart in our faith, it was troubling, and I could see that on their faces.

"To be clear in my words, I am not asking you to abandon the old gods," clarified Olaf. "I am asking you to add a new god to those you worship."

"Speak plainly," called Ulf. "What is it you require of us? Are we to lay down our weapons and become priests?" He scoffed.

"We are to be baptized," said Olaf.

The murmur climbed.

"And if we choose not to be baptized? What then?" asked Dragomir.

Olaf stiffened. "Then I will release you from your oath." Steel edged his voice. He did not like to be challenged like this, but I cared not a whit. It was only fair that the men knew what awaited them.

"By when do you need our decision?" asked Sveinn.

"Before my betrothal to Gytha," Olaf responded.

Sveinn looked at me and I at him. Others grumbled or left the hall. Still more turned back to their food, albeit in silence. My eyes shifted to Olaf. His menacing eyes glared at me. I rose, turned, and marched from the hall.

Two days later, twenty of us rode from Presota-Tun on horses that once belonged to Amounderness's lord and headed west into country that Godric expected would show favor to a lord from the North. As we rode, Godric told us of the steadings, of the walls and wells and lakes and streams that divided each, and of the taxes Olaf could expect to collect. He showed us where the hunting and fishing were good and how to navigate the numerous waterways that lined the area. And he pointed out the boundaries of the land, which were marked by rivers and were easy enough to identify.

Understandably, the people hid from us when we approached, at least until Olaf introduced himself as the area's new lord, which was not entirely true yet. Most had heard of the former lord's passing and of Gytha's thing to find a new husband, though few knew a new lord had been chosen or that he was a Northman by birth. It was news the people accepted with a mixture of emotions. Those who lived closer to the coast and waterways had come from Dyflin or the islands of the Sudreyjar and had Northern blood in their veins. These folks accepted Olaf more gladly than the English locals who lived just inland and were more guarded in their reactions.

The following day, we rode inland into a wind that blew down from the hills in the distance. Heads down, our mounts trod the remains of a Roman road that paralleled the Rippel to a village Godric called Rippelceaster. Like Presota-Tun, the village stood inside the skeleton of an ancient Roman fort that looked like it might have held some import all those years ago. Now though, nothing remained but a square embankment atop which stood a wooden gate and banner-bedecked watchtowers. Several hovels and smaller steadings stood around the town. South, along the banks of the Rippel, was a dock and several fishing skiffs, though judging from the piles of stones along the shoreline, a bridge might have stood there once.

"This is a crossroads," called Godric above the wind. "In ancient times, trade and soldiers headed north and south through this fort, or west to Presota-Tun. Today it stands in defense of Amounderness, for this is the border with Blackburn. Everything east and south of here belongs to Alfvin."

We sat astride our steeds and gazed with watering eyes east along the unsettled Rippel.

"So Alfvin controls this portion of the river?" asked Olaf.

Godric pointed. "Everything east of here."

"And the hills?" I asked.

Godric looked north, where the old road climbed into low hills that stretched east toward higher mountains. "Contested," he said. "Here, the road belongs to us, but it becomes Blackburn farther on."

"Does the Rippel continue east?" Olaf asked. "Toward Jorvik?"

Godric shook his head. "No. Not far from here it turns north toward its source in the mountains."

"Is there a path from the river's bend to Jorvik?" asked Olaf.

Godric shrugged. "I have not been that far east, lord."

Olaf grunted. "Then we must find someone who has."

"That does not remove the problem of Blackburn," Berse added.

"No," Olaf responded. "It does not. But I have other ideas for that. Come. Let us get out of this wind and find some warmth in the village."

Olaf turned his mount toward the gates, followed by Godric and the others. But I remained in my spot, staring into the distance and into the wind, feeling that this was more than an ancient crossroads. This was *our* crossroads — Olaf's and mine. From here lay Olaf's future — his success or his failure. But I did not share in that dream, in part because it involved compromises I could not stomach. And in part because I now felt the tug of something different in my gut. Something nebulous, but a pull all the same. I turned my mount and gazed down the valley through which we had just ridden, back in the direction of Presota-Tun. Or was it Dyflin? My black hair lashed my face. My steed fidgeted beneath me. But I ignored them and focused instead on the memory of Deidre that my mind had suddenly conjured. I blinked and the memory vanished, but the pull of her remained.

And with that thought lodged in my head, I turned my mount toward Rippelceaster.

That night, a man came to me. Stared at me in the murk of the Rippelceaster hall. His stony face and stern eyes judged me, and the dread of it cascaded through my body. He bore no resemblance to anyone I knew, though somehow I understood to fear him. Behind him, in the dark hall, Olaf's men drank and joked and slept, oblivious to the man who stared down at me in silent judgment. I would have called to them, had my wits been about me, but I could not find my voice.

The man turned slowly and vanished into the darkness.

Once again I was in the hall at Rippelceaster. Only this time there was no revelry. The others snored and coughed and shifted in their sleep as the glow of the hearth fire played upon their resting forms. I lay motionless, too afraid to move, and cast my gaze at the sleeping men. Had they not seen the man?

It was a dream, I told myself. Nay, a nightmare. Yet still my heart hammered at the memory of the man's face. What had he been trying to say to me? Was it a threat or a warning? Or was it something else?

Whatever his message was, it frightened me.

22

"So," said Olaf when we finally found ourselves alone. "Have you decided?"

It had been nearly half a moon since our visit to Rippelceaster, and the wedding was set for the following morning. Given the preparations for the ceremony and the growing number of men and petitioners constantly in Olaf's midst, it had been nearly impossible to find time with him. Even now, a steward worked on the sleeve of his tunic to prepare it for the following day.

At my silence, Olaf shooed away the steward. "Speak," he said as soon as the door to the room had shut.

I took a deep breath to steel myself. "I cannot," I said.

Olaf's brows slanted. "You cannot what?"

There was an edge in his tone that dared me to defy him, and so I did. "I cannot be baptized. I will not."

His scornful eyes studied me. "Why?"

"Because I swore an oath to your parents and to my father to protect you, but I cannot swear against my gods. I will not."

Olaf's jaw tightened as crimson crawled into his cheeks. "To a man, the others have agreed to baptism. Only you have not given me your commitment. How hard would it be to place a cross next to the hammer on your necklace? They are almost the same."

I set my jaw.

"Not hard," barked Olaf. "That is the answer. Yet you cannot, Torgil, because life to you was, is, and will always be black or white."

"Because I do not compromise my ideals for power? Or wealth?" My fingers had balled into fists at my side.

He snorted. "Your ideals did not keep you from profiting off the backs of slaves."

The words stung, but I could not deny them. "Yet another mistake I made because of my oath to protect you. But this is different. I will not forsake my gods for you." I spat.

Olaf shook his head and raised his arms as if to encompass the world. "Look around you, Torgil. The Christian god is everywhere. Whether we like it or not, He is rooted in this land. So we can fight it or we can embrace it."

"So you would turn your back on your gods?" I challenged him.

"No. As I told you before, I would add Him to the others who rule the sky and earth and world in which we live."

The sourness in my face made Olaf laugh.

"Do you remember when we were lads, Torgil? Digging for iron ore in that cursed Estland swamp?" He did not wait for my answer. "How in the mud and grime we found wealth for our masters?"

I nodded ever so slightly, though I knew not where the thread of his words was headed.

"The reason you refuse to accept this new faith is because you have no space in your head for complication. Complication muddies the water for you. Yet," he pointed at me, "it is in that mud where much wealth can be found. Unlike you, I have learned to wade through the swamp and shit and complications of our world to find that which will make me richer. And aye, more powerful. So, if the price for more land and wealth and power is one more god in the pantheon of gods we worship, I will gladly pay the fee."

I had no answer to that, though the crazed priest in Dyflin crossed my mind.

"Do what you must, Torgil. Wade into the river on the morrow and add a cross beside Thor's amulet, or turn your back on me in the name of your gods. The choice is yours." He turned to the door.

My jaw fell open. "Are you casting me aside?"

"No." He stared at me. "I am giving you a choice."

"You would relieve me of my duty to you?" I said, stunned.

He shrugged casually. "As you said not so long ago, my father and yours are dead. Only my mother remains, and I think she will not mind. So if that is your wish, I have plenty of others willing to make such sacrifices to serve me."

His words robbed me of speech. All I could do was work my mouth like some dying fish.

He shooed me away with a backhanded wave. "Now, if our business is done, I have more pressing issues to deal with." He turned to the door. "Steward!"

The steward stepped into the room, and I spun on my heel. Out into the antechamber I stormed, ignoring those whose eyes followed me, then out of the hall and into the town. When I finally stopped, I was on the edge of the Rippel, not far from where our ships lay and most of our men still camped. And there I fumed, my heart racing, my cheeks inflamed. I had protected Olaf his entire life. Had dedicated all to him, as was my oath to his father and my own. I had lost a wife and a child to follow him. Had pursued him through ill-advised battles and reckless decisions. Had lost friends because of his hunger for power and his headstrong ways. And my reward for all of it had been this: to be spit out like some disagreeable piece of gristle.

This was the crossroads I had seen coming, only it had unfolded in a way I had not expected. I had known we might butt heads. We had done so many times before. But to be cast aside if I didn't forsake my gods? This, I had not foreseen. It was almost violent in its callousness. After all we had done together? All we had lived through? All I had given? Just a backward wave of his hand was all it had taken to destroy everything.

I spat into the shallow water. Curse the bastard if that was the value he placed on our history. Curse him to Hel.

I did not attend the baptism of Olaf and his men. Nor did I attend his betrothal to Gytha, which took place in Presota-Tun's largest church. Instead I stood alone in the shadows of the trees that lined the feast ground where Olaf's union with Gytha would be celebrated. It would be a crowded affair, with most of the Amounderness, Lonsdale, and Leyland nobles and warriors in attendance, as well as the priests and townspeople of Presota-Tun. Alfvin of Blackburn, of course, had declined the invitation, which was a shame for him. Judging from the banners and garlands and decorated tables, it would be beautiful. I doubt Amounderness had ever seen such a rich affair in their lives.

The merrymaking began with the ringing of church bells, which accompanied Gytha and Olaf out into the feast field. As sour as I was, I could not deny their radiance or the pleasure that each displayed. It was written in their manner and the smiles on their faces as they walked hand in hand at the head of a long procession.

Not wishing to be seen, I retreated to the camp down near the shore-line. It was there, in the shadow of my tent, that I found Sveinn, who waited for me with two cups and a pitcher of ale.

"You missed your chance to earn a fine white dress today," Sveinn said.

I smirked. "I heard those garments are hard on skin as delicate as mine."

"Not after the priest dunks you in the water. It softens the dress. It's quite nice, actually. Oh," he said as he plucked the cross from his neck-lace and showed it to me, "and this gold thing. You would have earned one of these, too."

I chuckled softly.

He poured a cup of ale and passed it to me, then poured a cup for himself. I did not feel much like drinking but lifted my cup to him nevertheless.

"How was the wedding?" I asked.

"Hot," he said, then added, "You were missed."

I shrugged, then took a sip of ale. It was warm.

"What are you going to do?"

I sighed and twirled my cup. "Head to Dyflin, I suppose. Padraic must return, so my hope is to go with him."

"To serve Iron Knee, or to scratch an itch?" Sveinn grinned.

I chuckled again. "To scratch an itch. I cannot stay here, so I may as well see if Deidre will have me. Besides, Dyflin is a harbor. From there I should be able to go elsewhere when Deidre sickens of me."

"Which she'll no doubt do," he said with a wry smirk before his gaze shifted to his wooden hand.

The silence stretched uncomfortably, punctuated only by the sounds of revelry in the distance.

"I am no oath-breaker," I said to him bluntly.

Sveinn looked up and studied me. "We have all sworn to him at some point."

I shook my head. "Not I. I swore only to his parents. He knows this. You need to know this too."

Sveinn nodded, then sighed. "The men are already talking. I can try to speak to them, but I know not what it will do."

His words did not surprise me. I knew my absence from the baptism and Olaf's wedding would spark rumors. It was unavoidable. "I do not wish to put you in a bad position, Sveinn," I said. "If the men think me an oath-breaker and you come to my aid, that will only cast you in doubt. You need to see to yourself."

He looked down again. "You know I would go with you if I had no oath to Olaf. Others might, too."

I nodded. "Thank you," I said to him. "It will be hard not to have you by my side." And I meant it. Of all the men in Olaf's hird, Sveinn and I were closest. He was more brother than friend.

He lifted his cup to me. "To your future, Torgil. Wherever it may lead. Sköl."

"Sköl," I answered, and drank of the warm ale.

He rose. "I should get back. I'll leave you with the ale."

I watched him leave, then lay upon my cot, my ears full of the nearby celebration and my nerves on edge. It was torture to listen to the cheers and shouts and laughter, though I had no better place to go, and so I endured it until my mind eventually wandered off to what might lay ahead.

The truth of it was that I had no idea if Padraic would take me to Dyflin nor, frankly, what I would find or do when I got there. Northmen weren't welcome, and who knew how one lone Northman would fare in a city so hostile. Not to mention, I had no idea whether Deidre might accept me back into her home or whether there would even be employment for me in that foreign place. But I could not stay in Amounderness, and England was more foreign than Dyflin, save for my brief visits to Jorvik in seasons past. At least I knew people in Dyflin, including the king, and besides, that was where Deidre was. If my plans collapsed, I was certain I could find passage on a ship to Jorvik and possibly even back to the North.

Feeling more assured, I relaxed into my cot with my head propped on my hand and watched daylight fade to evening. I looked over at my cup, tempted to drink more despite the ale's warmth, but a sudden scream tore me from my thoughts. The ring of steel and the shout of men quickly followed.

I shot to my feet, my hand slipping unconsciously to the axe at my belt as I grabbed my shield. I dislodged my blade from its clip as I exited the tent, then rushed forth into the darkening night. More shouts and blade-song reached me as I threaded my way to the camp's inner edge, where I stopped and peered across the meadow to the ceremonial field. I saw no exterior threats. No men or horses attacking. The commotion seemed to be coming from the feast itself.

I raced forward to see what had befallen my friends without thought of my exile. I suppose nearly thirty seasons of protecting Olaf and fighting by the side of my hird-brothers had conditioned me. It was only as I neared the celebration that I suddenly remembered my changed status, so I circled left and slowed my pace. Still seeing no enemies, I pressed on, crouching now. Doing my best to stay in the shadows.

Fifty paces before me, a man broke loose from the gathering and scrambled for the trees. But he never made it. A spear took him in the back, and he fell dead beneath the boughs. I stopped and knelt, confused now. The man's killer emerged from the throng and yanked the spear shaft from the corpse's torso.

Berse.

Was he the cause of the screams? Had he threatened Olaf? I knew not the answers to these questions, so I crept on.

Berse returned to the crowd, and I edged right and into the commotion, though I lowered my shield and axe so as not to cause more concern among the guests. Slowly I wove my way forward until Olaf's head came into view. He was alive, as was Gytha, who stood by his side. Though I could not say the same for the lords of Leyland and Lonsdale, who dangled from the end of ropes not ten paces behind the newlyweds.

I inched forward. Other corpses lay on the ground before Olaf, like hunting trophies on display. Several women cried or hugged each other for comfort. Priests prayed on their knees. Other warriors stood bound by ropes, their faces red from exertion or, mayhap, fury. These were the noblemen and women of Amounderness's neighboring lands and the priests who had accompanied them to this peaceful affair. Olaf's guests.

Standing about the dead were a group of Olaf's warriors. Men who I recognized though whose names I did not know. They looked to be under the command of Berse, who prodded one of the corpses with his bloody spear, a self-satisfied smile on his stupid face. Standing to one side were Padraic and the rest of Olaf's hird, as well as Gytha's own warriors, including Godric. Their dark frowns, averted eyes, and silence spoke clearly about the whole wretched affair. Around me, the other guests stared in horrified silence or else sobbed in fright and consternation. To my right, a little girl hugged the leg of her mother, whose own arm draped protectively over her daughter. Seeing them all stoked my outrage.

It was not the sight of the dead that bothered me, nor the actual killing itself. Guile, surprise, and bloodshed were the trademarks of the

Northmen who called themselves Vikings. No, what bothered me was that Olaf had done it all so publicly and with such disregard for the people and warriors he would now rule — people who were clearly troubled by his ghastly exhibition and would undoubtedly fear him forevermore. This was not the Olaf I knew. This was not the man who drew people to him like honey draws bees. This was a lord to be feared, and mayhap even hated, by his people. This was an Olaf I had not seen before.

As these grim thoughts came to me, Olaf stepped up to his first captive and drew his sword from its sheath. "You men have a choice," he began as he ran his thumb down the edge of his blade. "Accept me as your lord and live, or reject me and die like your brethren. You." He pointed to the man standing just before him. "What is your decision?"

The man spat on the grass at Olaf's feet. It was the last action he took in this life. Quick as a blink, Olaf removed the man's head from its shoulders with the swing of his blade. He swung so hard and so cleanly, the man stood upright for several moments, as if his thoughts had not yet registered that his head and body were no longer connected. Finally his body dropped like a sack to the ground, accompanied by the shocked gasps of the wedding guests. Still, it was not as clean a stroke as Olaf might have liked, for the blood of it spattered on his fine new cloak and across Gytha's dress, a mishap that drew a surprising smile from his new bride.

I had seen enough. Sensing no danger to my own welfare, I threaded my way back through the crowd and to my tent, where I sat heavily on my cot and rubbed my face to clear my senses of the killing I had just seen. Eventually I sighed and lay back on my bed with a singular thought in my mind: the man I grew up alongside was no longer the man I knew.

Things had changed, and it was time to go.

23

The sudden turn of events at the wedding feast put an abrupt end to the celebration, save for Olaf's men, who continued on for days as I waited, like a chained hound, for release. I used the time to work on my gear and to bury a portion of my silver. While I knew not if I would be back, I did know that I could not take it all to Irland. So west of the town I found a barren tree, under whose roots I planted a bag of coins and rings.

Finally Sveinn informed me that he was taking Padraic back to Dyflin and that I was welcome on his ship. Perchance he had organized it this way to ensure my safety, but I would never know — outside of the offer and thanking me for the silver I paid him for the spot, he spoke not a word to me. No one did. I sat alone in the ship's bow with my sea chest, all but ignored by the crew and by Padraic. Alone, I should say, in my banishment. For that is what it was — banishment — though Olaf had never used the term.

Two days and one night upon the summer sea brought us to the harbor beneath Dyflin's walls. It had only been a moon or so since we had left, and the place looked much the same. I hauled my sea chest up onto the quay and gave Sveinn a brief nod of thanks. He nodded in return as the other crewmates looked on. Many could not look at me, though whether in shame of me or pity for me, I could not tell. I swallowed my dismay, then turned and followed Padraic up the dock, dragging my chest over the rough boards behind me. I must have made a pathetic sight.

My reception in Dyflin was as cold as the day was gray. Padraic left me as soon as we disembarked, not bothering himself with a "farewell." Locals stared at me and then at my sea chest, though none offered to help. I sighed and reminded myself that I was not here for their good graces. I hailed a man with an empty cart, and using gestures and the scant bit of the local language I remembered, explained that I needed help getting to a specific location. He regarded me and my chest dubiously until I showed him a coin, at which point he nodded. I climbed up in the bed and pulled the chest behind me. He did not help.

In truth, I was nervous to head to Deidre's, but with my possessions, I could not chance an inn. The gear, clothing, and remnants of my wealth that lay within the chest were all I had and were, frankly, worth a fortune. If anyone was to discover it, or know I possessed it, I was as good as dead.

With calls and hand signals, I guided the man through Dyflin's narrow streets to a spot not far from Deidre's abode. I dared not stop beside her place in the event that the man see me enter. People talked, and I knew that sort of attention would not go well for her. Which is why I waited until he disappeared to drag my chest to the doorway I remembered so well.

My stomach twisted as I knocked softly. I did my best to suppress the all too familiar doubts that flooded my mind. Would she still remember me? Would she turn me away? The answers to those questions would have to wait. Deidre did not seem to be at home, which posed another dilemma. What now? I could not haul my sea chest to the town's center. Nor could I wait in the street for her — it would attract unwanted attention.

I cursed and looked about. The street was empty, and so I pressed on the door. To my relief, it opened. Quickly, I turned, grabbed the handle of my chest, and yanked it inside. Then I closed the door quietly behind me until I stood alone in the dark space with the scent of Deidre's dry herbs bathing me. Only when my eyes adjusted to the gloom did I slide my chest beneath the worktable and take a seat on the bench.

Hunger and boredom quickly descended on me. As did fatigue. I had slept little on the ship. To fight off the trio, I paced and, more times than I can count, asked myself whether I was a fool. Each time, the same answer came back to me: there was no other option. I could not have stayed in Amounderness. Nor could I have gone elsewhere in England. All that was open to me, by virtue of Padraic's return to his king, was Dyflin. Which suited me fine. I needed to see Deidre again. I needed to understand if my feelings for her were as serious as they felt. And so I waited until, at last, the door creaked open.

I froze as Deidre stepped into her home, a loaf of bread in her hands. She did not immediately see me, but when she did, she jumped in surprise and nearly dropped the loaf. Only when she recovered did a grin stretch across her face. I crossed the room to her.

"You came back," she said in the Northern tongue as she quickly closed the door.

"I did," I confirmed as we hugged. "I needed to see you again."

She looked up at me, her smile stretching the long scar on her right cheek. "Are you with the others?"

"No. I am alone."

She stepped back and her brows tilted above her caring eyes. "What of Olaf? I thought you were his man."

I pursed my lips. "It is a long story. Have you any food? I have not eaten since yesterday."

"Of course," she said. "I will make you some cheese and bread, but only on the condition that you tell me what happened." She waved the loaf at me to accentuate her point.

I grinned and raised my hands in surrender. "You are a hard negotiator, but you have a deal."

"So what happened?" she asked as she moved to the table. Then she stopped abruptly. "What is that?"

"It is my sea chest," I said softly.

"You left Olaf," she guessed as she turned back to me. Her voice was filled with astonishment.

"I did not leave him," I grumbled, doing my best to keep my voice level despite the anger building inside of me. I was not angry at Deidre, mind. It was the memory of being cast aside that inflamed me. "He abandoned me."

"Why?"

I tensed. "Because I would not accept his new god."

Her head tilted slightly. "And what god is that?"

"The Christian god."

An audible gust of air escaped her mouth. I prepared myself for a tenser discussion, but Deidre did not bother herself with the details — she flew instead to the conclusion. "So now you are lordless. And homeless."

The words hurt, especially when delivered so bluntly.

"What will you do now?"

I shrugged. "I know only one thing, Deidre, and that is how to fight."

In the long pause that followed my words, I felt as if I was being appraised. As if Deidre was calculating in her mind what to do with me and whether it was worth her effort to keep me about. I did not blame her. She was no longer a young girl, and this was not young love. There was no doubt that we cared for each other, but she had carved out a life that she valued — a life I had left and suddenly returned to as a lordless, homeless man. There was much to consider. As for me, I did not want her pity. If we were to remain together, I wanted only her acceptance and mayhap, if things progressed, her love.

Without a word, she turned to the table and cut the loaf. Then she sliced the cheese and laid a piece atop the bread. Handing it back to me, she said, "I am glad you are back, Torgil. I missed you."

I accepted her words and her food gratefully. "And I, you, Deidre."

"Come." She motioned to her bench. "Let us sit."

I straddled the creaking bench.

"Tell me what happened," she said as she handed me more bread and cheese.

I told her of Olaf and his change and of how his thirst for power had muddled his thinking. I laid bare my convictions to the old ways, thinking it best if she knew me fully, despite the cross that hung from her neck. To her credit, she listened without comment, save for the occasional question.

"I am sorry," she said and laid a gentle hand upon my thigh. "Truly. It is not easy to lose a friend so dear."

"No," I admitted. "Nor to be cast aside so easily by that friend. But enough of me," I countered, having sickened of the topic. "Tell me of happenings in Dyflin. How do things here fare?"

She shrugged and smiled. "It has not been long since you left, so there is little to tell. Things have been quiet in Dyflin since the defeat of Domnall and Ivar." Her smile slowly vanished as a new thought came to her mind. "I suppose I cannot say the same for Iron Knee, who has been busy laying waste to the land of Leinster, taking cattle and thralls for our use in Dyflin or else to sell for profit."

Her words turned my mind instantly to Amounderness, which stood to eventually benefit from Iron Knee's trade if Olaf could open the way to Jorvik.

"When he's not raiding," she was saying, "he is chasing young thrall women or feasting. The young king has an appetite..." Her voice trailed off.

I grunted my understanding.

She sighed. "There is another way, Torgil."

"What do you mean? Another way for what?" I asked, confused by her strange and rather sudden comment.

"Another way to live. For you, I mean."

"And what is that?" I asked, as I moved a curl from her face with my finger. Thus far, I had resisted my desire to move closer to her, but I could not help myself with the errant curl.

"You need not fight."

I smiled patiently. "And what would I do?"

"Farm. Fish. Be a carpenter." She shrugged. "There are many honest professions."

"Heal?"

She giggled and tapped my nose. "No. For that, you need much training."

I smiled. "As I would for the other professions. It is not so easy to simply take up fishing and make a living. One must do these things from youth. As you did."

She pouted. "But it is possible."

I grunted. "We will see."

I leaned forward and kissed her gently on the lips. She smiled but did not return the gesture as I had hoped. Feeling suddenly awkward, I looked up at the roof, for the gentle pitter-patter of rain had begun.

Deidre was not wrong in her thinking. I had lived for six and thirty summers and was getting older. The pain of my many battles lingered in my bones and frequently made me wince. Nightmares and sudden thoughts plagued my mind. I had given much to Olaf and those I had served. Perchance now was the time to put away my fighting axe. Besides, the thought of approaching Iron Knee and asking for his charity did not appeal to me. Nor did I think I would receive it. Not with Padraic by his side, whispering in his ear of my falling out with Olaf. Still, fighting was my skill. I was good at it, and it had earned me much in my life. If I were to stay in Dyflin and not waste my days or burden Deidre, fighting would be my best chance to sustain some sort of life.

"I should go," I said to Deidre.

"Go where?" she asked in return.

I shrugged. "To find a place to sleep. I did not sleep on the boat over."

She chuckled. "Can you not sleep here? In my cot?"

I grinned. "There is nothing I would rather do, Deidre. I just did not wish to outstay my welcome. You have been kind to feed me and listen to me prattle."

She slid closer to me and kissed me softly. "I like your prattle. And your company. I would like you to stay."

Deidre was gone when I awoke, and so I dressed and walked into town. I thought to head to the town's center, but then a thought sprang on me, and I turned toward the harbor. Just inside the walls sat several inns that catered to sailors and traders. It was a rougher area, not far from the stench of tanners and fishing stalls, as well as the pens and trading blocks used for thralls. Here, the air stank of piss and vomit and rotten fish. It reverberated with peals of laughter and the shouts of drunken men, not to mention the cries of seagulls and accosted women. Red-faced priests did their best to maintain peace as they stood on their boxes with their accusing fingers and angry words. They received nothing but lewd gestures for their efforts.

I walked the slick boards of the street, skirting the men who staggered past me as I searched for an establishment. I had in my mind two thoughts. The first was that fights in these streets were frequent and second, there was no place better to find information about the world than from the loose tongues of drunken men. And so I studied the inns and settled on one that I thought held promise.

Pushing my way in and through the inn's patrons, I found an empty table and studied the activity around me. Thugs, gamblers, drunkards, whores — not much different than any other inn that I had frequented.

"Ale?" a deep voice shouted from my left. It belonged to a barrel-chested Vestmann with a bald head and a bushy red mustache. He held in his hand a pitcher and a cup. I nodded. He smacked the pitcher onto the table, spilling some of its contents, then shouted more words at me, but I did not understand.

"Do you speak the Northern tongue?" I asked him in his language.

He scowled. "Aye. A little."

"Are you the innkeeper?"

"Aye," he confirmed. "Why?"

"I seek employment," I said bluntly. With so many people in his inn, I wasted no time on pleasantries.

His bushy brows slanted toward his broken nose. "What do you do?"

"Fight."

"I have men," he said as he nodded at a big fellow near the door.

"Not like me," I countered.

He scoffed. "That'll be a penny for the ale."

I had no penny, and so I gave him a small chunk of hack silver worth far more than his price. He examined it in his fat palm, then left without a word.

I huffed at the man's back, thinking my first attempt to present myself had failed horribly, and then I poured myself some ale. It was decent. As I sat, I took in the place. Unlike most other inns, it had a bit of a fishing decor to it, with oars and fishing nets and even an eel spear hanging from the walls. From the rafters above hung willow cones, which I took to be fishing traps. On the far end of the hall was a hearth in which peat burned, throwing its warmth over patrons who, judging from the words spilling from their drunken mouths, were all Vestmenn. Were it not for the intrusive stares I received from those same patrons, I might have called the place pleasant.

Five sips into my ale, I noticed a slight shift in the crowd to my right. I glanced in that direction and saw two men approaching, both large and both eyeing me. The first, I recognized from the door. The second, I had never seen. Knowing not what these two ruffians wanted, but seeing the malice in their eyes, I shifted my hand to my axe and unhooked it. I then grabbed the handle of the pitcher in my left hand and poured a bit more ale into my cup as I hooked my left foot around the leg of my table.

There was no introduction. No words or shouts. The first man — black-haired and scar-faced — simply reached for the bicep of my right arm as if he intended to haul me away from behind the table and to my feet. I smashed my axe head into his forehead. Not hard enough to kill him, mind, but hard enough to stun him. As he fell to the floor, I used my foot to slide my table into the path of the second man as he rushed at me. He bent toward me as the table struck his thighs, and I smashed the clay pitcher into his temple with my left hand. The clay shattered, and he rolled sideways. With the table no longer obstructing me, I pounced on the man and smacked his head as I had done to the first, knocking him unconscious. Then I hopped to my feet and readied myself for another attack.

None came.

The crowd had fallen away, silent now as they stared at me and the men at my feet. The innkeeper pushed through his stunned patrons and looked at the groaning guards just now pushing themselves to their knees. He laughed and clapped.

"Well done, Ostman. Those were my two best. Come back on the morrow, and we will discuss your wish further." He tossed me my silver. "This is yours."

And so I began my employment at The Drunken Gull.

PART III

"All these thoughts of love and strife
Glimmered through his lurid life,
As the stars' intenser light
Through the red flames o'er him trailing,
As his ships went sailing, sailing, ..."

The Saga of King Olaf
Henry Wadsworth Longfellow

24

D*yflin, Irland, Spring, AD 989*

My banishment to Dyflin was not a pleasant memory.

It began well enough, with Deidre and me happy in our renewed life together. But her work took her frequently from our home, leaving me to myself and my thoughts, sometimes for days. I remembered this from before, but it was harder on me now because I had no outlet, no friends, and no activities to fill my days.

I had only work.

The Drunken Gull and its inebriated clientele became my life. Not all at once, mind — it took a few seasons. But eventually, the smells of stale ale and sweat and wet wool, the sounds of laughter and intoxicated conversations — all of it and more became as familiar to me as any hall in which I had spent my days. Like my old comrades, those drunken patrons told me of their hopes and dreams and, aye, their failures. They invited me into their conversations and their lives and little by little, I embraced them as friends.

I believe, too, that those patrons filled a void left by the absence of my old comrades and that of Deidre, who was so often tending to the needs of others. But that was only the start of it. Ale, I learned, is even better at filling voids, as my father before me knew. I had tried hard in my life to avoid the weaknesses that had plagued my father, but in the end, I fell victim to its same allure.

I know not when my drinking began in earnest. One day I had an ale, and that ale soon became two, and then three, and then more. At first, seldom did I stumble home drunk late at night, but over the course of my third season in Dyflin, that random drunkenness became more frequent, and then a nightly occurrence. Deidre did not chastise me at first, but eventually she could no longer hold her tongue. Our fights became so common that I took to sleeping at the inn rather than face her wrath after a night among friends. Until one morning when she too banished me. Just like Olaf.

It did not happen as I thought it might. There was no horrid war of words or rain of tears. I simply came home the morning after one of my raucous evenings, my stomach roiling and my head throbbing, and found Deidre filling my sea chest with my belongings. I know not what she had intended to do — perchance leave it on the street outside her door — but whatever it was, she gave up her toil upon seeing me.

"It is time for you to go," she said. There was a sadness in her eyes but also a resoluteness, and so I did not try to argue.

"I will finish packing my things," I mumbled as the suffering in my stomach slid to my chest and then my heart.

She gave me the briefest of nods, then skirted past me and out the door.

The shame washed over me as I stared down at the piles by my feet. Not for losing Deidre, mind — her life had little room for me in it. No, I was ashamed because I knew I was better than the ale that filled me. Better than the floundering, wasting man I had let myself become. And at that moment, as I tossed the remnants of my things into my sea chest, I knew I had a choice to make: remedy the situation, or dwell in the bitterness of my loss.

I want to say I chose the prior — that I rolled up the sleeves of my tunic and sucked the cleansing air into my chest — but I did not. Instead, I hauled my sea chest across the wet boards of Dyflin's town, head bent in disgrace, and plodded to the pain-numbing refuge of The Drunken Gull. There, I worked out an arrangement with the owner, Conall, for a room and a cot, then I drowned my remorse in even more ale.

The next two seasons passed in a haze of laughter and whores and fights and regret. I saw naught of Deidre nor, frankly, of Dyflin. My life condensed to the four walls of The Drunken Gull and the patrons who walked through its doors. But I was not completely lost. I could still fight. Even when I could remember nothing of my exploits — which was often — I heard of them later. The regulars feared me, and those newcomers foolish enough to test me quickly learned it was best to keep the peace. I was compensated well for this gift. Conall fed me and kept me well-supplied with ale, though the whores took their share of my earnings.

Nor was I completely oblivious to the happenings in Dyflin. Working in an inn had its benefits, one of which was loose-tongued patrons whose feelings and secrets spilled from their mouths as readily as the ale went in. Dyflin was changing, and the Dyfliners were none too happy about it. My old friend Olaf, it seemed, had opened the way to Jorvik, and Iron Knee had ramped up his efforts to supply the world with the wealth of Irland. The increase in trade brought more foreigners to the city, sparking the old resentment of Northern rule. It was gradual, but Dyflin was moving in the wrong direction, at least according to the banter of drunks. And worse, Iron Knee cared not at all. Word was, he was more concerned with reaping the bounties of his newfound fortune. The stories of his feasts and the women he took to his bedchamber bordered on legendary, though commonly told with a tinge of bitterness.

I listened and nodded politely to their gripes, even though it did not concern me. I cared not if more Northmen came or if Dyflin closed its walls for good. I wanted only to disappear and live a life away from damned princes and their damned oaths and battles. Even when I heard of Olaf's successes in controlling ever-larger swaths of land. Even when Olaf's ships came to Dyflin for thralls and trade goods. Even when Iron Knee's wealth grew and his feasts became infamous affairs. None of it concerned me. All I wanted was some ale, some food, some laughs, and mayhap a whore to enjoy. That was my life. Simple. Or, as Olaf might say, uncomplicated.

That is, until Sveinn, Dragomir, and Ulf walked into The Drunken Gull.

I recognized them instantly. Sveinn with his long hair and wooden hand. Dragomir with his dour face and keen eyes. Ulf with his girth and smile. They were no longer the young men they had been, but despite their graying hair and thickening bellies, I could not mistake them.

I cannot say that they identified me as quickly. I suppose I had changed much since my departure from Amounderness. Unlike them, I was no longer a warrior. I was a simple Vestmann in clothing, hair, and manner, with gray snakes in my black beard and a body turned soft by easy, besotted living.

I followed my former friends to their table and asked them for their order in the Northern language when they sat.

"Ale, and lots of it!" Ulf called to me, still not seeing me for who I was.

I nodded and was turning to go when Sveinn grabbed my arm. "Wait."

I turned back to him.

"Where did you get that?" He nodded at my axe, then raised his eyes to my face. "Torgil?"

I nodded. They frowned and exchanged glances. It was possible they still hated me for what they believed to be my oath-breaking, but when they looked back at me, I saw something else. Disbelief? Pity perchance?

Sveinn stood slowly, and I stepped back, not knowing what to expect. He opened his arms. "Torgil, you bastard. It is good to set eyes on you."

I hugged my former shield mate. "It is good to see you, Sveinn." And I meant it. I then nodded to Dragomir and Ulf, who were also standing. "It is good to see all of you!"

"We thought you had gone back to the North," said Dragomir as he hugged me. "Gods, man. You stink of ale."

"I came here and never left," I told him, indicating The Drunken Gull and, more broadly, Dyflin.

Ulf grabbed my wrist in the way of warriors and tousled my graying hair. "You look it! Dyflin has chewed you up and shat you out." He said this with a smile, but there was truth behind his words.

I ignored his comment and beckoned to the table. "Sit. I'll get some ale."

I returned to the table with three frothing pitchers of ale and four cups, all of which I purchased for my friends. After filling each, I raised my cup to them. "Sköl."

"Sköl!" they called to me.

"So you are not angry with me?" I asked, meeting each of their eyes in turn.

Ulf shrugged. "Was for a time, but Olaf finally told us the truth. Said you broke no oath to him. Though you did walk out on us. He's still bitter about that."

I grunted. "You all would have killed me, had I not."

Dragomir grunted. "True. We might have."

It was a bitter draught to swallow. "What made Olaf tell you?"

Sveinn shook his head. "The gods only know. Caught him in a weak moment? He was deep in his cups, as I recall. Perchance he felt it safer once you were gone for good."

"Safer?"

"Aye, safer," Sveinn said flatly. "Do you think Olaf wanted the leader of his hird challenging his decision? Whispering in the ear of his men about the fallacy of the god he had chosen? Do you think Gytha wanted that?"

I drained my cup to give myself time to think. It was hard to accept that I would ever be a challenge to the man I had protected his entire life. We had many differences of opinion, but never once had I challenged his rule. Nor would I.

"Let us talk of better things," I said after draining my cup. "I heard Olaf opened the route to Jorvik. With your help, no doubt."

Sveinn glanced at my empty cup as Dragomir responded. "Of course with our help," he said. "Ousting Alfvin and taking Blackburn were no small feats, nor was quelling the uprisings in Layland and Lonsdale. Turns out, their lords were popular and Olaf was hasty. Navigating the kingdom of Jorvik was the easiest part of the whole damned campaign. Once the jarl realized what he had to gain from an overland route, the rest was easy."

Ulf belched under his breath and poured himself another cup.

"And the others?" I asked, as the stench of his burp reached my nose.

Sveinn smirked. "You'll be glad to know that not much has changed. Old Crowbone is just as unpredictable as always. Orm still has his finger lodged in his nose, and Berse still has his nose lodged in Crowbone's arse. It's a wonder he can breathe at all. Hauk rules Lonsdale and Finn rules Leyland, both in Olaf's name. It pays to be related to a prince, eh?" He nudged me. "There's been some trouble since we quelled the uprisings, but nothing those two can't handle with a little help from us. Olaf even married them off to some local wenches, so they're fat and happy. Hauk's a father, by the way. You forgot to send him a gift."

"A father…" I said, shaking my head. "That is a hard one to believe."

"Harder to believe he didn't crush the poor woman when he sired his whelp," Ulf quipped, which made us all laugh.

"Hey." Sveinn smacked my arm. "Did you know Olaf is a father?"

"Truly?" My mind flew back to Wagria and that sad night in Geira's hall. I was glad for him, even if we were no longer friends. "That is good news."

"The lad is coming on a full circle of the sun," added Dragomir.

I grinned. "A lad, you say?" Olaf had always wanted a son. "That is good."

Dragomir smiled. "Good for him. Bad for us. Now we have two of those headstrong bastards to contend with."

We chuckled. Ah, it felt good to be back with them. I had missed it.

"Enough of us," Sveinn interjected. "What of you? Living a life of fame and fortune, I see. How fares Deidre?"

The mirth evaporated. "Neither fame nor fortune. And sadly, no Deidre."

"So I was not wrong," said Ulf. "Dyflin *has* shat you out."

I shrugged. "It's not all bad. I have the inn and ale and women."

Sveinn nodded at my cup. "Since when have you liked ale?"

"Since discovering what good ale tastes like," I said a bit too testily. He sounded like Deidre.

Sveinn rolled his eyes, and I switched the subject. "So what brings you all here? It must be a rare occasion to draw Olaf's hird to an affair."

Sveinn looked at the others, then back at me. "Trade," he said. "Nothing more."

But there was more, and I saw it in Sveinn's look. Still, I played along. "Trade must be good," I said, then held my tongue.

"That it is, my friend." He raised his cup to me.

I drank the dregs from my cup, then my eyes shifted to the others. All seemed suddenly on edge, as if I had hit on a sour subject. "Something is amiss," I said as I lowered my cup. "What is it?"

Sveinn looked again at the others, then his eyes fell on me. "Not here. I will find you on the morrow, and we will speak then."

As if by some unspoken signal, the conversation ended and my old comrades rose. I rose with them.

"It is good to see you hale," Sveinn said and patted my shoulder.

The others nodded to me as they left, and I, confused by their sudden departure, watched them go.

Seeing me suddenly free, others in the inn invited me to join them at their tables, but I refused and drank only sparingly until the inn closed its doors that night. Rather than head to my room, I walked to the town walls and climbed to the parapets so that I could look down upon the harbor. Just that small exercise left me winded. Or mayhap it was the sight in the harbor that took my breath away, for tied to the quay were five of Olaf's ships, including my old friend *Sea Wolf*.

Something was amiss.

∽

I rose early the following morning, bathed in the river to the south of town, dressed in a clean tunic and breeks, and purchased a roll of warm bread from the baker I liked. I then retraced my steps to the town's parapets, where I engaged a guard in some friendly banter.

"A good morning to you," I said to him. "Bread?"

I tore a piece from the portion I held in my hand and offered him some. He took the bread with a grunt of thanks.

"Strange to see so many Northmen here," I said to him casually. "Is there trouble?"

"Aye," he said as he popped the bread into his maw. "I've never liked those bastards, but we'll be grateful for their help nonetheless."

"Help?" I asked. "Why is it needed?"

He looked at me as if I lacked a brain. "Ivar of Waterford is on the move again. Have you not heard?"

I shook my head, remembering back to that foggy battle and Olaf's wound. I had heard in the inn of Ivar and his raids throughout the Irland Sea and around the island, including the land around Dyflin. He was a constant threat, but with Iron Knee firmly planted in the city, enjoying the support of both Malachy and Olaf, Ivar had kept his distance.

"The bastard doesn't give up," he grumbled.

"Is he with Domnall?" I asked, meaning the king of Leinster with whom he had been allied when he last marched on Dyflin all those summers ago.

"Domnall? He's dead, man. Killed years ago by rivals in southern Leinster. No, he marches with the kings of the Isles and Ellan Vannin," said the guard, meaning the Sudreyjar. "The brothers Maccus and Godfraid — God curse those traitors." And he spat to emphasize his disgust.

I frowned as I recalled the island warriors beside whom we had fought against Ivar and his men. "I thought Maccus and Godfraid supported the kings of Dyflin."

The man shrugged and glanced at me. "The winds have shifted."

"Why?"

The man shrugged. "Only God knows." He crossed himself.

So there it was. Sveinn had not lied. This *was* about trade. Maccus and Godfraid controlled the islands off Dyflin's coast. With them and Ivar patrolling the Irland Sea, the waterways were not safe. Olaf, it seemed, had come no doubt at the behest of Iron Knee, but certainly to protect his own interests as well. It made sense, though there was still much I did not know.

I stared at the fleet, though my thoughts lingered on my future. It seemed that, yet again, I was at a crossroads. How easy it would be to ignore the upcoming fight and vanish into my uncomplicated life. Even if Ivar succeeded and Dyflin fell to him, life for me would almost certainly go on as it had before. Who would bother me as I sat in the shadows of The Drunken Gull?

But could I let that happen? Could I ignore my old friends if it came to a fight? Perhaps. After all, Olaf had cast me out and they had turned their backs on me. But they had done so based on an assumption. Had they known the full truth, would they have exiled me so readily? That was an answer I did not have, nor did I think I ever would. And yet, that was the crux of my anger and the answer I needed.

I sighed. Life had turned complicated yet again.

25

In the end, I did not need to seek the answer — it came to me in the form of Sveinn.

That very morning, as I approached The Drunken Gull after my discussion with the wall guard, Sveinn stepped out of the shadows and into my path. I had not even seen a figure standing there, and his sudden appearance made me jump.

He looked at me strangely.

"You surprised me," I said, even as I chastised myself for not noticing him.

"You'd be a dead man if I were a thief," came his sour retort.

I scowled at the truth in his words.

"Never mind that," he said, switching subjects. "We should talk. Come." He grabbed my arm and turned me around.

I shrugged free of him. "Olaf's battles no longer concern me."

"You know?"

Had I not known, I certainly did now. "The town's guards know, Sveinn. It is not so hard a riddle to solve."

He nodded as we walked. "We could use your help," he said.

I almost laughed. "Do not include me, Sveinn. I have no interest in helping Olaf protect his interests. This is not my fight. Besides," I lifted my arms to show him my softness, "I have not fought in a battle in many summers, in case you have forgotten."

He frowned at me. "What has become of you, Torgil? You were a fighter."

I scowled. "I *was* a fighter. I was Olaf's fighter. But he released me, or do you not remember?"

"I remember," he said almost in a whisper, then cast his eyes left and right to ensure we were alone. "Still, this is Dyflin's fight. If Ivar and his army succeed, there is no telling what they will do to the citizens of this city. Think of Deidre and your friends at the inn."

That gave me pause. Though Deidre and I had parted on poor terms, and we had not crossed paths in some time, I still cared what happened to her. And to my friends at The Drunken Gull.

We moved aside to let a cart roll past. "There is talk of arming the citizens," he continued when the cart's owner was out of earshot.

"Why? Is Ivar's army so vast?"

Sveinn's face sobered all the more. "The odds are not in our favor, Torgil. Iron Knee seems as lost as you to his ale and women. And Malachy?" He shrugged. "We have messengers out to him, but he is taking his time."

I forced my mind from the insult and tried to focus on Sveinn's words. Iron Knee's feasting and womanizing were well known, but I had not heard that they impaired his decision-making.

"So you would have me join you?" My tone dripped with mockery. "What would the others say? Most think me an oath-breaker. A nithing. Odin's balls, man — Olaf cast me out."

He shrugged. "So join Iron Knee's men. I care not. Just arm yourself, Torgil. You are worth ten men or more, even in your sorry state."

I bit my lip. "When is Ivar's army expected?"

He shrugged. "Half a moon. Less. I know not, though I do know he is on the move. Give it serious thought, my friend. I do not want you caught with your head in your cup."

And with that, he nodded and left. I watched him go, my mind and my stomach astir, the bread in my hand all but forgotten. I cast my eyes on my belly and knew that I was in no condition to fight. Yet I knew, too, that I could not run or hide. I would not. The shame of cowardice alone would kill me.

And so I decided.

With Olaf's warriors in the streets and setting up camp in the harbor, as well as the increase in guards along the walls, it did not take much to deduce that something was awry. By that afternoon, word of Ivar's advance had spread within Dyflin's walls. And where news spread, so too did rumors. Iron Knee was fretting, some said. Others had heard that he did not think the threat was real. Still others shrugged off the news, for this, they said, would be like all the other times Ivar had harried near Dyflin. He would take his booty and leave.

Only this was not like the other times, and I knew it.

It was true that Ivar had plucked slaves and cattle from the lands around Dyflin since Iron Knee's ascension to the throne. But large armies did not form around a king to win only thralls and livestock.

Nor would the brothers Maccus and Godfraid break their alliance with Iron Knee unless the prize was great. No, they came for something better. They came for Dyflin. Olaf and Iron Knee knew it too, or Olaf would not be here with his fleet.

I did not share that grim thought with my friends at the inn. There was no telling how they might spread the word and what fervor those words might create. Though Dyflin was large, word traveled quickly, and I did not want to create more fear than already drifted through the streets. Instead, I nodded and offered a few opinions but kept most of my thoughts to myself.

That very night, I battled the urge for ale and the invitations of my friends to join them and instead went to my room to check my war gear. I knew not if I might need it, but I was glad I took the precaution, especially after seeing the condition of my shield. Dust and cobwebs clung to the rim, while the leather had decomposed in spots and revealed the loose boards beneath. Thankfully, my armor, helmet, and seax had been protected by the sea chest and the wool bags in which I had stuffed them, though dust and spots of rust were still visible. Had my father been alive, he would have flayed me for allowing my gear to fall into such disrepair, and deservedly so.

The very next morning, I purchased the items I would need to repair my gear, though with my shield, I did not bother. I had not the tools, space, or time to construct a new one, so I sought a shield among the stalls of Dyflin. It took some time, but eventually I found one with the size, balance, and weight I preferred. I paid the shield maker and turned to leave.

"So you are a warrior now?" came a woman's voice.

I turned and found Deidre staring at me. She was older now and more deeply lined at the corners of her brown eyes. Gray coils fell among the red and framed her scarred face, which seemed somehow more severe. Whether that severity was from age or the sight of me, I knew not, nor did I care to hazard a guess.

I looked at my new shield and shook my head. "No."

In her hand was a basket containing several bundles of herbs and fresh cloth. The tools of healing. "Off to see someone in need?" I asked.

I meant it cordially, but Deidre took it differently and frowned. I suppose my words recalled the rift that ended us.

"Aye."

We stared at each other awkwardly. I knew not her mind, but I was trying desperately to find words to fill the silence.

She nodded at the shield. "I thought you laid down your shield and blades."

I looked at the shield again. "We should speak."

She shrugged. "So speak."

"Not here, Deidre."

The grooves in her face deepened. She motioned with her head. "Come, then."

I followed her from the market, noticing instantly the weight of the shield, how it banged against my thigh, and the pressure it placed on my wrist as I maneuvered it through the crowd. It felt at once familiar and yet foreign.

"So what is it you need to say?" she asked over her shoulder.

"Can you stop for a moment?"

She faced me, her body tense.

I approached her and looked about. We were alone for an instant, though townsfolk walked in our direction. They would be upon us soon. "I heard from old friends in the camp that Ivar is coming for Dyflin," I hastened to say. "But this time he has help from the kings of Man and the Isles. I worry for Dyflin and its people. I worry for you, Deidre. Do you have a place to go?" I should not have cared, given our history, and yet I did. Despite all the arguments and pain and loneliness, she was still in my thoughts.

Deidre laughed coldly. "You worry for me? After summers and winters locked in your inn among your friends, lost to your ale cup and your whores? How many times has Ivar come to our lands and threatened us, and now is the time you worry?" Crimson blotches appeared on her cheeks.

My own ire flashed, but I had not the time to respond before a couple walked past. Once they were out of earshot, I rasped, "How would you know about my worry? You were never around to hear it."

"I came to the inn many times to pull you from the mire," she hissed as she pointed in the direction of the harbor. "And still you returned. Still you left me. Your concern?" She snorted. "It is laughable."

"And every time I returned to you, you left. Sometimes for days. Strange that you know how to heal people and yet you left our relationship to shrivel and die."

People stopped nearby to stare at us. It brought me to my senses, and I let out a large sigh. She was not so willing to acquiesce, and her nostrils flared. I held up my hands to calm her.

"Our life together was not meant to be, Deidre. I have accepted that." I picked my way through my words as one might step on wet stones while crossing a stream. "It is past. But that does not mean I have no care for you. Nor think of you. Which is why I tell you these things now and ask the question that I did."

The onlookers lost interest and moved on.

Deidre's eyes locked on my face, her shoulders rigid. "I will be here, Torgil. No matter what happens, Dyflin is my home and these are my people. I will not leave them, especially if things are as bad as you let on."

Of course she would not. I was a fool to doubt her dedication or her courage. And so I argued no more and instead, nodded.

Her features suddenly softened. "I wish you well, Torgil. Wherever life takes you."

"And I, you, Deidre. May the gods protect you."

She turned and left with her basket of herbs and strips of cloth. And as she retreated, part of my heart went with her.

I slept poorly in the nights that followed. Despite practicing in my room with my axe and shield and working up a good lather, my worry overwhelmed any weariness I might have felt in my body. I was not so foolish to think that I could reclaim my skill and strength in a handful of days, but at the very least, I hoped to reclaim the movements that had once been a part of my every day. My motions, of course, did not come so easily. They felt stilted and clumsy, and it worried me. So much so that I tossed on my cot and often rose to pace in the night.

No longer did I have the luxury of a mind and body numbed by drink. Quite the opposite, if truth be told. Thoughts and emotions haunted me. Chief among those were the actions I would take in the coming days. I would fight — there was no question of that — and I would most likely die, for my skill had left me. Strangely, the thought of that did not bother me. So long as I died with my face to the enemy, I would be at peace. And mayhap, if I fought well, the Valkyrie would choose me for Valhall, where once again I would see my friends and my father.

No, I was more concerned about throwing my life away frivolously. I wanted to be smart about my decision of how and with whom I might fall. The Vestmenn were good fighters, but I would be alone among them. At least with Sveinn and the others, I would be among men I knew. But I knew, too, that I could not return to Olaf unless he himself asked. And that I doubted he would do. It would mean admitting he was wrong, and he was too bullheaded and prideful for that. Which left me with no answer and no plan…

Beyond my own welfare were my concerns about Dyflin. I knew Deidre's choice now, but what of my friends at the inn? When should I tell them of the danger they faced? Would they be safe? Could I protect them? And what of the other citizens of Dyflin? Did I care for them too? Should I? I knew I did or I would not ponder these questions, yet I had no answers for protecting them and it frustrated me.

Three nights of sleeplessness led me to the day the fires appeared on the horizon. I knew naught of them until a man entered The Drunken Gull and shared the news, which, of course, drove everyone to the walls.

Beside me, Conall muttered something and crossed himself.

I did not begrudge him. Beseeching his god seemed appropriate, given the amount of black and gray smoke billowing across the southern horizon. We could see no enemy from where we stood near the northern portion of the wall, but we need not have. The fire told the story.

"Iron Knee will be looking for warriors," said one of the inn's patrons.

Another snorted. "If he can pull himself out of bed and away from his women."

"Padraic will get him on his feet," Conall remarked. "I trust that man."

I did not. He seemed a capable enough warrior, but he always seemed distant to me.

"What will you do?" I asked Conall. "With the inn, I mean." What I really wanted to know was what he might do if Dyflin fell to Ivar, but I could not utter the words. I did not want to bring bad luck.

Conall laughed and smacked my arm. "Do? I will do nothing. War is good for business. It brings refugees and warriors. We will have more work than we can handle." He laughed again and walked away.

I glanced at him, then at my friends. "And you?"

Most shrugged. Some shook their heads.

Fergal, with whom I was closest, seemed surprised. "Do you ask if we'll fight? Ha! We are not fighters, Torgil. If Ivar takes the city, the only thing he'll see of me is my arse as I head out the gate." He barked a laugh. The others chuckled.

I just stared. It was a mindset I did not understand.

If Fergal or the others saw my expression, they did not address it. Perchance they were already too ale-addled to notice it. Instead, Fergal just patted my shoulder and walked past me. The others followed him, putting me in mind of ducklings following their mother. A parade of drunken ducks.

I turned my gaze back to the billows of smoke and wondered briefly if Ivar had the courage to attack Dyflin's walls, or if he would besiege the city. If Malachy truly was coming, it would behoove Ivar to strike quickly and decisively. And if Iron Knee were smart, he would bolster his defenses and let Ivar come to him. I was certain Olaf would agree, but then, who knew what was in Olaf's head? He had surprised me too many times for me to truly know his thoughts.

My thoughts drifted to Malachy, the king who had placed Iron Knee in his seat. I was certain he knew of Iron Knee's appetite for food and women, as well as for slave trade, but would that deter him from helping his half-brother? I doubted it. For all of his supposed failings, Iron Knee had brought riches to Malachy. Surely that spoke well for him. But then, where was Malachy and his army? Without them, we would be stuck in Dyflin, and I, for one, had lived through enough sieges to know how bad life could get.

I cursed. It was frustrating not to have the answers. Which, in turn, brought my thoughts to Sveinn. Perchance he knew more and could tell me what I needed to know. And so I promised myself to seek him out the following morning.

But events deteriorated faster than that.

26

I awoke the following morning to a city in chaos. Horns blared. Shouts echoed. Footfalls thumped on the wooden streets outside The Drunken Gull. Suddenly alert, I rolled from my cot and quickly dressed, though I did not shrug into my armor. I needed to know what the matter was before I did.

That answer came soon enough.

Sunlight had not yet fallen on the streets as I rushed out the door and toward Dyflin's walls. Ascending the steps, I was greeted by a sight both terrifying and impressive. At least twenty ships rested on the water outside of Dyflin's harbor. Their tall masts and sweeping, beast-headed prows rose above the mist. The shouted threats of hundreds of spear warriors echoed across the water to Dyflin's warriors, who stood on the walls, mesmerized in their dread. How they had arrived so suddenly — without so much as a call of warning — was astonishing in its own right. They must have come at night, a feat both perilous and bold.

More horns blared behind me, and I spun. So too did the men beside me. It was hard to see Iron Knee's guards to the south in the early morning gloom, but word traveled to us quickly. Ivar and his army had appeared to the south, and based on the reaction of the warriors beside me, not one man had known they would come so quickly. But he had come, and I knew it was because Malachy was not yet there.

Which meant one thing: the battle was upon us.

Olaf's men knew it, too. Below the walls, in the harbor and in the camp, his warriors scrambled to don their armor and grab their shields and weapons. I could see my old friend in their midst, calling out orders as he wove through the camp. As hard as it must have been, he was right to abandon his ships. What chance would five ships have against twenty? Though it did make me wonder: if Olaf knew about Maccus and Godfraid, why did he bring so few men? Perchance he did not believe them capable of an army so large?

Olaf's men retreated slowly through the northern gate, not far from where I stood, and so I left the wall and returned to my room, where I shrugged into my tight-fitting armor and cinched the belt around my waist. I added my seax and my axe, pulled my worn glove onto my shield hand, slipped the helmet over my head, and hefted my shield. The exertion of dressing left me sweating, and I cursed myself for ever having slipped this far from who I truly was.

I had not thought of my plan for leaving The Drunken Gull — I thought I would have time to do so — so I merely waved to Conall and walked out the door as he shouted at me to come back and get to work. I turned right toward the gate though, in truth, that was as far as I had planned. I still knew not whether I would merely join the Vestmenn or try to slip in among Sveinn's crew.

That issue resolved itself as soon as I reached the main street that headed from the northern gate into town. There, Olaf's Northmen were congregating, and so I simply slipped in among them. There was no more thought to it than that. Some looked at me, but I ignored them and focused instead on locating my former comrades. They were there, I was sure, but not near the group with whom I stood.

With a call, we trod past the marketplace and into the inner courtyard surrounding Iron Knee's hall, where his own guards readied themselves for battle. Olaf disappeared through the doors of Iron Knee's residence with Berse by his side, and Olaf's men removed their helmets and milled about, waiting for instructions. Some leaned on their spears. Others checked the sharpness of their blades. Ulf rested on the head of his massive battle axe, his red hair flowing over his shoulders. He had not had time to braid it for battle. Beside him stood Sveinn and Dragomir and Orm, laughing at something. I know not why, but when I rested my gaze upon them, I felt a wave of regret wash over me. It was hard to see them standing there among Olaf's men, and harder still to be standing on the periphery, looking in.

Olaf and Berse reemerged from the hall with Iron Knee between them. I had not seen the Dyflin king in many seasons, and his appearance alarmed me. Though still tall, the lad had gained weight. His face was pudgy and blotched. His hair was disheveled. He seemed out of sorts and was still struggling with his belt as he stepped onto the porch. Noticing the gathering before him, he gave up and gazed at the crowd.

"Men!" His voice cracked, and he cleared it, then tried again. "Men! The enemy is at our gates, but fear not! Our walls are stout, and you are stouter." He spoke in the tongue of the Vestmenn, which satisfied his men but left Olaf's warriors confused. "They may try to breach this city's walls, but they will never take it. Not while we man the gates!" He bunched his fist to show his fervor, and his warriors cheered.

"We have with us the mighty Olaf Tryggvason and his army, who will guard the northern gate against the men of the Isles. We, men of Dyflin, shall hold the southern gate against Ivar and his army. Remember as you go forth: we have God on our side. We will prevail!" He pulled his sword from its sheath and raised it above his head. And again, his men cheered.

The young king turned and beckoned Olaf forward. "Olaf Tryggvason."

Olaf nodded his thanks, then gazed out at the crowd. Next to the bedraggled Vestmann, he cut an imposing figure in his burnished armor. "I will speak plainly and leave the fancy words to King Iron Knee." His men chuckled. "We will guard the northern gate. Our job is simple: keep the island men out of Dyflin. I need not tell you of the challenge that faces us, but I will be by your side and lead you against the foe."

I rolled my eyes. As if he alone could protect us.

"Let us fight like giants," he continued, "so that Dyflin and history remember our names."

Though they had not received as impassioned a speech as Iron Knee's, his men nevertheless cheered just as loudly. I too found myself riled up by his words, though I refrained from shouting and satisfied myself with that long-forgotten pulsing in my veins. Gods, was it good to feel that fire again.

Olaf marched from the courtyard, and I followed with his men. My hope was to pull Sveinn aside and find a spot among my old friends, though I knew it would be tricky. In a battle such as this, they would stand near Olaf, and I could not. Still, I looked for a chance, and it came when we reached the northern gate. Sveinn did not climb the steps near Olaf, but rather saw to the less experienced warriors, directing them to various spots along the wall.

Being the last in the long line, I waited for Sveinn to notice me. When he finally did, his mouth stretched into a broad smile. "You look like an overstuffed sausage," he said.

"My girth makes me stouter," I retorted with the faintest of grins.

"And slower," he replied.

"Careful," I said to him. "I still know how to use my axe."

He chuckled. "It is good to have you with us, Torgil. I have missed you."

"And I, you, though I know not why." I winked at him. "Where do you want me?"

"With Berse's lads, off to the left there."

I frowned.

"Would you rather stand beside Olaf, with us?"

I snorted.

"Just stay far off to the left. End of the line beside the Vestmenn." He pointed to the western side of the north wall where it bent southward. "Berse will be on the right of his group, here above the gate. Your paths won't cross."

"And where will you stand?"

"Here, over the gate. Where else would Olaf have us stand?"

I nodded and climbed onto the first step. He patted my shoulder. "Like old times, eh?"

I snorted. "Far from it."

He laughed and followed me up.

I need not have worried about being noticed. The Northmen's attention was not focused on me nor on who passed by their shoulders. They were focused on the water, where the drums thumped and the cries of the island men grew more fevered.

I found a spot at the end of the Northman line just as the enemy ships turned their prows toward shore and glided under oar through the morning mist and into the harbor. Though the light was dull, its weakness could not hide the spear tips and helmets lining the ships' prows.

We watched helplessly from our perch as those same prows glided to a halt just beyond an arrow's range. Strangely, they did not come closer than that. Nor did Maccus or Godfraid do more than stand on the dock and survey the walls as their crews cast curses upon us. Several of the

Dyfliners let loose with their arrows, but they fell pitifully short of the mark, which only served to elicit more laughs and jeers from our besiegers.

"They'll come on the morrow," said a voice to my right. It was Dragomir, who carried a wooden cup in each hand. "Ale?"

Oh how I wanted it, but I resisted. "No. Thank you."

"I'll have it," said a man to my right.

"Get your own," Dragomir growled at him as he passed the man. He then drank one of the cups in five large gulps, burped loudly, and placed the empty ale cup on the ground between us. "Your loss," he said to me with a smile.

I looked at the barren cup, then at Dragomir. "You are cruel to tempt me."

"No one ever said I was nice." Dragomir chuckled.

I turned my gaze back to the harbor. "On the morrow, you think?"

My former comrade rested his arms on the low wall beside me and tapped his cup on the wood. I tried to shut my mind to the barley smell but failed. Gods, was it tempting. "Aye."

"Why not today?" asked the man to my left.

I looked at him. He may have been half my age, with eyes a bit too close together, a long nose, and long brown hair. He was not what I would call handsome. "What is your name?"

"Dufgall," he said. "Why? What is yours?"

My brows lowered. "What kind of name is that?"

"He's from Amounderness," Dragomir said, pointing his thumb at the lad. "Dad's a Northman. Mom's from the isles somewhere."

"So why not today?" asked the man again.

I ignored his question, for I knew not the answer.

Dragomir responded in my stead. "Well, Dufgall, look at the warriors." He nodded at the ships. "Many of them wear their armor, but some sit on their decks and sharpen their weapons. Does it look like they are ready for war?"

I had not noticed these things either, and that concerned me. Still, I held my tongue and nodded all the same.

"So, either they will attack tonight," said Dragomir into the silence, "which is hard, given the lack of visibility, or they'll attack on the morrow when it is cooler and they have more time to fight. If I had to wager, I'd say it will be morning."

I nodded. "It's harder to sail at night, but that didn't stop them from coming."

"True," conceded Dragomir. "I guess we will see." He slapped my back. "Let me know if you need anything."

I snorted. "I wouldn't ask you if I did."

He chuckled and looked at Dufgall. "You're a lucky lad, Dufgall. He might look past his prime, but he'll keep you safe. Just follow his lead."

As Dragomir walked away, Dufgall squinted at me with his strange eyes. Appraising me, no doubt.

"Torgil," I finally said. "My name's Torgil. Torgil the Lucky."

"Why do they call you 'the Lucky'?"

I grunted sourly. "The gods only know."

He kept silent after that.

～

We slept that night on the walkway atop Dyflin's walls. We dared not remove our armor or leave for more comfortable quarters and so we slept on the wood in our metal and leather. Thank the gods it was a cloudless night — one of the few we had had that spring. We took turns sleeping, though I did not trust Dufgall. I did not think he would fall asleep — he seemed too frightened for that. Rather, I worried that his inexperience would befuddle his hearing and he might misidentify the sounds of attackers if indeed the island men decided to come that night. And so I rested only lightly, which is why I jumped so quickly to my feet when the frantic blare of horns rose from across the city.

It was morning, but just barely. My first instinct was to grab my axe and peer over the wall, expecting to see a mad rush of warriors coming for us. But I saw nothing, at least not at first.

"Where are they?" Dufgall asked beside me. There was panic in his voice.

More horns filled the air. I turned my gaze south and listened but could not hear the sounds of battle. No shouts. No cries of dismay. No ring of steel. I looked left, toward Olaf's position. His tall form towered in the midst of his men but did not move.

And that is when I heard it. A low rumble of voices to my right, coming closer. I waited as the voices grew in clarity — until I could hear them distinctly — and my heart nearly stopped.

Iron Knee was dead.

27

"How could that be?" men asked, and indeed, I had the same question. Had he gone to the wall and an arrow struck him by happenstance? Had he tripped and fallen on his sword? Had he drank too much?

The answers came soon enough, albeit in snippets whispered by the Dyflin warriors. "Murdered. A slave. Last night. In his bed."

"What is happening?" Dufgall was frantic now, for he did not understand the language of the Vestmenn. "What are they saying?"

I looked at him. "King Iron Knee is dead. Murdered."

His mouth fell open. Beside him, the other Northmen began to chirp and the word of Iron Knee's death traveled farther.

My mind raced. Something was wrong. A king murdered on the eve of a battle. It was too perfect.

And just as that thought hit me, so too did the din of fighting at the gate. Thinking the island men had crept up to it in the night, I smacked my colleague.

"Come, Dufgall," I called and ran for the steps that would take me below.

But what I found when I reached the ground was not what I expected at all.

Berse was there with a group of his men. Rather than fighting off an attacker from without, he and his men were assailing the gate guards within. I gawked, my mind racing, but in my heart, I knew what had happened. Berse fought for Ivar and his allies. And knowing Berse could do nothing without Olaf's blessing, that meant Olaf had switched sides.

"What are they doing?"

Dufgall's desperate question brought me to my senses. "Go back to your post!" I yelled at him, knowing he could not fend off Berse or his men.

My shout, however, alerted Berse to our presence. He struck down a Vestmann and ordered two of his men to open the gate. Then he turned to me and Dufgall.

I'm not certain which of us was more stunned, though I'd had time to process the situation and so acted faster. "Get back, Dufgall," I ordered him and pointed at the wall. "Now!"

He hesitated.

"Now!" I ordered him again.

"If it isn't the oath-breaker!" Berse called to me, as the massive gate creaked open and the island men flooded forward from the harbor. Horns blared on the walls. I didn't prepare to fight. Instead, I spun and ran.

Berse's laughing call chased me as I stumbled away. "Run, you nithing!"

His words seared me, but I did not stop. Instead I headed to The Drunken Gull and burst through the door.

"The Northmen have breached the wall!" I shouted into the cavernous space at the shocked faces. "Run!"

As I raced on, shouts erupted upon the walls. So did the ringing of steel and the cries of the wounded. The Northmen had turned on their Dyflin brothers.

Had they all known? I asked myself as I raced through the streets. *Had Sveinn and Dragomir known? Is that why they wanted me with them? To save me? But if so, did they really think I would turn against the Dyfliners?*

More screams rent the air, pulling my thoughts back to the present. The air grew hazy with smoke. Citizens ran from their hovels and crowded the streets, though when they saw me in my Northern armor, they turned and ran. I ignored them. I needed to reach Deidre, to at least warn her of what horror had befallen the city, for I knew Ivar would give the Dyfliners no quarter.

I turned onto Deidre's street and sprinted to her door. Again, people avoided me, which suited me fine; I meant them no harm. I pushed the door inward and stared into the shadows. Deidre screamed when she saw my armored shadow before her.

"Deidre, it's me," I hurried to calm her.

"What is happening?" she asked as she scraped instruments and bandages and herbs into a basket. Her hair was disheveled, as if she'd just awoken. Or mayhap she hadn't slept.

"Iron Knee was murdered. Olaf broke his alliance. He's let Ivar and his men into the city. You must leave."

She spun on me. "I cannot leave!" she yelled at me. "The people. They'll be slaughtered."

"And so will you!" I roared back. "Please. You must."

Her expression was stricken, as if I'd slapped her face.

"Do you know of a place where you can go? An exit that is not the gates?" I asked her.

"Aye," she whispered. "I think."

I reached out my hand. "Come. Leave the basket. You won't need it."

She stared briefly at the basket, then set it on the table.

"Grab a knife. A sharp one."

This she did, then followed me to the door.

I poked my head into the street, then grabbed her hand and stepped into the flood of people.

"This way," she said and turned left against the crowd.

Together we wove through the rush. It was not hard. People recognized Deidre, or else avoided me in my Northern armor, and cleared a path.

Ahead of us, four Vestmenn warriors appeared. They were young and bloodied and retreating desperately from something that came behind them.

"Here," I said and pulled Deidre down a side street.

She took the lead again and turned right at the next cross street. We were nearing the west wall. Above us, on the fighting platform, a small knot of Iron Knee's warriors huddled behind their shields, their spears keeping Olaf's Northmen from the stairs that led down to the city. The air rang with their frantic shouts.

Deidre stepped into a doorway and pointed ahead, toward the base of the wall where a closed postern door stood. It was used for the pedestrian traffic that trickled in from the various tracks and paths on the outside of the wall. There, two Northern guards struggled against the people who pressed against them as they clamored for release. In their desperation, the guards simply cut people down to keep them back.

"Come," I said as a plan formulated in my mind. "Get behind me."

I hefted my shield and pressed into the back of the unruly group, carrying my axe in my right hand. Seeing my armor, people moved aside quickly to let me through so as not to be harmed. When I reached the front of the crowd, I charged toward the warrior on my left with my axe in my right hand, ready to strike. It was a crude plan, I will admit, and one rooted in surprise, but I had no time to consider anything else. In moments, the Northmen on the wall would gain the steps into the city, and once they did, this exit would be blocked for good.

My shield thudded against the Northman with such force, he fell back and away. As I went with him, I hacked wildly at the leg of the man on my right, just below the line of his byrnie. The man beneath me hit the ground, and I collapsed on top of him in a heap of armor and weapons and shields. I had no time to rise before the citizens roared and pressed over us. As they yanked the latch from the door, their feet trampled my legs, my back, and my head. Someone stepped on my ankle and twisted it. Others thumped on the old wounds in my ribs and shoulder. I lost count of the times my head smacked the earth. I am certain I yelled or cursed, but their screams overwhelmed my own.

When the pounding on my body finally ceased, I felt a tug on my arm.

"You must rise. Torgil. They are coming!" It was Deidre's pleading voice in my ringing ears.

"Leave," I croaked.

"Please," she begged.

"Go." There was a tang on my lips. Blood.

The tugging stopped, and she ran off. I listened to her footfalls until they faded.

I know not how long I lay there. I was too exhausted and injured to rise, yet my wounds could not block the horrid screams and wicked laughter, nor the smell of death in my broken nose. Eventually, I pushed myself to my knees. The man below me no longer had a face. It was a mess of blood and shattered bones. To my right, the other warrior moaned, though I sensed from the strange angle of his limbs that he too would eventually die. I thought to end his life and show him mercy and then withdrew the thought. He had earned his fate.

Taking a deep breath, I grabbed my axe and pressed myself to my feet. The pain of that effort made me hiss and spit a wad of bloody phlegm from my mouth. Beneath me, my right ankle protested mightily, and I gritted my teeth against the misery. Then I turned my eyes slowly to the chaos of Ivar's victory. I thought to see flames licking the sky, but Ivar was more clever than that. He wanted wealth and control and revenge. And so, rather than fire, I was greeted with corpses and blaring horns and the screams of those unlucky enough to have fallen victim to the Northmen. The city was finally his to ravage.

As I stared at the wreckage, axe dangling at my side, I forced my aching head to devise a plan. Running made little sense. Where would I run to? I was never a Vestmann and could not pretend to be one. And with Deidre now gone from my life, I had nowhere to go. Besides, my body was too broken to get anywhere. Still, the thought of remaining and serving Olaf sickened me. Yet again he had trod on friends and allegiances. And for what? More silver? More power? Why else would he break his alliance with Iron Knee if not to strike a better bargain with Ivar?

"If it isn't the nithing," called a familiar voice from above me. And with that voice, my chance at escape left me.

I craned my sore neck to gaze up at the sneering bastard on the wall. The arse-licking Berse. At his feet lay the corpses of Iron's Knee's warriors who had tried to hold out.

I turned to him as he began descending the steps into the city. "I am surprised you could pull your prick from Olaf's arse long enough to walk the walls, Berse. It must be lonely."

"Oh, it's not so lonely," he said. "I have my men," he gestured to the warriors with him, none of whom I recognized. He reached the ground and faced me. "You look injured. What luck."

I shifted my weight to my better foot and raised my axe. "Why luck?"

He smiled as his men spread around me. "Because it will make your capture all the easier."

"You will not capture me," I vowed.

He snorted. "Of course I will. A valiant death is much more than you deserve."

I crouched, feeling my anger pulse. "Then come, Berse. Try to capture me."

He waved his sword toward the other men. "Oh, I don't plan to capture you. That honor I will save for my men."

I lifted my axe and charged the bastards.

But I never made it. Not three steps had I gone before my head rang from a violent blow and my legs faltered beneath me. I do not remember hitting the ground, but I do remember the triumphant smile on Berse's face as I slipped from consciousness.

28

W ater splashed upon my face, and I sputtered to consciousness.
I tried to lift my hand to wipe the moisture from my eyes but
found it tied to my other wrist. So instead, I used my bicep to sleeve
the drops away and to see who had thrown the water upon me. I meant
to curse the fellow, but the words caught on my tongue. For there,
standing above me, was Olaf. I had not seen him up close since he had
cast me out of Amounderness. His face had somehow elongated in his
maturity, as if someone had stretched his skin to highlight his cheek-
bones and his newly forming wrinkles. Where there had been a twinkle
in his eye, there was now only a flat coldness. Or mayhap he had
reserved that stern countenance for me.

He knelt before me and studied my face. As he did, my gaze flicked to
the cross dangling from his neck. There were no other talismans now,
no vestiges of the old gods at all.

"You have changed, Torgil."

"As have you," I responded sourly.

"It's a shame. You could have had riches and fame, had you stayed loyal to me. Now look at you. A forgotten old warrior." He shook his head. "What was it your father used to say? Where oaths break, doom follows."

I snorted. "Aye, and the gods will curse you for turning your back on them."

He chuckled. "Says the man in bonds. The old gods gave me nothing. This god," he lifted the cross at his neck and showed it to me, "has given me all, and I will honor Him for it. Just as the priest foresaw."

I squinted at him as if he, too, had lost his wits. In truth, I was stricken. He had been as close as a brother to me. Oh, there were plenty of times I wanted to box his ears for his wild schemes and bullheaded ways, but at least I understood those. This new Olaf, I did not recognize, and it pained me to my core.

Olaf laughed. "You think me mad. I see it in your eyes. But you need not. The Christ God smiles upon me. Where you are lost and hopeless, I am wealthy and powerful." He looked at the others in the pen, then back to me. "But," he leaned closer to me, "it need not be like this, Torgil. I can release you from this place. You know this."

His words incensed me. "And what bad bargain must I make for my release?"

"Allow yourself to be baptized, and swear your fealty to me. That is all. That is not bad, is it?"

My anger ignited in me and before I could control it, I spat at Olaf so that it splattered on his face. I thought he might cut my throat then — was convinced of it, really — but somehow, he restrained himself, sleeved the spittle from his face, and stood. "Rot in thralldom, Torgil."

"Curse you and your damned god," I roared at him.

He turned and marched from the pen, and I glared at his retreating form until he vanished among the tents. I then glared at the others around me. I recognized some of them from my time in Dyflin, but I ignored their slack-jawed stares. We were doomed, and I, for one, was in no mood for kindness.

It was then that a cheer rose from the wall and forced my gaze upward. A commotion brewed above the gate that I did not understand until I saw the spear rise and the gore-slick thing stuck to the point of it. Iron Knee's head. A foulness made all the more profane by the treachery that had caused it.

Day stretched into evening, and more Dyfliners entered our pen. We received no food and only a few small sips of dirty water from our guards. There was no privacy for shitting or pissing. No escape from the mud or the kicks from our drunken guards. We were nothing more than penned animals, though it was hard to say who was treated worse. At least we would not be slaughtered for the tables, though I am certain that some of the women who were taken away for the enjoyment of the guards might have preferred that.

As night fell, my thoughts turned to the North and to my daughter. I had hoped to see her again someday but knew now that the chances were slim. My future was unknown, though I was certain of one thing: I would not die as someone's possession, broken and forgotten, in some foreign household. I would escape, or I would die in the attempt. There were no other options. And so I set my mind to developing a plan…

"Psst," came a whisper. It was late, and the sudden but soft noise surprised me. I jerked, thinking the man to my right needed my attention, but he slept. I turned farther and found Sveinn's face near my shoulder.

"Here," he said, passing me an object in the darkness. "Place it in your boot."

I took the thing in my bound hands, realizing with a start that it was the handle of a sheathed knife.

"The gods give you luck, my friend," he whispered. Then he vanished.

The spit of rain upon my face woke me. I blinked and opened my eyes to the sight of my lap and the puddled mud between my legs. I had slumped in my slumber, and now my neck and shoulders ached from the discomfort of it. Around me, others woke. Some yawned and stretched their limbs. Others stood in the mud and patted life back into their arms, their hair plastered to their skulls, their clothes tight from the moisture. A few of the younger captives cried. And all the while, the guards looked on with weary boredom.

My thoughts turned briefly to escape. On the inside of my worn boot was Sveinn's knife. Removing it and killing a tired guard might not be so hard, but with my throbbing ankle, the gods only knew how far I would get. Besides, where would I go? There was nothing for me in Irland. And so I looked away and stretched, and I did my best to ignore the painful emptiness in my stomach.

Sometime later, new guards gathered us from the pen and divided us into lines.

"What are they doing?" asked a lad behind me in the tongue of Vestmenn.

I did not turn to answer. "Taking us away."

"Where?" he asked.

I shrugged. "I know not. Mayhap to other markets, like Jorvik. Or other towns here."

"To be sold?" he asked, his voice a pathetic squeak now.

"Aye, lad. To be sold as thralls."

A whimper seeped from his lips, and I ground my teeth. I knew his pain and the future that awaited him, and it squeezed my nerves like a vise.

The guards marched us to one of Olaf's ships, where they kicked and prodded us until we sat as a group near the mast. And there, finally, we were given a slice of bread to eat with butter smeared upon it. To this they added dried strips of beef and three pitchers of water to share between us. I suppose the bastards could not have their thralls starve — it was bad for business.

As we ate, the crew boarded the ship and took their seats. I wondered briefly if I might recognize anyone, though thankfully, I did not. That is, except for one man, who came after the others and gazed down onto the ship's deck from the dock. His eyes scanned his cargo until they found me, at which point he laughed.

"Ah," Berse said as he climbed down onto the deck and stood before me, "the old gods are cruel to you, Torgil. Are they not?" He knelt before me and smiled. "Oh, it is fine to see your downfall, Torgil. I have waited a long time for it."

I glared at that sniveling whoreson but bit my tongue. It would do me no good to spit my fury at him.

"Have you lost your voice along with your luck?" He laughed, then looked around him, as if hoping others might also laugh at his jest. A few men chuckled, though most looked perplexed, for they did not know me as Berse knew me.

"Well," he said with a backhanded wave, "I am certain you will find both again when your new owner lashes you. I would do it myself just to hear your scream, but sadly, Olaf has forbidden it."

"Because you're a good little lapdog, aren't you?" I croaked, unable to restrain myself.

Berse backhanded me with a force that rang in my ears. Then he stood and marched to the aft deck, where he called to the crew to ready the ship. As he stood there with his barrel chest and his gleaming armor, I wondered briefly how I might slip the blade from my boot and drive it into the bastard's belly. It might be worth my own death if I succeeded, but I knew the chances were slim. And so it remained a dream — a wish that took my mind off the grim future before me.

We departed just as the sun peaked through the gray clouds and a gentle breeze began to blow — a breeze that changed to a gusting wind as soon as we reached the ocean. Sea spray showered us as the waves rolled against our hull and rocked the vomit from the stomachs of my fellow thralls. I growled and cursed at those who retched, especially when the remnants of the morning meal slid and sloshed in my direction or the wind carried the spume into my face. The Vestmenn were too sick to care about my protests, but the crew roared with delight at my misery, especially Berse. Seeing the futility of my outcry, I turned my anger inward and focused on my escape. It would happen, of that I was certain. It might end in my death, but even death would be better than thralldom. At least I would be free.

The wind calmed at night and settled, if only slightly, the torment my neighbors disgorged upon me, but it did not end my agony. My body ached from sitting. My crotch stung from urine. My nose struggled to find the salty bliss of sea air in the midst of the rancid spew and body odors. I slept, though I do not remember falling asleep.

The wail of a horn woke me. My eyes stung and my temples thumped. We had arrived somewhere, for the ship sat still and the crew had pulled in their oars. Dark clouds and fog lay like a mantle upon us. I sat up and winced, for in my slumber, I had fallen sideways against a lad named Murchad. To his credit, he had let me sleep, though I could tell he had not. He, like many others, was green with his sickness, which had rivered down his chin and chest. He probably had not even felt me against him. Still, I nodded my thanks and stretched my neck and back.

"Up, you swine," yelled Berse.

With groans then forlorn silence, we obeyed his order and stood upon the slimy deck. A brief glance about told me we had arrived in Amounderness. Though the day was dark, I recognized the river and the sloping beach as well as the stone wall that surrounded the nearby town. From here, I knew, we would be sold to locals or, if we showed strength, marched to Jorvik.

"Where are we?" whispered Murchad to me.

"A place called Amounderness," I responded, "though I know not what it is called in your tongue."

The guards pulled us onto a new dock and marched us down to a small field where another pen waited. The last time I had been to this place, Olaf's army had camped in that very spot. It sickened me to contemplate just how far I had fallen from my previous arrival in this place and just how inglorious was my return. Perchance Olaf was right. Perchance the gods had abandoned me.

I cast the thought aside and focused on Murchad, who now walked before me. "If you get a chance, lad," I said as the guards shepherded us into the pen, "run. Get free."

"Is that what you will do?" he murmured back to me.

"If I can," I said.

I limped into the pen and found a spot in the mud to sit. As I did, another ship arrived, bringing with it more captives from Dyflin. And together, we wretched prisoners spent yet another afternoon and night caged in a guarded sty. How long we would remain was impossible to say, but I knew that the weaker I became from my hunger and lack of sleep, the harder it would be to make good on my promise to leave. Throbbing ankle or no, I had to escape. And so, as others chatted away the day, I slept. And when they slept, I awoke in the darkness.

29

I waited and let my eyes adjust to the deepening shadows. The field in which we sat was flat and devoid of trees. To the south of us, the land sloped down toward the river. It would lend some protection, but I knew, too, that it was rocky there. Navigating those stones would be tricky in the dark, especially with my ankle. Which meant it had to be the field. And it had to be quiet.

I turned my attention to the guards. There were six of them encircling the pen, none of them vigilant. Why should they be? Their captives were weaponless and forlorn and bound, and so they stood in bored silence. Half warmed themselves at a small fire. A few drank from their skins. Others focused on their hands or clothes or whatever thing offered some modicum of distraction.

I waited. Waited until the shadows deepened even further. Waited until their fire began to die. Waited until a light sprinkle began to fall. And then I moved.

With my heart thudding in my chest, I inched my hand to my boot. Slowly I worked the blade up my ankle until the sheath came into view. I worked the blade loose, then sawed its edge against the hemp at my wrists until the rope fell away. The movement sounded like thunder in my ears, but my neighbors slept on, and so I consoled myself that, perchance, it was only my anxiety that made the noise seem louder.

I sat back against the post and scanned the guards. Still six. Still bored. Still distracted. And, if I was lucky, even wearier than before.

My mouth was dry now. I would need to be quick, yet I was older, heavier, and wounded. Doubts filled my mind. The top of the pen was not too high. With luck and the help of my hands, I could vault it and run, but it would need to be fast and silent.

The guards gazed at us again, then turned away. I exhaled, crouched, and waited. Nothing. No sounds of alarm. No calls. I turned and planted my good foot on the lower crossbeam with my hands on the upper. There was laughter behind me. I vaulted the beam and landed with a thud on the opposite side, gritting my teeth with the pain of it. I glanced quickly at the guards. Still nothing.

Crouching, limping, I slipped into the night.

I thought to head to the town and slip my blade into Berse, but the fates had not woven that tale. Instead I stumbled through the darkness westward, toward the coast, staying close to the old Roman road beside which stood a few farms I remembered. And just as important, close to the tree under which I had buried a bag of my silver.

The landscape was more marshy and barren here, though there was enough foliage to offer some cover. The air was chilly and salty from the nearby sea, but still my brow dripped with sweat and my legs ached from crouching and hobbling from shrub to shrub and tree to tree.

Eventually I reached a farm and scanned it for what I sought, but the farm was poor and had not what I needed. I moved to the next, and then a third, and there I found it. Leaping a low fence, I yanked an axe from the wood pile, then tore the saddle off the beam of the horse pen. This I placed slowly on the larger of the sleepy horses as I tried to ignore the hound barking in the farm's hall and the startled prancing of the beast. With gentle words and pets along its muzzle, I slowly worked the saddle and tackle into place. Then I climbed onto the horse's back and urged it gently forward. With the farm's gates now in view, I coaxed the steed into a trot and prayed the barking hound would not bring the farmer.

But my prayers went unheeded.

"Hey!" yelled a voice behind me, just as the dog's barking increased in intensity.

I did not turn back. Cursing, I bent low in the saddle and kneed my mount into a gallop. The horse reacted to my urging and bolted through the gate.

I moved off into the night and did not stop until the hound's bark was but a whisper in my ear. I made my way quickly to the tree where I had buried my silver and dismounted. Using the blade of Sveinn's knife, I pried loose the stones at its base, yanked the sack from its hole, and tied it to the saddle. Then I clambered back onto my steed and headed east, skirting the towns of Presota-Tun and Rippelceaster as I headed into the mountains.

I was free of thralldom, at least for now, but I was not free of my burdens. Before me stretched the long journey to Jorvik that I had never made. It would take effort, and luck, to get there, but I had to try. It was all I had left. For there I might find a ship to take me to the North, and to my daughter…

I did not remember many of Godric's words about the direction to Jorvik, only that it lay to the east and that one could follow the Rippel in that direction, at least until it turned north into the mountains. A new bridge now crossed the Rippel at Rippelceaster, but I did not cross it for fear of being spotted by the guards on the town's walls. Instead I circumnavigated the town and stayed clear of the hovels around it so I would not draw any attention to the strange sight I must have made by riding a horse in my old tunic and soiled breeks.

I stayed in sight of the dark line of the river as I moved eastward into the night. The horse I rode seemed contented enough, though in time that would change as thirst and hunger overcame it. It was no different for me. Hunger gnawed at my gut and my tongue felt thick and chalky in my mouth, but I rode on. Only when I felt I'd put enough distance between me and Berse would I allow myself to rest.

East of Rippelceaster, I regained the old Roman road as it meandered beside the water, heading northeast toward higher elevation. Here the land rose more sharply on my left, which unnerved me. I liked not the idea of someone watching me from above, though I reminded myself that it was still dark and I was but a shadow in the landscape. Still, I listened intently for noises that did not belong in my surroundings, a skill that Lodin had taught me as a youth and that I had honed over the decades. The metallic clink of iron, the methodic thud of a wooden shield upon a warrior's back, the grate of loose gravel and stones beneath a boot — these were the sounds of men, not nature, and I knew them well.

Eventually the shadow of the hills to my left moved away and I descended to a fork in the river. The line closest to me bent northward. The other continued in a northeasterly direction. I decided on the latter, even if it meant crossing the river. Though more dangerous, it afforded me and the horse a chance to drink, as well as to bathe — two things I desperately needed.

The river here was blissfully slow-moving and calm, or so it appeared at night with the moonlight stretching across its surface. But it also proved to be deep. So while the drinking and bathing went well enough, I struggled to get my steed into the river past its belly. Like a mule, it resisted my every effort, until I finally smacked a branch across its rump. Thankfully, I clung to the lead line as I did, for it bolted into the water like a rabbit evading a hound.

The horse swam to the opposite shore as I swam along behind it, trying hard to keep my head above the waterline. As soon as the steed's hooves touched the muddy bottom, it bucked from the water and ripped the lead line from my grasp. It ran off with my silver and axe still attached to its saddle. I gave chase but had not the energy to run it down. What a fool I must have appeared to be, limping across an empty field in the dark of night as water squished from my boots and poured from my clothing.

Eventually, and by the luck of the gods alone, the beast's hunger overcame its fear, and it bent its muzzle to the grass on the opposite side of the field into which it had run. I gave the animal some time to relax and feed before taking its line yet again and walking it back toward the river.

With the darkness fading around me, I paused to consider my options. My eyes stung from lack of sleep, a mighty hunger gnawed at my gut, and a chill had settled upon my skin. I thought to stop and build a fire, but I had no tools for that, and so I pressed on.

Not long after, I came to a scattering of hovels and animal pens divided by a narrow lane. Above it, to the east, sat an old circular fort of stone, though whether a lord lived there now was hard to say. I saw no one upon its walls. The town, if I could call it that, was different. People toiled in their gardens and milled about the place. I questioned whether to show myself, but my hunger was too great now. I needed food before I collapsed. So I pulled some hack silver from my sack, did my best to straighten my rough clothing, then rode into town.

I hailed an old woman who stood beside the stone wall that marked her home. "Gōd morgen," I said in what I presumed to be her tongue.

She nodded at me but did not speak.

"Do you have any food?" I asked her. "I can pay."

"Northman?" Her old gray eyes examined me. She must have heard it in my accent.

I shrugged. "Does it matter?"

My response made her squint. "Aye. To me."

"I was born in the North but have not been home for many seasons."

She grunted. "Thought so. Plenty of your kind about. Far as I am concerned, your lot can all starve."

I bit my tongue and moved on. More eyes fell upon me as I rode up the lane. Some were curious, but most regarded me with a malignancy I could not ignore. At the far side of the town, I mustered my nerve and stopped again to ask for food and, once again, was turned away. So fierce was the pain in my stomach, I had a mind to take food by force, but I resisted. There were not many men about, but there were enough, and I could not fight them all.

I cursed the town and its people as I followed the Rippel out into the land. The sun rose to my right and cast its brilliant glow upon the valley before me. Dew sparkled like tiny jewels on the tips of hay that ruffled in the field. Mist crouched in the green trees that blanketed the hills to either side of me. A bird of prey — perchance a buzzard by its lines — circled overhead, its eyes on a stone wall where rabbits hopped. If I did not eat soon, mayhap that same bird would feast on me.

The river gradually wound northward and vanished into a forest. Though there was a track beside it, I was not keen to enter, and so I stopped to speak with a shepherd who was bringing his sheep out to pasture.

"Eoforwick, you say?" the grizzled old shepherd asked, using the English name for Jorvik.

I nodded.

"Then it is good you stopped to ask," he said as he leaned on his staff. He seemed a friendlier fellow than the townspeople. "The river will take you north into the mountains. But that old track there" — he pointed to a small cart path that veered off to the right, not ten paces from where we stood — "will take you east below the Dales to Eoforwick."

"Have you been that way?" I asked.

"I have never been as far as Eoforwick, but there's a band of your type who come through regularly and take that route."

"A band of my type?" I struggled to sound unconcerned.

"Aye. The bastards bring their thralls and trade goods through." He spat. "Not real welcome in these parts, as you can guess."

I tossed the fellow a piece of hack silver, which he watched drop in the grass at his feet. "I thank you, friend."

The man picked up the silver and dropped it in a pouch.

"If you have any food, I have more silver," I ventured.

He scratched his stringy beard, regarding me closely. I knew his thoughts. It was beyond odd for a rider to be headed so far without food, proper clothing, or any idea of how to get to his destination. Mayhap to him I looked no better than many of the thralls who came this way. Still, he seemed to come to some sort of agreement with himself and gave a curt nod. "Can you stomach a bite of stale bread and hard cheese?"

I smiled at the graybeard. "I've had worse."

The man fished in his sack as his small flock bleated and munched in the field around him. He handed me his simple fare, and I gave him more of my silver with a bow of thanks.

"You have been kind," I added.

"You watch yourself," he said in return.

I did not wait to eat. So famished was I that I devoured the cheese and hardened bread before the shepherd had time to turn away.

He smiled politely and gave me more. "It seems you might need this more than me."

I took it gratefully and devoured it, too. Crumbs fell like snow on my lap, and I picked at them when I had finished the main course. The shepherd never moved his eyes from me. With a final burp of satisfaction, I nodded yet again at the old man, grabbed my steed's reins, and left the Rippel behind.

"God be with you," he called to my back.

The morning stretched into midday with not a soul in sight save for birds and a few rabbits. Still, I proceeded with caution and watched for people. I did not worry much about farmers. They would not tussle with an armed man. It was warriors and bandits I worried about, for I knew nothing of the land through which I walked and felt blind to the trouble I might encounter. Adding to my concern was my weariness, which made concentration difficult. Several times, I caught myself nodding off and smacked my cheeks to wake myself. The final time, after nearly falling from my saddle, I determined that it was time to rest. I could go no farther.

I led my steed into the next line of trees I encountered and found a spot deep within the foliage, though not far from the track. I tied my horse to a branch, curled up on the ground, and promptly fell asleep.

And that is where the men found me.

It was the whispers and the rattling of gear that woke me. It came from the direction of the road. I crawled quickly to the edge of the trees and peered out at the field. Four young men hastened toward me, not thirty paces away. Each stood about ten paces from the other. None were armored, and all carried shoddy weapons, save for the leader, who brandished a hand axe. I recognized one of the men from the village through which I had traveled.

These thoughts registered in my head as I scurried to my left, in the direction of the man who seemed to be leading the others. In my hand I carried the axe I had taken from the farm. Kneeling behind a boulder close to my horse, I exhaled to calm my quickening breath.

I did not see them enter the trees, but I heard the breaking of branches and their whispers. I gripped my axe and peered carefully out from behind my shelter. The men stood in a semicircle, gazing at the spot where I had slept. They must have thought to surprise me and, seeing the vacant area, relaxed. For the briefest of moments, I thought to warn them away, for I was not keen to kill them. But I dispelled the thought as quickly as I entertained it — the men had come to kill me. They deserved no better.

My attack was swift. Their leader only had time to turn and flinch before my axe cleaved his head from his shoulder. The ease with which my blade traveled through the man's neck tossed me off-balance. Still, I regained my feet in time to spin my blade above my head and take the next man low in his gut with all the force I could muster. He folded over my blade, then collapsed to his back. I yanked the blade free just as his friend's screams rent the air — screams that ended as soon as my axe split his skull.

My strategy had been to shock the attackers, and it had succeeded. The last man — a lad, really — did not wait to learn his fate. He flew from the woods and out into the field, stumbling as he turned to see if I gave chase. But I did not. I was too winded and my ankle too sore. And so I watched as the boy regained the path and scurried back in the direction of the town.

I spat what little saliva I could conjure from my dry mouth. Chest heaving from exertion, I dropped my axe and bent quickly to the corpses to see if they had any food or silver upon them. There was none, though each had a skin of water that I stripped from their bodies. I drank thirstily from the first skin, then stopped myself and tied both to the saddle of my steed. I knew not how far Jorvik lay, but I sensed I would need to ration it. I then checked their weapons. The hand axe of the leader was smaller than mine and well-balanced. I slipped it into my belt. Then I grabbed the reins of my horse and led it from the woods and down to the cart path.

The light was fading, which was good. It would give me darkness through which to travel. Rested now and with water to drink, I kneed my mount into motion and pressed on.

I did not get far before a new sound filled my ears. Horses. A group of them, and coming at a gallop. I knew without looking what it meant. And I knew, too, that it was futile to run. Not that I would have. As physically unprepared as I was, it was time to stand my ground.

And so I turned my steed.

30

B erse rode at the head of a small group, his travel cloak flowing out behind him as he bobbed in his saddle. With him were eight others, all of whom I recognized from the ship, though none of whom I knew by name. I breathed in deeply of the grassy scent in the air, though I know not why. Mayhap it was to calm myself or mayhap it was to etch this time and place in my thoughts, for this moment had been a long time coming. Perchance, if the gods were kind, I might have a skald make a song of this and listen with a smile in the later seasons of my life.

I lifted my arms as Berse and the others slowed their steeds before me. Mud spattered their clothing and skin. Dark circles hung beneath their eyes. They had ridden hard to catch me.

"I commend you, arse-licker," I called to Berse. "You found me. Now what?"

"Now I kill you, Torgil," Berse called to me as he dismounted and pulled his shield from his back.

"Because that is what your lord, Olaf, commanded you to do?"

He scowled. "Olaf knows not of this, though I am certain he will not be too dismayed. I will be sure to cut out your tongue and bring it to him as a gift for your oath-breaking. And for all the times you've called me 'arse-licker.'"

"I broke no oath, but I suppose that matters not to you. So a duel between you and me it is," I replied as I, too, climbed from my horse and slid the longer axe from my saddle. "Or do you need the help of your men?"

He laid his cloak across his saddle and handed his shield to another warrior, then he pulled his sword free from its sheath, "Do not interfere," he said to them. "This will be quick."

The bastard was confident, and he had reason to be. I was a soft, aging man with an aching ankle, and he was a muscled warrior who had never stopped fighting. Oh, I had guarded an inn and thrown drunkards to the street, but it was not the same as fighting with weapons in a battle. In strength and weapon skill, he had the advantage, but as my father had told me often, a wise man will not stake too much on his strength. If I were smart and, aye, lucky, I might find a way to use his confidence against him.

I pushed my mount off the path and took stock of my gear. In my hand was the longer axe I had taken from the farm. My new hand axe hung from my belt. And strapped to my right boot was Sveinn's knife. I had trained with none of them and knew not how they would fare in a fight. Conversely, Berse approached with his sword in hand and a seax on his hip. Both of them were fine weapons and both he knew as well as he knew his body.

He slashed an X in the air before him. "Come then, Torgil," he called to me. "Let us end this."

I crouched and circled, my axe steady in my right hand. My limbs tingled with an energy I welcomed, for I would need it. Berse moved closer, his blade lifted and pointed at my left. He lunged at me, blade seeking my ribs. A feint that I easily backstepped. He followed it with a sidestep and a slash at my left shoulder. I dodged beyond the blade's trajectory and let it pass my torso, then I followed behind it with a strike at his arm, though my ankle protested the sudden move and threw off my balance. My swipe came too slowly, allowing him time not only to evade but also to twist his wrist and strike back at my head. I dodged awkwardly and stumbled sideways. Seeing me off-balance, he came again and swung heavily at my neck. My body merely reacted, and I lifted my axe to protect myself. It caught his strike, but not perfectly, and so his blade swiped across my cheek. The force of it dislodged my weapon from my grip and knocked me to the ground.

Berse could have easily ended me at that moment, but he did not. Instead he relented, though I know not why. Perchance it was his confidence, for it could not have been his respect for me. He had none. "Get up," he snarled at me with disgust.

I rose to my feet and pulled my new hand axe free. It was shorter than the other, which meant I would need to work inside his sword strikes, a difficult task at best. But it was also lighter and, therefore, faster. I crouched again and huffed to steady my breath. Sweat stung my eyes. My cheek was aflame. Blood dripped at my feet. My ankle was aflame. Was I a fool to think I could defeat Berse?

I had no time to answer the thought, for Berse came again in a barrage of quick swipes at my head and upper body. He roared as he came. It was a visceral sound — the sound of hatred and fury. The attack pushed me back toward the group of horsemen, but my cheek wound had focused my thoughts, and I did not lose my wits. Rather, I concentrated on a response, and so, step by step, I gave ground and waited.

And then I saw it. A mistake. A sword lifted too high in order to keep the momentum of his swings. Back I retreated and on he came, his swipes becoming more errant as he advanced. I struck. Just as his sword swiped past my face, right to left and up to reset, I stepped toward him and hacked up and under his arm. The blade was not as sharp as it could have been, but it bit into his flesh all the same. He grunted and blinked at the shock of it, but I did not relent.

Now at close quarters, I used my seasons at The Drunken Gull as an advantage. Without thought, I smashed my left palm into his nose. He staggered backward like a drunk, and I followed at speed. Stunned, he retaliated with a feeble swing, but I was too close now and blocked his arm. And this time, I did not release it. Instinctively, his hand fumbled for the seax on his belt, but I struck first with a blow that lodged my axe deep in the bastard's forehead, killing him instantly.

For a long moment I stared into Berse's lifeless face, and then I let him fall. With a leaden thud, he hit the dirt. Only then did feelings rush back to me. The throb in my cheek. The ache in my ankle. The sweat in my eyes. They hit me like a wave of icy water upon my skin.

So too did the thought of the other warriors watching their leader die. I turned toward the others. Though Berse had told them to stay clear, I knew not what they might do now that their leader was dead. But they did not move. So great was their shock that they merely stared at me in silence.

"Tell Olaf what has happened here today," I said as I wiped some spittle from my lips, "and that I am a free man now. I seek no quarrel with him or any of you. I wish only to live in peace."

The men did not respond, but I did not need them to. I needed only to leave. And so I gathered Berse's cloak and shield and weapons, and the food on his saddle, which were now mine by right of Berse's defeat. Then I went to my horse and climbed slowly, sorely, onto its back.

31

S igurd's Estate, The North, Late Fall, AD 989

The rain thundered down as I rode my horse onto the estate that had once belonged to Sigurd. I say "once" because I knew not if he yet lived. After all, it had been twelve turns of the sun since I had last rested my eyes on the rolling green that defined his lands. Yet, to my eyes, not much had changed. Flocks of sheep still dotted the sodden hills. His borg still stood where I had seen it, though its walls were now a blur in the driving downpour.

A man challenged me with a spear at the borg's gate. I did not recognize him, but soaked to the bone as he was, the poor sod looked worse than I felt.

"Torgil Torolvsson," I replied when he asked my name. "I am an old friend," I added.

The man shouted over the rain at his comrade, who ran up the muddy path to the hall in the distance. I waited patiently. Beneath me, my horse shifted its feet impatiently, then rocked its head in a futile attempt to shed the moisture. I soothed him with a stroke on his muscled neck. He was a new steed I had purchased in Kaupang after traveling across the sea in a trade ship. A gentle beast whom I had grown quickly to like.

In time, the runner returned and motioned me through the gate. I walked my mount up through the sucking mud to the porch of the main hall, where two forms waited in their heavy furs. My heart lightened to know that Sigurd and Turid were alive.

And then it promptly plunged.

I stared at the two, unable to speak, and so it was Turid who spoke first. "Welcome, Torgil," she said loudly, but stiffly. "It pleases me to know you are alive and hale. Please, come in out of the rain."

"Aye, be welcome, friend," called Sigurd's brother, Jostein, with a grand sweep of his arm. He was a handsome man with a frame nearly as large as Hauk's, a well-groomed beard of brown and gray, and eyes as blue as his brother's.

I dismounted and passed the reins of my mount to a servant who had appeared from my left. The fellow hastened away, and I was suddenly glad that I had buried my wealth not far from the estate.

I steeled myself and climbed onto the porch with a smile for my hosts. "Thank you for the welcome," I said formally and nodded at them.

"Please, come inside," Turid said with a forced smile on her freckled face. It was with a pained heart that I returned it. Not because of the strands of gray in her red hair or the deepened grooves at the corners of her eyes, but because I sensed there was something more that lay upon her. Stress or worry. Or fear.

My hosts ushered me into the cavernous hall, where thralls moved like wraiths in the firelight and a handful of men sat along the walls. Their conversations ended abruptly as I strode into the place and removed my dripping cloak. I kept my axe on my belt, however. Just in case.

"Tell me," said Jostein as he escorted me to a table near the high seat. "What news of my sons, Finn and Hauk?"

His men returned to their conversations, but I did not speak, for my eyes caught sight of a giant carved cross hanging from the rafters behind Jostein's lordly seat — the seat that had once belonged to Sigurd. The sight of it threw me for an awkward spell, and I could not find my words.

"Forgive my haste in asking," said Jostein. "You must be travel weary. Please sit. Eat."

I turned my head away from the cross and sat at the table, my thoughts spinning like a spool. A thrall placed a pitcher and a plate of bread before me. I poured a cup and drank deeply of the ale. Its headiness relaxed me and gave me time to collect myself as Jostein and Turid sat across from me.

"Finn and Hauk are well," I finally responded, "though the last I saw of them was many springs ago. I have heard, though, that Olaf has seen nicely to their care and their upbringing."

Jostein grinned. "That gladdens me. It has been many seasons since I've seen them. They must be capable men now."

"Oh, aye," I responded. I took another deep draught of my drink and cast my gaze around the hall. "They are lords now of their own lands, with wives. And Hauk is a father."

Jostein laughed and clapped. "That is wonderful news. Wonderful. Oh, I would like to see them again."

Not knowing what to say, I nodded and cast my gaze about. There was not a familiar face among the men. "Forgive me for asking, my lord, but what has happened to Sigurd? To his hird?"

Jostein pursed his lips and grunted. "It is a fair question. Sadly, my brother died."

"It was an accident," Turid added a bit too quickly.

The news hit me heavier than I expected. I had loved Sigurd as a lord and a comrade, and though he had stolen my wife, my hatred of him had long since transformed from a visceral passion into a smoldering memory, like a fire whose heat had grown cold. To think I would not see him again in this life stabbed me like an unexpected blade.

"And his hird?" I queried hesitantly.

Jostein shrugged. "Sadly, age claimed Ulrik. Bolek and the others withdrew to other places. I offered them a place among my men, but they decided to sheath their swords for good. It is unfortunate. They were good men."

The news of their absence was nearly as hard to hear as the news of Sigurd's death, especially Ulrik, whom I had come to love and respect despite his rough edges. He had often seemed unbreakable, and yet, age claimed us all. But there was something more that troubled me about the news. It was the way Jostein delivered it. Stilted it was, as if it were rehearsed or untrue, and I struggled not to peer at him with questions in my gaze. Aware that I was gawking, I looked down at my cup and shook my head. "That is sore news, indeed. When did all of this come to pass?"

"Several summers —" Turid began.

"Three summers hence," Jostein interjected.

I looked from one to the other.

"Aye," repeated Turid. "You are right, husband. It has been three summers now."

I wanted to ask why Jostein was here with Turid and what had happened to his own wife, but my mind was already twirling like a whirlpool. So I changed the subject quickly. "And your daughters?" I asked Turid.

She brightened at the question. "Sigrunn is a woman now. Newly married. She is a beauty, Torgil. You would not recognize her. And

Astrid is blossoming into a young lady. The lord and lady of Jel — your old home — foster her."

I was glad to hear of Sigrunn, but the news of young Astrid chafed me. "My old home" had been taken by force from my father, and the news of its new owners turned the corners of my mouth downward.

Seeing my sudden anger, Turid added, "Sigrunn and her new husband will come for the Yule feast. Will you stay?"

The question caught me by surprise, and I paused. "I cannot," I finally said, "but I thank you for the offer. I will be leaving as soon as the rain lets up. I am on an errand for Olaf," I lied.

"I see," said Turid.

"That is a shame, Torgil," added Jostein. "Though I hope you will be back soon enough. Perchance you can encourage Olaf and my boys to come with you next time, eh?"

I forced a smile to my lips. "Perchance."

I left that afternoon, after filling my belly and waiting for the rains to abate. It had been difficult to stay that long, but to leave earlier would have been strange and rude. Turid escorted me to the hall's porch, where I bade her a stiff farewell.

"You are wise to leave," she whispered to me as we stepped outside. "Sigurd died at Jostein's feast, and Jostein took all that was his. Ulrik protested and died for speaking his mind. Bolek is in Kaupang. Seek him there. I know nothing about the others." She then smiled as Jostein appeared at the threshold behind her. "Take care of yourself, Torgil," she said to me with a sudden shift in her demeanor. "And come back when you are able."

"Aye, my friend," called Jostein as I shrugged into my damp travel cloak. "You are always welcome."

I brushed the head of my axe and had a mind to use it, but restrained myself. "Thank you once again for the food and shelter," I forced myself to say. "Despite the troubling news, it was good to see friendly faces."

I rode from my former wife and from Sigurd's hall, both of which now belonged to Jostein because of Sigurd's death. I had labored so hard to reach this place of my dreams, where my daughter and Turid and Sigurd and my old comrades laughed and dined and played the pan flute to the roar of the hearth fire. But it had all been an illusion, a mist that scattered to reveal a truth both familiar and foul, with Jostein's men sitting at its benches and the cross of the Christian god hanging from its rafters. Had I not already fought so hard against that god? Had I not already lost dear friends and comrades because of him? What more would he take from me? What more did I have to give?

None of it was what I imagined save for one thing: the riddle of my future. And so I decided to point myself toward it and press on.

THE END

THANK YOU

Dear reader,

Thank you for reading *Riddle of the Gods*. I hope you enjoyed it. Please take a moment to leave a review, even if it's a short one. Your opinion is important to me.

If you have not yet read the other books in *Olaf's Saga*, you can find out more about them on my website: https://www.ericschumacher.net

If you would like to know when one of my books is available for pre-order or a discount, please consider joining my Readers Club at https://www.ericschumacher.net/readers-club/.

Thanks again for reading!

HISTORICAL NOTES

Little is known of Olaf's exploits during this long period in his life. During his years on the move, the sagas and historians place Olaf in Frisia and the coasts of France, England, and Scotland, as well as in Ireland. I could have written a travelogue of all of his journeys, but I chose instead to focus on an event upon which most historians agree: his conversion. Olaf's conversion is murky, and to be honest, it may not have even happened during the period that this book covers. However, it is believed that it happened while he was abroad.

The sagas tell of his conversion by a hermit. Records in history, such as the *Anglo-Saxon Chronicle*, tell of his conversion as part of a deal made with the English king. Some believe he may have been baptized by the hermit and then re-baptized later by the English king. The truth may never be known, but one thing is clear: he became zealous in his pursuit of this new religion. As a result, I picked a time in Olaf's history that not only offered a plausible reason for converting, but a suitable backdrop filled with other adventures, too.

On that note, King Iron Knee existed, as did the turmoil between the other Irish and Norse kings. According to the ancient chronicles, Iron Knee was killed by a slave when he was drunk. That was roughly in

AD 989. Medievalist Benjamin Hudson suggests that the reports of the killing in the Irish annals, and the sudden changes thereafter, suggest that Iron Knee was most likely killed as a result of factional infighting in Dublin. I chose to focus on that idea for Iron Knee's fall. Never one for missing an opportunity, I placed Olaf in the midst of it all.

Related to that was Olaf's marriage to a princess who, according to *Heimskringla*, was the sister of Olav Kvaran (Iron Knee's father). However, it is more commonly believed that Gytha was Olav Kvaran's daughter and Iron Knee's sister. *Heimskringla* places her in England, but in no specific area. I decided to place her in Amounderness, as it is almost directly across from Dublin and on the path to York (Jorvik). As Olav Kvaran had ruled both York and Dublin during his life, presumably to create a trading route between the two, it made sense to place Gytha there, though there is no record I could find to support or refute that.

As for the ongoing hostility between the "old gods" and Christianity, this is known and accepted. What was then Germany, France, England, Denmark, and other kingdoms all had Christian kings. This did not mean that they were docile, peaceful kingdoms. It meant that it put those kingdoms at odds with kingdoms who had not yet accepted the new ways. That, too, made for an interesting layer of tension in the story.

I hope you've enjoyed reading this novel as much as I've enjoyed writing it. Torgil the Lucky (or Unlucky, as I've begun to see him) has found a way to survive despite his hardships, and now that he has shed the yoke of Olaf, he will soon find a way to thrive.

ABOUT THE AUTHOR

Eric Schumacher (1968 –) is a historical fiction author of multiple best-selling novels set in the Viking Age. His fascination with Vikings and medieval history began at a young age, though exactly why is not clear. While Los Angeles has its own unique history, there are no ancient monasteries or Viking burial sites or hidden hoards buried in fields. Still, from the earliest age, he was drawn to books about medieval kings and warlords and was fascinated by their stories and the turbulent times in which they lived.

Schumacher now resides in Santa Barbara with his wife and two children and is busy working on his next novel.

www.ericschumacher.net

Printed in Dunstable, United Kingdom

68235577R00171